DESTINED

Also by Aprilynne Pike

WINGS

SPELLS

ILLUSIONS

DESTINED

APRILYNNE PIKE

An Imprint of HarperCollins*Publishers*

HarperTeen is an imprint of HarperCollins Publishers.

Destined
Copyright © 2012 by Aprilynne Pike
All rights reserved. Printed in the United States of America.
No part of this book may be used or reproduced in any manner
whatsoever without written permission except in the case of brief
quotations embodied in critical articles and reviews. For information
address HarperCollins Children's Books, a division of HarperCollins
Publishers, 10 East 53rd Street, New York, NY 10022.
www.epicreads.com

Library of Congress Cataloging-in-Publication Data is available.
ISBN 978-0-06-166812-8

Typography by Ray Shappell

12 13 14 15 16   CG/RRDH   10 9 8 7 6 5 4 3 2 1
❖

First Edition

To Neil Gleichman, who taught me the
importance of finishing strong.
I hope I have.
Thanks, Coach.

ONE

TAMANI PRESSED HIS FOREHEAD AGAINST THE chilly windowpane, fighting back a wave of exhaustion. Sleep wasn't an option, not while the only thing between him and an angry Winter faerie was a thin line of table salt.

Tonight, he was *Fear-gleidhidh* twice over.

The old word was one he normally wore with pride. It marked him as Laurel's guardian, her protector. But it had a richer meaning, one that went beyond the more traditional *Am Fear-faire*. *Fear-gleidhidh* meant "warden," and Tamani was charged with not only keeping Laurel safe but making certain she accomplished the mission Avalon had given her as a child.

Now he played prison warden too.

He looked over at his captive. Yuki's chair sat on the scuffed linoleum in the middle of a circle of white, granular salt. She slept, her cheek resting on her knees, hands cuffed loosely behind her. She looked uncomfortable. Beaten.

Harmless.

"I would have given up everything for you." Her words were hushed but clear.

Tamani felt Shar stiffen at the sound of her voice, breaking the thick silence.

Not sleeping after all. And she could never be harmless, he reminded himself. The small white flower blooming from the middle of her back, marking her a Winter faerie, was proof enough of that. It had been more than an hour since David cuffed her to the chair—an hour since Chelsea had exposed the irrefutable proof that she was, in fact, a Winter faerie—and Tamani still hadn't gotten used to the sight. It filled him with an icy fear he had rarely felt before.

"I was ready. That's why I stopped you before you brought me inside." Yuki looked up and unfolded her legs, stretching as best she could under the circumstances. "But you knew that, didn't you?"

Tamani held his tongue. He *had* known. And for a moment he'd been tempted to let her make her confession. But it wouldn't have ended well. Yuki would eventually have discovered that his affections were a sham, and then he would be at the mercy of a Winter faerie scorned. Better to cut the charade short.

He hoped he wasn't deceiving himself about that. She posed a threat; he shouldn't have felt any guilt about lying to her in the first place, much less now that he knew she'd been lying too. The power Winter faeries had over plants also made it possible for them to sense plant life at a distance, so from the instant Yuki had met Tamani, she had known him for a faerie. Known Laurel, too. The Winter had played them all.

So why did he still wonder whether he'd done the right thing?

"We could have been so good together, Tam," Yuki continued, her voice as silky as her rumpled silver dress, but with a malicious edge that made Tamani shiver. "Laurel's not going to leave him for you. She may be a faerie on the outside, but inside she's all human. David or no David, she belongs *here*, and you know it."

Avoiding his captain's eyes, Tamani turned back to the window and peered out into the darkness, pretending to look at . . . something. Anything. A sentry's life was full of viciousness, and Tamani and Shar had both seen each other take extreme measures to protect their homeland. But always against an obvious threat, a violent attacker: a *proven* foe. Trolls were their enemy—had always been. Winter faeries were the rulers of Avalon, and though Yuki had deceived them, she'd never actually *harmed* them. Somehow, putting her in chains felt worse than killing a hundred trolls.

"You and me, Tam, we're the same," Yuki continued. "We're being used by people who don't care what we want or what makes us happy. We don't belong with them; we belong together."

Reluctantly, Tamani glanced at her again. He was surprised to see that she wasn't looking at him as she spoke—she was staring past him, out the window, as if at some bright future she still imagined possible. Tamani knew better.

"There isn't a door in this world that can be closed to us, Tam. If you vouched for me, we could even go peacefully to Avalon. We could stay there together and live in the palace."

"How do you know about the palace?" Tamani asked reflexively, knowing even as he did that he was snapping at her bait. A barely audible sigh came from Shar, and Tamani wondered if it was directed at Yuki's stupidity or his own.

"Or we could stay here," she continued calmly, as though Tamani hadn't said anything. "Anywhere we wanted to go, anything we wanted to do, we could. Between your power over animals and mine over plants, the world would be ours. You know, the pairing of a Spring and Winter would work really well. Our talents complement each other perfectly."

Tamani wondered if she understood just how right she was—or how little it tempted him.

"I would have loved you forever," she whispered, bowing her head. Her dark, lustrous hair fell forward, veiling her face, and she sniffled quietly. Was she crying, or stifling a laugh?

Tamani started when a knock sounded at the door. Before he could take a step, Shar moved silently to the peephole.

Knife in his fist, Tamani tensed—ready. Was it Klea? That's what everything was for—the circle, Yuki in cuffs—an elaborate trap to snare the scheming Fall faerie who *might* be trying to kill them.

And might not.

If only they could know for sure.

Until they did, Tamani had to assume they were a threat—a lethal one.

But with a shimmer of a grimace, Shar pulled the door open and Laurel entered the room, Chelsea close behind.

"Laurel" was all Tamani managed to say, his fingers falling from the knife. Even after loving Laurel for as long as he could remember, and lately becoming something . . . something *more*, he still felt a leap of joy every time he saw her.

She had changed out of her dark-blue formal—the one she'd worn when he'd held her in his arms over a year ago at the Samhain festival, when he'd kissed her so passionately. It seemed far away.

Laurel wasn't looking at him now; she only had eyes for Yuki.

"You shouldn't be here," Tamani whispered.

Laurel arched one eyebrow in response. "I wanted to see for myself."

Tamani clenched his teeth. In truth, he *did* want her there, but his own selfish desires were at odds with his concern for her safety. Would he *ever* be able to satisfy both?

"I thought you were going after David," Tamani said to Chelsea, who was still in her deep-red formal. She'd ditched her heels somewhere, so the bottom of the dress pooled at her feet like blood.

"I couldn't find him," Chelsea said, her lip quivering almost imperceptibly. She looked at Laurel, who was still studying their silent prisoner.

"Yuki?" Laurel said tentatively. "Are you okay?"

Yuki looked up, glaring at Laurel with steel and fury. "Do I look okay to you? I've been abducted! I'm handcuffed to a metal chair! How would *you* be?"

The Winter faerie's venomous tone seemed to hit Laurel like a breaking wave and she took a step backward. "I came to check on you." Laurel glanced at Tamani, but Tamani wasn't sure what she wanted. Encouragement? Permission? He offered her a pained grimace and a tiny, helpless shrug.

Laurel turned back to Yuki, the Winter faerie's expression unreadable, her chin held high. "What does Klea want from me?" Laurel asked.

Tamani didn't expect her to answer, but Yuki met Laurel's gaze and simply said, "Nothing."

"Then why did you come?"

Yuki smiled now, a crooked, mischievous smile. "I didn't say she *never* wanted anything. But she doesn't need you anymore."

Laurel's eyes darted to Tamani, then to Shar, before returning to Yuki.

"Laurel, listen," Yuki said, her voice quiet, comforting. "This whole charade is completely unnecessary. I'll talk to you if you just get me out of here."

"That's enough," Tamani said.

"Step in here and shut me up," Yuki said, glaring at Tamani before turning back to Laurel. "I've never done anything to hurt you and you *know* I could have. I could have killed you a million times, but I didn't. Doesn't that count for anything?"

Tamani opened his mouth, but Laurel laid a hand on his chest, silencing him. "You're right. But you're a Winter faerie. You hid that, even though you had to know about us. Why?"

"Why do you think? The moment your soldier friends found out what I was, they cut off my power and chained me to a chair!"

Tamani hated that she was right.

"Okay, well, maybe we just need to start over," Laurel said. "If we can figure this out before Klea shows up, even better. If you could just tell us—"

"Tamani has the keys," Yuki said, looking over at him, malice gleaming in her eyes. "Let me out of here, and I'll tell you *whatever* you want to know."

"No deal," Tamani said, doing his best to sound bored.

Laurel spoke to Yuki again, cutting them off. "It's probably safest for everyone if—"

"No!" Yuki shouted. "I can't believe you're even a part of this! After what they did to you? To your parents?"

Tamani frowned; what did Laurel's parents have to do with anything?

But Laurel was already shaking her head. "Yuki, I don't like that they made me forget. But I can't change the past—"

"Forget? I'm not talking about memory elixirs. What about the *poison*?"

"Oh, come on—" Tamani blurted.

Laurel shushed him. "Yuki, do you know who poisoned my father?"

Tamani was pretty certain of the answer, and he knew Laurel was too—it had to have been Klea. But if Laurel could convince Yuki to confirm their suspicions . . .

"Your father?" Yuki looked confused. "Why would they poison your father? I'm talking about your *mother*."

Again Laurel looked at Tamani, and he shook his head with a tiny shrug. What was Yuki playing at?

"You don't even know, do you? Big coincidence that the couple who *happened* to own the land around the gate just *happened* to be childless—waiting for a little blond baby to pop into their lives. How . . . convenient. Wouldn't you say?"

"That's enough," Tamani said sharply. He should have guessed—more games. Yuki was just looking for ways to get them doubting themselves—and each other.

"They did that," Yuki said. "Fifteen years before you even showed up on their doorstep, the faeries made sure your mother was baby-hungry enough to take you without question. They damaged her, Laurel. Made sure she could never have her own children. They ruined her life and you're siding with them."

"Don't listen to her, Laurel. It's not true," Tamani said. "She's just trying to get into your head."

"Am I? Why don't we ask *him*?"

8

TWO

LAUREL FOLLOWED YUKI'S EYES TO SHAR, WHO
stood as still as a statue, his face betraying nothing.

It couldn't be true. It *couldn't*. Not Shar, who had been her
unseen guardian since she first left Avalon.

So why isn't he denying it?

"Tell her," Yuki said, straining against her chair. "Tell her
what *you* did to her *mother*."

Shar's mouth stayed closed.

"Shar," Laurel begged quietly. She wanted to hear him say
it wasn't true. *Needed* him to say it. "Please."

"It was necessary," Shar replied at last. "We didn't choose
them. They just lived there. The plan had to work, Laurel.
We had no choice."

"There's always a choice," Laurel whispered, her mouth
suddenly dry, her chin quivering with anger. Shar had poisoned her mother. Shar, who had been watching over her

even longer than Tamani, had *poisoned her mother.*

"I have a home and family to protect. And I will do whatever it takes to keep Avalon safe."

Laurel bristled. "You didn't have to—"

"Yes, I did," Shar said. "I have to do a lot of things I don't want to do, Laurel. Do you think I wanted to sabotage your human parents? Wanted to make *you* forget? I do as I'm told. It's why I watched you every day, before Tamani came along. Why I know everything there is to know about you. The heirloom bowl you broke and lied about. The dog you buried outside your window, because you couldn't bear to have him farther away. The time you spent with Tamani, out at the cabin in October."

"Shar," Tamani said, his voice a clear warning.

"I gave you what space I could," Shar said quietly, his voice at last holding a hint of remorse. But the tiny apology was clearly extended to Tamani, not to Laurel; the sudden urge to stride across the room and slap Shar across the face was stifled only by her paralyzing rage.

Yuki's smile faded. "This is the force you've allied with, Laurel? I may not have always been truthful with you, but even I thought you were better than these monsters." She looked down at the salt encircling her chair. "A little swish of your foot and I can put a stop to this. I'll take you with me and show you how wrong Avalon is. And you can help me make it right."

Laurel stared at the salt. Part of her wanted to do it, just to lash out at Shar. "How do you know about Avalon?"

"Does it matter?" Yuki asked, her face unreadable.

"Maybe."

"Set me free. I'll give you the answers they've been keeping from you."

"Don't do it, Laurel," Tamani said softly. "I don't like it either, but letting her go doesn't make anything better."

"Do you think I don't know that?" Laurel snapped, but she couldn't tear her eyes away from the white circle at her feet.

Tamani drew back, silent.

Laurel wanted to kick the circle—she *did*. It was an irrational urge, one she knew she'd never act on, but hot tears pooled in her eyes as the desire burned in her throat.

"Laurel." A soft hand touched her arm, pulling her back to reality. She turned to a white-faced Chelsea. "Come with me. We'll talk it over, take a drive, whatever you need to cool down."

Laurel stared at her friend, focusing on the one person in the room who had never hurt her, never wronged her. She nodded, not looking at anyone else. "Let's go," she said. "I don't want to be here anymore."

Once they were outside, Chelsea closed the door then stopped. "Damn it," she cursed softly. "I put my keys down somewhere. Stupid dress with no pockets," she muttered, gathering the hem so she wouldn't trip on it. "I'll be right back."

She turned and the door opened before she could touch the knob.

"Keys," Chelsea explained as she pushed past Tamani.

He pulled the door shut, leaving the two of them alone on the porch. She fixed her gaze on the stairwell, suddenly unwilling to look at him.

But then, he wasn't meeting her eyes, either.

"I didn't know," Tamani whispered after a long pause. "I promise."

"I know," Laurel whispered. She put her back against the wall and slid down to the ground, hugging her knees. Her voice was flat even to her own ears. "My mom was an only child. Her dad left when she was a baby. It was just her and her mom. And then Grandma died too. Mom always wanted a big family. Five kids, she told me one day. She wanted five kids. But it never happened."

She didn't know why she was telling him this, but talking made her feel better somehow, so she kept going.

"They went to a ton of doctors and no one could figure out what was wrong. None of them. That basically cemented her mistrust of doctors. It also wiped out their savings for a long time. And it doesn't even matter, because Mom would have kept me even if she had other kids," Laurel said firmly. "I know she would have. Shar didn't have to do it at all."

She was silent for a while. "You know what *really* makes me mad?"

Tamani had the grace to shake his head silently.

"I have a secret now. I tell them everything. Everything. It hasn't been easy, but being open and honest has been the most wonderful part of my life the past year or so. Now, I have this—this *thing* that I can't tell them ever, because they would never look at me or faeries the same way." Her anger flared, white hot. "And I hate him for that," she whispered.

"I'm sorry," Tamani said. "I know how much they mean to you and . . . and I'm sorry they got hurt."

"Thank you," Laurel said.

Tamani looked down at his hands, an emotion sketched across his face that Laurel couldn't quite decipher. "I resent that I didn't know," he finally said. "There's so much I don't know. And I don't think Yuki is going to tell us anything. Half of what she says contradicts the other half. I thought maybe, once we had her trapped, we'd finally get the answers we've been looking for, but . . . if something doesn't happen soon . . . I'm not sure what Shar will do."

"Shar . . ." What was it he'd told her? *I will do whatever it takes to keep Avalon safe.* "He won't hurt her, will he? To get more information?"

"He can't. Even if he were so inclined, he can't enter the circle."

"There are things he could do without entering the circle," Laurel said. "He could—"

"I won't let him," Tamani countered firmly. "I promise. I'll watch out for her. Lies or not, she was my friend. Maybe she still is, I don't know. Besides, even Shar wouldn't risk the penalties he would face for . . . for torturing a Winter faerie."

Laurel wasn't sure she believed that.

"He's not a monster," Tamani continued. "He does what has to be done, but that doesn't mean he likes it. I understand you can't trust *him* right now, but please try to trust *me*."

Laurel nodded glumly. Like she had a choice?

"Thank you," he said.

"Can it really hold her, Tam? The circle?"

He was silent for a moment. "I think so."

"It's just salt," Laurel said quietly. "You were with me in the Winter Palace; you felt the power in those upper rooms. Containing that kind of magic with something that's currently sitting on my dining-room table doesn't seem possible."

"She walked into it of her own accord. Shar says that's where the power comes from." His eyelashes rose and his pale green eyes met hers. "Never underestimate the power of a situation you put yourself into."

She knew he was talking about more than just the salt circle.

After a moment of hesitation Tamani joined her on the ground, settling a comforting arm over her shoulders.

"I'm sorry for everything," he whispered, words weighted with regret. She turned her face and leaned in, wanting to lose herself in him, to forget everything else, just for a moment. Tamani exhaled shakily and brought his face close to hers. Laurel lifted her hand to his cheek and drew him forward the rest of the way. Their lips had scarcely touched when the door opened and Chelsea stormed out, keys jangling in her hand.

"Shar had them the whole time," she complained loudly. "He stood there and watched me look all over for them and then—" Her eyes zeroed in on Tamani's arm around Laurel's shoulders. "Oh, duh," Chelsea said, clearly realizing Shar's intent now. Then, softly, she added, "Sorry."

Laurel rolled down her window, letting the wind caress her face as Chelsea drove through the empty, darkened streets. For nearly half an hour Chelsea said nothing further about their short bout in the apartment or her ill-timed appearance, and Laurel appreciated the effort her friend must have put into keeping quiet. Silence certainly did not come naturally to Chelsea. She was probably dying to rehash their visit with Yuki, but all Laurel wanted to do was force it to the back of her mind and pretend it had never happened.

"Hey, is that . . ."

Chelsea was already pulling over when Laurel realized that the tall guy walking down the side of the road, silhouetted by the streetlight, was David. His eyes were wary as the headlights flashed across them, but recognition—and relief—dawned as Chelsea pulled her mother's car alongside him.

"Where were you?" Chelsea demanded when David crouched to peer through the passenger window. "I drove all over the place."

David studied the ground. "I stayed out of sight," he admitted. "I didn't want to be found."

Chelsea glanced over her shoulder in the direction he had been walking. Toward the apartment. "Where are you going?"

"Back," David growled. "To make things right."

"She's doing okay," Chelsea said, her eyes serious.

"But I put her in there."

"She's figured the circle out," Chelsea insisted. "It's not like it was. She's not hurting herself anymore. She just sits there. Well, sits and talks," she added.

But David was shaking his head. "I've been running away from my part in this and I'm done. I'm going back to make sure everything stays humane. Or, you know, whatever the plant equivalent is."

"Tamani said he would make sure she was safe," Laurel said.

"But his—and Shar's—definition of *safe* may not quite match up with mine. Ours." He looked between them. "*We* put her there. All of us. And I still think it was the right decision, but if it wasn't . . . I don't want to stand by and let it get worse."

"What are we supposed to do?" Laurel asked, not willing to admit that she didn't want to go back either.

"Maybe we can take shifts. One of us, one of them," David said.

Chelsea rolled her eyes.

"Someone would have to stay all night," Laurel said. "Which my parents would probably let me do, but—"

"Staying up all night isn't really your thing," David said, voicing Laurel's concern.

"I can text my mom," Chelsea offered. "I told her I'd probably spend the night at your house anyway—makes total sense after a big dance. And she never checks up on me."

Laurel and Chelsea both turned to look at David. "I'll think of something," he mumbled. "What about Ryan?"

"What about him?" Chelsea asked, finding something interesting to examine on the steering wheel.

"He's going to wonder why you keep running off at strange hours. You can't always use Laurel as an excuse."

"I don't think he'll notice," Chelsea said.

"You can't just assume that," David retorted. "Don't underestimate him. You *always* underestimate him."

"I do not!"

"Well, he's going to notice *something* if you suddenly start being 'busy' all the time. And he's going to want to spend time with you over the break. Especially after you ditched him almost every day last week to study for finals," David said.

"Somehow, I don't think that's going to happen," Chelsea said ruefully, leaning back against her seat and meeting his eyes at last.

David just shook his head. "I don't understand you. You were so worried about him when Yuki or Klea or whoever slipped him that memory elixir and now it's like you don't care at all." He kicked the dirt at his feet. "Why don't you just break up with him?"

"I did," Chelsea said quietly.

David's eyes darted from Chelsea to Laurel and back again. "You *what*?"

"How else was I supposed to justify running off in the

middle of the dance . . . with you," she added in a mumble.

"I was kidding!"

"I wasn't. I was going to do it anyway."

David looked to Laurel. "Did you know about this?"

Laurel glanced at Chelsea before nodding.

"Why?" David asked. "What went wrong?"

Chelsea opened her mouth, but no sound came out.

"It was just time," Laurel said, coming to the rescue. This wasn't something *anyone* needed to talk about yet. Certainly not right now.

David shrugged, his face a mask of nonchalance. "Whatever. We've got to get back there. It's going to be a long night."

THREE

"SO YOU JUST SIT HERE?" CHELSEA ASKED TAMANI, her voice cracking a bit as she tried to hide a yawn.

The apartment was dark and quiet. Shar had taken the opportunity to lean his head against the wall and was getting a little much-needed sleep. That left Tamani chatting quietly with Chelsea, who had insisted on taking the first shift.

"Pretty much," Tamani replied. "You can get some sleep if you want to; the carpet is soft. Sorry the furniture is so . . ."

"Nonexistent?" Chelsea offered, straightening up in the simple wooden chair that normally sat, unused, at the kitchen table. "It's okay, I'm really not that tired. Just kinda bored." She paused before leaning close to Tamani. "Doesn't she ever talk?"

"Yes, I *talk*," Yuki hissed before Tamani could respond. "It's not like you haven't heard me talk a million times before. Remember back in the day, when we went to school

19

together? I know *last week* must seem like ancient history now, but I thought you humans could at least remember back that far."

Chelsea was still with her mouth agape before snapping it shut and muttering, "Well, sooor-ry!"

"Don't feel sorry for me," Yuki said, fidgeting in her seat. "I'm stuck here for a couple days at worst. You're stuck for the rest of your life."

"What do you mean?" Chelsea asked, turning more fully toward Yuki.

"Don't listen to her," Tamani warned. "She just likes to get under your skin."

"Chelsea Harrison," Yuki continued, ignoring Tamani. "The perpetual third wheel. Always so close to what you desperately want, but never quite there."

"Really," Tamani said, shifting to place himself between Chelsea and Yuki. "She has nothing to say that you want to hear." He couldn't help but feel protective. The human girl had wormed her way into his good graces the last few months and he didn't want her to be hurt by whatever was going to come out of Yuki's mouth next.

"You really think you can compete?"

But Chelsea's curiosity was almost as infamous as her honesty and she leaned forward so she could see Yuki again. "Compete with *who*?"

"Laurel, of course. Fact of the matter is, she doesn't have to choose David—which she will," Yuki added, doubtless for Tamani's benefit. "But even if she doesn't, you still lose.

Let's say everything happens like you dream. Laurel leaves David behind, and one day he turns around and realizes, for the first time ever, that you've been standing there the whole time, just waiting to be noticed."

Chelsea's face flushed red, but her eyes never left Yuki's.

"Suddenly you're everything he never knew he always wanted. He adores you and—unlike your flaky boyfriend—is willing to go to college anywhere you want."

"Who told y—"

"You go to Harvard, you move in together, maybe you even get married. But," she said, leaning forward as far as she could, "Laurel will always be there in the back of his mind. All the adventures they had, the plans they made. She's prettier than you, more magical than you, just plain *better* than you. Face it, you have no hope of ever being *anything* but a rebound. And you'll have to live your life knowing that if it had been up to David, he would never have even gotten a chance to be with you. Laurel wins."

Chelsea's breathing was ragged. She stood, avoiding Tamani's eyes. "I . . . I think I need some water."

Tamani watched her disappear into the kitchen, just out of sight. He heard the tap start to run—and run. And run some more, much longer than necessary to fill a cup. After a full minute he stood and shot a glare at Yuki, who looked smug.

Shar lifted his head at the sound of Tamani's footsteps. But Tamani waved a *Be right back* sign at him.

Keeping Yuki in the corner of his eye, Tamani followed Chelsea to the kitchen, where she stood, facing away from

21

him, arms braced on the sink. There was no cup in sight.

"You all right?" Tamani asked quietly, his voice just louder than the hiss of the faucet.

Chelsea's head jerked up. "Yeah, I . . ." She gestured aimlessly. "I couldn't find a glass."

Tamani opened a cupboard right in front of her and retrieved one, handing it to her wordlessly. She filled it under the flowing water and started to reach for the tap to turn it off, but Tamani stopped her. "Leave it on. Less likely she can hear us."

Chelsea looked down at the running water—probably fighting the urge to not waste it—then nodded and withdrew her hand. Tamani stepped a little closer, half an eye still on Yuki's blossom, barely visible around the corner.

"She's wrong," he said simply. "She makes everything she says sound true, but it's twisted until it's not really truth at all."

"No, it's absolutely true," Chelsea said with surprising confidence. "Laurel is so much more than I will ever be. I hadn't thought about how her effect on David could linger like that. But it will. Yuki's right."

"You can't think that way. Laurel is very different from you, but you, you're amazing all by yourself," Tamani said, surprising himself by how much he meant it. He hesitated, then grinned. "You're funnier than Laurel."

"Oh, good," Chelsea said dryly. "I'm sure a couple of well-timed jokes'll win David's heart over to me forever."

"That's not what I mean," Tamani said. "Listen, seriously,

you can't compare yourself to a faerie. We're plants. Our perfect symmetry is something you humans value for some reason. So on the outside, yeah, she's going to look different from you. But that doesn't make her better, and honestly, except for maybe in the beginning, I don't think that's what David saw in her."

"So she's better on the inside, too?" Chelsea muttered.

Now she's being deliberately knot-headed. "No, listen, I just want you to understand what makes Yuki so wrong. In Avalon, everyone has the same kind of symmetry Laurel and I have. We do have a range of . . . beauty, I guess, but there's nothing special about Laurel's appearance. She even has a friend at the Academy who is practically her mirror image. If David somehow met Katya, or some faerie more beautiful than her, do you think he'd stop loving Laurel?"

"I gotta say, you're really bad at this," Chelsea grumbled.

"Sorry." Tamani grimaced. "I didn't mean to imply that he would never stop—"

Chelsea interrupted him with a small, pitiable sound. "It's okay, I know what you're trying to say. Really, the last thing you need to be doing is trying to convince people that Laurel's nothing special. I don't believe it; you don't believe it. And considering the fact that you stealing her away is my only hope for any chance with David in the future, I hope you never do."

"No, that's not it at all." He paused, thinking. "Laurel was gone for a long time, Chelsea. And even though she always had my love, I've looked at other girls in the past."

He couldn't help but feel a little silly, making the confession. "There was one really beautiful faerie who I . . . danced with a couple times, at festivals. I haven't seen her in years, but I have to tell you, since being able to really be with Laurel—to get to know her all over again—I haven't thought of that faerie once. Seriously," he added with a grin when Chelsea raised her eyebrows. "I barely remembered her enough to bring her up. I love Laurel, so she *becomes* the most beautiful faerie in the world to me, and no one else can compare."

"Yes, I think we've established that Laurel is awesome," Chelsea drawled. "I think so too. That's kind of the problem."

"No, I . . . Forget Laurel for a minute. Just listen to what I'm *saying*. I don't know if David will ever love you. But if he does, if he *really* does, it won't matter how pretty or exciting someone else might be. If he really loves you, you can't possibly lose. Because he won't see anyone as even remotely comparable to you."

Chelsea looked up at him with her big gray eyes—eyes that begged for his words to be true. "Would you forget about Laurel, if you fell in love with me?"

Tamani sighed. "Sure, if it were possible for me to love anyone but her. I don't think it is, though."

"How does she resist you?" Chelsea asked, but her smile was back.

Tamani shrugged. "I wish I knew. How does David resist *you*?"

She laughed, for real this time, dissipating the tension that had filled the small kitchen.

"I wish you success with him," Tamani said, serious now.

"How altruistic of you," Chelsea replied, rolling her eyes.

"No, really," Tamani said, laying a hand on her arm and leaving it there until she looked up at him. "My own hopes aside, I know what it feels like to pine for someone. I know the pain it can bring." He paused before whispering, "I wish us both success." As they walked out of the kitchen together, he offered her a grin. "And the fact that the one depends on the other, well, chalk it up to a happy accident."

FOUR

THOUGH LAUREL'S EYES WERE OPEN WHEN HER alarm rang, its shrill buzz still made her jump as it cut through the early morning half light. December 22. Normally this was a day she would spend helping her parents in their stores, or putting up last-minute decorations, listening to Christmas music, maybe making some holiday treats. She suspected this year wouldn't be nearly so festive.

The sky was still murky as Laurel opened her closet and reached for one of her faerie-made shirts—it seemed fitting today, when she was truly fulfilling her role as an agent of Avalon. As she slipped the pink peasant top over her head, it felt more like armor than simple, gauzy fabric.

Just outside the front door, Laurel was met by a green-clothed sentry she didn't recognize—there were just so many of them now!—looking very much like he wanted to stop her. "Sun's coming up," Laurel said, without waiting to hear

26

what he had to say. "And I'm going to Tamani's. You can check up on me in about five minutes. Now move."

To her surprise, he did.

She glanced at the house as she was backing down the driveway, eyes lighting on her parents' darkened window. She still hadn't told them what was going on, but that couldn't last much longer. "It's almost over," she said, hoping she was right.

After a short drive Laurel knocked on the apartment door and waited for someone to let her in, bracing herself for the possibility of Shar answering. Not that it mattered; Shar was here somewhere, and she would have to face him eventually. But later was better than now and Laurel was relieved when Tamani's face appeared behind the door.

"Everything go okay?" Laurel asked as she ducked in, keeping her voice low.

"If by *okay* you mean *uneventful*, then yes," Tamani replied, looking down at her with a warmth in his eyes that she hadn't seen since they captured Yuki. She wondered what Tamani and Chelsea had talked about and if there was any way to request they talk about it more often.

"I guess that's *okay*," Laurel replied, dropping her backpack on the floor. But she knew they were all hoping something *would* happen. It had now been almost eight hours since they'd first captured Yuki. It felt too long—and Klea did not have a reputation for tardiness.

Chelsea was sitting in a chair near Tamani, looking tired— still in her rumpled dress—but sporting a smile. Tamani had

27

lost his bowtie, shoes, and jacket—though because of Yuki, not his gloves—and his shirt was unbuttoned halfway down his chest. The two of them looked like they had been at an all-night party rather than sentry duty.

The sound of running water reached her ears and Laurel realized Shar must be taking a shower. Six months ago such mundane, human-like behavior from the captain might have made her smile. Instead, every moment she spent eyeing the door to Tamani's room ratcheted up the tension in her neck and shoulders. How could she face him again, knowing what he had done to her mother?

"I'll stay with you when he comes out," Tamani said, his breath tickling her ear. She hadn't even noticed he'd stepped so close.

Laurel shook her head. "You need sleep too."

"I dozed here and there. Trust me," he said, his fingers soft on her shoulders, "I'm fine."

"Okay," Laurel whispered, feeling inordinately better that he would be with her.

They both turned as Shar emerged from the bedroom, his hair still damp. He paused when he saw Laurel but met her gaze evenly before she lost her nerve and looked down at the floor.

"Anything happen in the past five minutes?" Shar asked, placing his hands on his hips as he stepped into the front room of the apartment.

"Not a thing," Tamani said, mirroring Shar's posture. Laurel suppressed a smile at how reflexively—and likely unconsciously—Tamani emulated his mentor.

Shar turned and looked at Yuki with a strangely neutral expression. Laurel wasn't sure how to read him at all. At times he seemed practically emotionless. She knew there was more to him than that—Tamani had told her stories, stories that made the both of them laugh to tears. But the faerie now observing his prisoner—so focused, so unaffected— made her question how anyone could get close to him.

"How much longer do we wait?" Tamani asked. "I'm starting to wonder if we were right the first time; that Yuki is nothing more than a distraction and Klea is letting her sit while she does . . . whatever it is she's planning to do."

"Unless Klea's plans threaten the gate, or Laurel, they are of no concern to us. We have Laurel under constant guard, and to truly threaten the gate, Klea needs *her*," Shar said, pointing—almost accusingly—at Yuki. "So until she comes to retrieve Yuki, we can assume the gate is safe. As safe as it ever is," he amended. "Our place is here, doing just what we're doing now."

"Do you think we should tell Jamison?" Laurel asked.

"No," Tamani and Shar said in unison.

Yuki looked up at them with a strange, focused expression.

"Why?" Laurel insisted. "It seems like he, of all fae, should know."

"Come with me," Shar said, turning back toward the apartment's lone bedroom. "Watch the Bender for a few minutes, please, Tam."

Laurel's throat tightened. She felt the soft fabric of Tamani's glove as his hand slipped into hers.

"I'll come stand in the doorway if it'll make you feel better," he whispered.

But Laurel shook her head, swallowing her anger as best she could. "I'm okay," she said, willing it to be true. "He's still the same Shar he's always been, right?"

Tamani nodded and squeezed her hand before letting it slide from his fingers.

"I'm going to go," Chelsea said wearily, before Laurel could follow Shar.

"Thanks," Laurel said, hugging her friend. "The house is unlocked." One bonus of having so many sentries surrounding her house was that Laurel never bothered to lock her doors anymore. "Try not to wake my parents. Trust me; you don't want to have to explain all this to them." She swallowed. The inevitable explanation would be *her* task, soon enough.

Chelsea nodded, stifled a yawn, and headed out the front door; Tamani bolted and chained it behind her.

Laurel walked into Tamani's bedroom, not bothering to flip on the light. The sun was halfway over the horizon now, casting a purplish glow through the curtainless window. It illuminated a sparse room where a single wooden chair draped with various articles of clothing sat beside a double bed with a mussed blanket on it. Laurel stared; it was Tamani's bed. It was strange to think that this was the first time she had seen it. The first time she had been in his room at all.

"Please close the door."

Laurel did, meeting Tamani's eyes for an instant before the door shut between them.

"We can't tell the other sentries what we've learned about Yuki, and we *cannot* go to Jamison," Shar said. He stood with his face close to hers, his arms crossed over his chest and his voice barely loud enough for her to hear. "For several reasons, but the main one is that we can't risk going anywhere near the gate. The only thing standing between Yuki and Avalon is that she does not know its exact location. As soon as she does, everything is over."

"But Klea worked with Barnes. She *must* have. She's got to know where the land is already."

"Doesn't matter," Shar said brusquely. "Short of cutting down that entire forest, the only hope she and Yuki have of accessing the gate is if they know its *precise* location and how it's disguised."

"But we could send someone. Aaron, or Silve, or—"

"And if they're followed? That could be the reason Klea has waited this long to rescue her protégée. She could be waiting for us to go for help."

"And what if she never shows up?" Laurel snapped. "We can't keep Yuki chained to that chair forever, Shar!"

Shar drew back.

"Sorry," Laurel muttered. She hadn't meant to speak so sharply.

"No, it's fine," Shar said, sounding bemused. "You're right. But it may not matter. As far as I'm concerned, the only way this ends well is if we keep Yuki as far from the gate as possible."

"So we just sit around?"

"We've come to a fork in the branch. Right now, all we have is one Winter faerie and a lot of strong suspicions. Say we go to Avalon. Assuming Klea doesn't know where the gate is, we might lead her to it. If she does know, she may have set traps along our path. Either way, we stand to lose a lot more than we stand to gain. And even if we make it to Avalon safely, what then? How will you feel if Queen Marion orders us to execute Yuki?"

Laurel swallowed.

"Believe it or not, that's probably the *best* we could hope for," Shar said grimly. "Our other choice is to wait here," he continued. "The circle will hold as long as it's unbroken, but make no mistake, it is a fragile thing. One misstep and Yuki is unleashed on us all. The only way to guarantee our safety is to put a knife in Yuki right now."

"What? No!" Laurel couldn't keep the panic from her voice.

"You're starting to see the problem," Shar said, his voice just a touch softer. "Yuki is clearly dangerous, but I don't think she's done anything worthy of death. Not yet, anyway. But no matter what we do, at some point it will almost certainly come down to us, or her. The only hope I have is that Klea does need Yuki, and that she will come to rescue her. And if we can just last long enough—if we can find some way to neutralize Klea *here*—"

"Then we confirm our suspicions, the gate stays safe, and nobody has to die," Laurel finished in a near monotone. She didn't like it, but she didn't have any better ideas. They were only three faeries and two humans trying to stand against Klea and whatever forces she had at her disposal. What would they face? A dozen trolls? A hundred? More faeries?

"Do you understand now?"

Laurel nodded, half wishing she didn't. She had to grudgingly admit that Shar's plan was, in all likelihood, the best one. For now. Without a word, she turned and left the room, Shar close behind.

"So . . . how does this work?" she asked, surveying the apartment and trying her best not to look directly at Yuki.

"We just sit. Or stand. Whatever you want," Tamani said. "Shar and I watch the door and the windows. I try to ask her questions, but that generally goes nowhere." He shrugged, the gesture seeming to be directed at Shar more than Laurel. "It's pretty boring, to tell the truth."

Yuki snorted, but none of them acknowledged her.

An electronic *ding!* sounded from Tamani's bedroom, followed by a murmured exclamation from Shar.

"Beastly, frost-blighted—"

Laurel smirked; Shar detested cell phones, and every time one went off, he swore at it. Quite creatively, most of the time. His dark mutterings were swallowed by the bedroom as he went to retrieve his "human trinket" from where he had almost certainly accidently-misplaced-it-on-purpose.

A knock sounded at the door and Tamani sprang to his

feet. "Chelsea probably forgot her keys again."

Shar stepped out of the bedroom carrying his phone. "It says Silve's name. What does 'text two' mean?"

Tamani pressed his eye to the peephole.

"It means you have two messages—" Laurel began.

But Shar's wide eyes were fixed on the back window of the apartment. "Don't!" he shouted, turning back to Tamani.

With a crack of gunfire, the door exploded.

FIVE

THE BLAST THREW TAMANI TO THE FLOOR AND shattered the security chain with a metallic zing. As Laurel spun from the stinging spray of debris, she saw the back of the apartment burst apart. Window glass and drywall skittered across the floor as the most massive troll Laurel had ever seen came crashing through—a lower troll, like the one she'd seen chained in Barnes's hideout. The misshapen, pale monstrosity thrashed about in an attempt to dislodge Aaron, who clung to the knives he'd embedded in its shoulders. The struggling pair rolled further into the kitchen, disappearing from sight.

As she turned back to Tamani, Laurel was horrified to see a bouquet of roses arcing through the air from the front door, shedding crimson petals like drops of blood as it floated almost leisurely toward Yuki's prison. The instant stretched to eternity as Laurel realized that in about half a second the roses were going to breach the salt circle, Yuki was going to be free, and if Shar was to be believed, there was a good chance she would kill them all.

A diamond-bladed knife cut through the air, pinning the paper-wrapped bouquet to the wall not an arm's length from the salt barrier that was keeping them all alive. Shar was already pulling another blade from a sheath at his waist as Yuki screamed in frustration and Laurel turned to the wrecked front door and the figure framed in it.

"Callista!" Shar exclaimed as Klea raised her face into the light.

A shadow of recognition passed over Klea's face and she looked at Shar, though her guns were pointed squarely at Tamani and Laurel. "Captain! Serendipitous."

"I watched you die fifty years ago," Shar said, disbelief heavy in his words. And then, "You're *Klea*."

"Shar!" Aaron stumbled in from the kitchen, flecked with debris and covered in troll blood. His left arm hung limp at his side. "There's more on the way; we tried to hold them back—"

Horror froze his features as his eyes lit on Yuki's rumpled blossom. "Goddess of Earth and Sky. Is that—?"

But the troll lunged at him from behind, and the two went crashing through another wall.

"I *told* you to cut that damn thing off," Klea snapped at Yuki. The gun in Klea's hand shook—almost certainly with anger rather than fear—but Laurel didn't dare move. "Now look what you've gotten yourself into."

Klea raised a defensive hand as Shar whipped another knife through the air. The blade knocked away one of her guns with a clang, but she turned the other at Shar and fired. Its sharp retort echoed in Laurel's ears and Shar staggered back, clutching his shoulder and slumping against the wall.

Seizing the moment, Tamani sprang at Klea, but she sidestepped his lunge and caught his wrist in her free hand, flipping him in the air and slamming him to the floor.

"Tam!" Shar's voice was strained as he struggled to stand.

But Tamani was already back on his feet, a long silver knife in his hand; Laurel hadn't even seen him draw it. Klea lunged at him with liquid speed, her movements so graceful they might have been a dance. She wove through Tamani's swipes untouched, then whipped the butt of her pistol across his face, leaving a ragged gash along his cheek. She landed another blow against his wrist and Tamani's knife seemed to leap into her hand as if of its own volition.

Tamani retreated two steps, evading most of Klea's jabs, but with nothing to parry her blows his shirt was soon a mess of ribbons, wet with sap from the shallow cuts accumulating on his arms and chest.

As Laurel looked for an opportunity to dive for Klea's dropped gun, something at the corner of her vision fluttered on ruby wings. With a sick twisting in her core she realized a petal had fallen from the skewered bouquet—drifting like a feather, its circuitous route was a ballet of twists and twirls in the breeze that wafted through the apartment. In moments it would enter the circle and then, under Yuki's power, the soft, innocent bit of flower would become a deadly weapon.

And Laurel was too far away—she'd never reach it in time.

"Shar!" she called, but he was between Klea and Tamani, wielding a chair as an improvised shield.

"Get her out of here!" Shar shouted, a kick from Klea twisting the chair from his grip. *"Now!"*

The world spun before Laurel's eyes as Tamani's arm clenched around her waist—rolling her straight to the destroyed wall—and then they were falling. A scream escaped her lips but was cut off as they hit the ground and the air was pushed out of her chest. They tumbled together along the ground and when they came to a stop, for a moment it was all Laurel could do to look up breathlessly at the hole Aaron's troll had made in the wall, ten feet above them.

"Come on," Tamani said, pulling Laurel to her feet before her head had completely stopped spinning. She followed him almost blindly, her hand tight in his as he wound around the back of the apartment building.

They paused when the squeal of splintering wood filled the air, accompanied by a sudden rush of wind. "Circle's broken," Tamani growled. The sound continued as they rounded the corner of the building, where Tamani immediately back-stepped, flattening Laurel against the wall. "It's crawling with trolls out front," he whispered, his mouth so close to her ear his lips brushed her skin. "We can't get to my car; we're going to have to run. You ready?"

Laurel nodded, the sound of snarling trolls reaching her ears over the deafening storm of splintering wood. Tamani gripped her hand tighter and pulled her along with him. She tried to look back, but Tamani stopped her with a finger on her chin and pointed her gaze forward again. "Don't," he said softly, sprinting across the open ground, slowing only slightly once they reached the relative safety of the trees.

"Will Shar be all right?" Laurel asked, her voice shaking as they ran through woods. Tamani was loping ungracefully, helping her along with one hand, the other clutched at his side.

"He'll handle Klea," said Tamani. "We need to get *you* to safety."

"Why did he call her Callista?" Laurel asked through heaving breaths. Nothing that had happened in the last few minutes made any sense to her.

"That's the name he knew her by," Tamani answered. "Callista's practically a legend among sentries. She was an Academy-trained Mixer. Exiled before you even sprouted. She was supposed to have died in a fire. On Shar's watch, back in Japan."

"But she faked it?"

"Apparently. Must have done a good job, too. Shar was thorough."

"What was she exiled for?" Laurel gasped.

Tamani's words were shaky as he picked his way through the trees and Laurel struggled to catch them. "Shar once told me she experimented with unnatural magic, faerie poisons . . . botanical weapons, basically."

Hadn't Katya told her, two summers ago, about a faerie

39

who had taken things too far? It must be her—Laurel's stomach knotted at the thought of an Academy-trained Mixer who created poisons so evil she'd been exiled for it. Klea was scary enough *without* magic.

They ran silently for a few minutes, finally finding the faint path Laurel knew Tamani must have taken a hundred times over the last few months.

"Are you sure he'll be okay?" Laurel asked.

Tamani hesitated. "Shar is . . . a master Enticer. Like the Pied Piper I told you about a few weeks ago. He can control humans from a distance, and his control is far greater than most Ticers. Way better than mine," he added quietly. "He—he can use them. To help him fight her."

"So he's going to . . . control them?" Laurel asked, not quite understanding.

"Let's just say that fighting Shar in a building full of humans is a very, very bad idea."

Sacrifices, Laurel realized. *Human barriers to lie in Klea's path, or soldiers attacking against their will.* She swallowed and tried not to dwell on that, concentrating on not tripping as Tamani continued to run almost too fast for her to keep up.

Soon she started recognizing the trees—they were nearing the back of her house. As he ran into the yard Tamani let out a high-pitched, warbling whistle. Aaron's second-in-command, a tall, dark-skinned faerie named Silve, came bursting from the tree line.

"Tam, they're everywhere!"

"That's not the worst of it," Tamani replied, gasping for air.

Laurel stopped, resting her hands on her knees and trying to catch her breath as Tamani explained the situation—with sputtering protests from Silve at the details Tamani and Shar had kept secret.

"There's no time for explanations," Tamani said, cutting Silve off. "Shar needs backup and he needs it *now*." The two sentries took only a few precious seconds to outline a plan for dividing forces, and Silve sprang into the tree shouting orders.

Tamani put a protective hand at Laurel's waist and guided her to the back door, his gaze returning to the trees the whole way.

Laurel's mom was in the kitchen, a light cotton robe tied loosely at her waist, concern in her eyes. "Laurel? Where have you been? And what . . . ?" She gestured wordlessly at Tamani's wet, torn shirt.

"Is Chelsea here?" Laurel asked, avoiding her mom's question. For the moment.

"I don't know. I thought you were in bed." Her eyes flitted to Tamani and his pained expression made her face go white. "Trolls again?" she whispered.

"I'll go check for Chelsea," Laurel said, pushing Tamani onto a barstool as gently as she could manage.

She hurried up the stairs and cracked open her bedroom door just wide enough to see Chelsea's unmistakable curly hair spilling across the pillow. She pulled the door shut and heaved a sigh, relief washing over her, melting her down onto the carpet.

She looked up at the sound of footsteps, but it was just her dad stumbling blearily down the hall. "Laurel, what's the matter? Are you okay?"

The avalanche of events that had buried her life in less than twenty-four hours forced her to blink back tears. "No," she whispered. "No, I'm not."

SIX

LIKE WATER SEEPING THROUGH A DAM, FIRST AS A trickle, then a torrent, Laurel found herself stumbling over her words as she explained everything to her parents, including the events of the past week that she'd been avoiding telling them. The words came more slowly as she wound down, explaining how Klea had attacked and that Shar was still in danger, and then at last she was done, feeling purged and empty—except for the smoldering memory of the one thing she could never let her parents find out.

"I . . . I didn't know how to tell you earlier," she finished.

"A Winter faerie?" her dad asked.

Laurel nodded.

"The kind who can pretty much do anything?"

She rubbed her eyes. "You have no idea."

Laurel's mom glanced up at Tamani, who had remained silent through Laurel's explanation. "Is my daughter in danger?"

"I don't know," Tamani admitted. "Despite being a Winter faerie, I don't think Yuki is a threat to Laurel personally. Klea, however, is another story. She does things that aren't even remotely legal in Avalon, and we still don't know what her end goal is."

"It's a shame we couldn't have just hit Klea on the head and dragged her away when she was here at our house last month," Laurel's dad said, only half joking.

"Do we need to take you somewhere, Laurel?" her mom asked.

"What do you mean?"

"Would you be safer if we took you and went away? We can be gone in an hour." She was on her feet, staring down at Laurel with an expression of such fierce protectiveness that Laurel wanted to laugh and cry at the same time.

"I can't leave," Laurel said softly. "This is my responsibility. If Klea was going to hurt me, she's had plenty of opportunities. I don't think that's what she wants from me."

"What *does* she want from you?"

Laurel shrugged. "The land, probably. The gate to Avalon. Like Tamani said, we just don't know."

"And we won't know much of anything else until Shar comes back," Tamani added.

Laurel noticed his tightly clenched fists and laid a hand on his arm. "He'll come back," she said softly, hoping she sounded more certain than she felt.

"You know," Tamani said quietly, not looking at her, "maybe your mother's right. We've done everything we can here. Jamison asked us to find the root of the troll problem. Klea brought trolls to rescue Yuki. I think that's proof enough that the root is her, so, mission accomplished. The rest is really up to Aaron and Shar, but if they aren't . . . successful . . ." Tamani paused, and Laurel could almost see him imagining the worst. "Maybe you *should* leave."

Laurel was already shaking her head. "With all the sentries in the woods, there's *nowhere* safer than right here." She turned to her mother. "I know you want to protect me. But I have a job to do and there are thousands of faeries in Avalon who are depending on me to keep their world safe. If Shar and Aaron can't stop Klea—if there's anything I can do, I have to be here to do it. I can't run away from that. I just . . ."

Laurel's mom was smiling at her, eyes shining with unshed tears.

Laurel shrugged helplessly. "I just want to help."

"We're not going to talk you out of this, are we?" her dad asked.

She shook her head, afraid her voice would quaver and inspire her dad to try just that.

"Maybe you two should go without Laurel," Tamani suggested. "I don't think Klea has any interest in you, but at least then Laurel would know you were safe."

Laurel's mom looked over at her. "If Laurel is staying, so are we."

Tamani nodded.

Her dad stood and sighed. "I'm gonna go shower. Clear

my head. Then we can make a plan."

"I have to call David," Laurel said, reaching for the phone as her dad tromped up the stairs.

"Why does David always have to be involved?" Tamani muttered, already starting to pace.

"Because he thinks he has a shift coming up," Laurel said pointedly, dialing David's number as Tamani pulled out his cell.

"He has an iPhone?" her mom whispered as the second ring sounded in Laurel's ear.

Laurel nodded. "I was saving that little tidbit for ammunition the next time we discussed *me* getting a cell."

Her mom was silent for several seconds as Laurel listened to David's voice-mail message. "Do they get . . . service? In Avalon?" she asked.

Laurel shrugged and left a brief message for David to call her when he woke up. She considered calling his home phone, but didn't want to wake his mom. After all, it was barely seven in the morning. She would have to wait.

Just like everyone else.

Tamani's hand lingered in his pocket and he walked back and forth across the kitchen floor until Laurel thought she might scream.

"Would you like a cup of tea, Tamani?" her mom finally said, with a tiny edge in her voice. Pacing was not a popular habit in the Sewell household. "Or perhaps you want to . . . clean up a bit?"

"Clean . . . ?" Tamani said, looking a little dazed. He

peered down at his tattered shirt and the scratches on his arms that were no longer oozing but remained shiny with sap. "That's probably a good idea," he said haltingly.

"Maybe something to eat, too?" Laurel suggested. "Considering this turn of events, I suspect even green stuff is back on the menu," she added, forcing a laugh. Tamani had been avoiding his favorite foods to keep from coloring his eyes and hair roots, but Laurel assumed it wouldn't matter anymore. She supposed, in retrospect, that it had never really mattered—Yuki had always known what he was.

Tamani nodded jerkily. "Yeah. Thanks. Broccoli, if you have it."

"I'll go up and find you a T-shirt," Laurel's mom said, turning to follow in her husband's footsteps.

"Thank you," Tamani whispered, though his eyes were on his cell phone again. Laurel could feel him willing it to ring.

Numbly Laurel grabbed a knife to chop up the stalk of broccoli she'd fished from the refrigerator.

Tamani turned his head slightly, listening to Laurel's mom's footsteps as she climbed the stairs and went into her bedroom. Then he seemed to melt onto the barstool, running his hands through his hair with a soft groan.

Laurel loaded several florets onto a plate and handed it to him, but he took the plate with one hand and her hand with the other, his gaze so intense it took her breath away. He slowly transferred the glass plate to the counter and pulled her close.

Laurel curled herself against his chest, grasping at what was left of his shirt. His hands were in her hair, then around her waist, his fingers pressing almost painfully against her back.

"I honestly thought that might be the end," he whispered in her ear, his voice gravelly. When his lips fell on her neck, her cheeks, and dotted her eyelids, she didn't pull away. Even when his mouth found hers, frantic and delving, she returned the kiss with the same fire and passion. It wasn't until that moment—feeling the desperation fueling his kiss—that she realized just how narrowly they'd cheated death. Not since he'd been shot by Barnes had Laurel seen Tamani lose a fight like that, and she clung to him, trembling with relief from a fear she hadn't even known she was feeling.

Laurel's fingers brushed the cut on Tamani's cheek, pulling back at his soft gasp of pain against her lips. But he didn't jerk away. If anything, he drew her closer. She wished there was more time; time to lose herself in his kisses, to forget that Shar was out there, somewhere, fighting for all their lives.

He finally lifted his mouth, his forehead pressed against hers. "Thank you," he said softly. "I . . . I just needed you for a moment."

Laurel twined her fingers through his. "I think I needed you, too."

Tamani met her eyes and stroked her face with his thumb. The desperation was gone now, and he was all softness and calm. His mouth brushed hers tentatively, as his hands had so often done. Laurel leaned forward, wanting more. Wanting to *show* him that she wanted more. She stopped listening for her mother's footsteps, for a sign of Chelsea coming out of her room, for anything but the soft purr of Tamani's breath on her cheek.

Only when the jangle of the phone sounded close to her ear did the world snap back into focus. It rang again as she tried to catch her breath. "That'll be David," she whispered.

Tamani stroked her bottom lip with his thumb, then let his hand drop and turned to his plate of broccoli as Laurel picked up the handset.

"Laurel!" David said, his voice bleary. "You're home. Did you oversleep? Do I need to get over there and cover for you?" She could hear him fumbling around, probably pulling on jeans and a T-shirt, ready to rush in and save the day.

"No. No, it's worse than that," Laurel said quietly. All rustling on David's end came to a halt as she explained what had happened.

"I'm coming over."

"I think there are enough stressed people in this house," Laurel argued.

"Well, I can't just sit around here and wait. I . . . I'll feel better if I'm over there, just in case. Is that okay?"

Laurel suppressed a sigh. She knew exactly how he felt and, if their positions were reversed, she would want the same thing. "Okay," she said. "But just let yourself in. Don't knock or ring or whatever. Chelsea's still sleeping and she really needs it."

"I won't. And Laurel? Thanks."

Laurel hung up and turned to face Tamani. "He's coming over."

Tamani nodded, swallowing a mouthful of veggies. "I figured as much."

"Who's coming over?" Laurel's mom asked from halfway down the stairs.

"David."

Laurel's mom sighed in half amusement as she tossed a clean gray T-shirt to Tamani. "I have to say, I don't know what that boy tells his mother."

SEVEN

TAMANI GRITTED HIS TEETH AS HE GINGERLY PULLED THE new—and rather too big—shirt over the binding strips Laurel had spent the last ten minutes applying. David had arrived and Laurel was sitting with him on the couch, filling him in on the morning attack. Tamani blocked out her voice; he was already replaying the events in his mind, looking for some way he could have been more prepared, more effective.

Especially against Klea.

He hadn't lost a round of hand-to-hand combat to anyone but Shar in years. To lose to a human-trained Mixer hurt almost as badly as the wounds she had left on him—and those stung plenty.

Laurel's parents had offered to stay home from work, but Tamani insisted it was better for everyone if they went to their stores and pretended it was a regular day. Before Laurel could even suggest it, Tamani had ordered half a dozen sentries to

51

tail each parent, just in case. The grateful look in her eyes had been a welcome bonus.

"So what now?"

Tamani looked over and realized David was talking to him.

"We're waiting to hear from Shar," Tamani grumbled. "Silve took a whole company of sentries back to the apartment to help with the trolls. They should sound the all-clear any time."

"And . . ." David hesitated. "If they don't?"

That was what Tamani had been fretting about for an hour. "I don't know." What he wanted to say was that he'd take Laurel somewhere no one could find her—not even David—and stay there until he knew she was safe. Last resort for any *Fear-gleidhidh*. But Laurel had already decided she wasn't going to run and Tamani probably shouldn't warn her that they might be running whether she liked it or not.

"I don't like the sound of that," said David.

"Yeah, well, neither do I," Tamani said, frustration heavy in his voice. "We're not exactly safe here, either, it's just safer than anywhere else at the moment." *But for how long?* He crossed his arms over his chest and looked down at David. "Would *you* like to leave?"

David just gave him a dark look.

Tamani's phone began vibrating in his hand. He looked down at the screen to see a blue box heralding the arrival of a text message.

From . . . Shar?

klea took yuki and ran. i followed.

Then the phone buzzed again—a picture this time. He'd been expecting to hear from Shar—perhaps *hoping* was a better word—but even though he'd been clinging to his phone since they'd arrived at Laurel's house, the person he'd assumed would call was Aaron. Maybe Silve. Shar had never managed to use the phone before; generally he refused to even try. Tamani slid a finger across the screen once, twice, three times before it recognized his touch and unlocked. He squinted at the minuscule picture for a second before tapping it to make it bigger.

Not that it helped.

He was looking at a log cabin with a white, tentlike structure sprawling out the back. There were two slightly grainy figures near the front door.

"What is it?" Laurel asked.

He beckoned her forward. "It's from Shar."

"Shar?" The disbelief in Laurel's voice was as heavy as it was in Tamani's mind. "He *texted* you?"

Tamani nodded, studying the picture. "He said Klea got away with Yuki. He followed them here." He slid his fingers over the screen, zooming in on the two figures, wanting to be sure before voicing his suspicions. "Those two guards," he said slowly, "I don't think they're human."

"Trolls?" David asked, still sitting on the couch.

"Fae," Tamani said, not looking up from the screen. "They don't seem to be trying to hide it either. This must be . . . I don't know. Klea's headquarters?"

"Should you call him?" Laurel suggested, but Tamani was already shaking his head.

"No way. If that's where he is, I can't risk giving him away."

"Can't your phone, like, find his with GPS or something?"

"Yeah, but I don't know that it matters. There's no text with this picture and for now I have to assume that means I should do nothing." He shoved his hands back into his pockets—one still clenched around his phone—and began pacing again.

The phone buzzed almost immediately. Another picture.

"What are they?" Laurel asked, squeezing in beside him to squint at the tall, green stalks.

Tamani's stomach twisted with a sick churning. It had taken the Gardener's son in him less than a second to recognize the distinct plant specimen. "They're sprouts," he said hoarsely.

"Sprou— Oh!" Laurel said, sucking in a breath.

"The plants faeries are born out of?" David asked, rising from the couch to look over Tamani's shoulder.

Tamani nodded numbly.

"But there are dozens of them!" Laurel said. Then, after a pause, "Why are so many of them chopped down?"

But Tamani could only shake his head as he glared at the picture, trying to understand Shar's message. Everything about this was wrong. He was no Gardener, but the condition of the growing sprouts was appalling even to the untrained eye. The plants were too close together, and most of the stalks were too short in comparison to the size of the bulb. They were malnourished at best and probably permanently damaged.

But it was the cut-off stalks that bothered him the most. The only reason to cut a stalk was to harvest it early. Tamani's mom had done so once in her career, to save a dying baby fae, but Tamani couldn't imagine Klea's motives were so maternal. And he had no idea why she would do it to so many. She had to be *using* them. And not for companionship.

His gruesome speculation was cut off by another picture, this one of a metal rack filled with green vials. There was no spark of recognition this time and Tamani tilted the screen toward Laurel. "Do you recognize this serum?"

Laurel shook her head. "About half of all serums are green. It could be anything."

"Maybe it—" His question was cut off by the phone buzzing again. Not a text this time; a call. Tamani sucked in a breath and held the phone up to his ear. "Shar?" he said, wondering if he sounded as desperate as he felt.

Laurel looked up at him, worry, concern, and hope twining together in her gaze.

"Shar?" he said, more quietly now.

"Tam, I need your help," Shar whispered. "I need you to . . ." His voice trailed off, and shuffling noises were loud against Tamani's ear as it sounded like Shar set the phone down.

"Don't move, or this whole shelf goes over." Shar's voice came through clearly, but with a slight echo. *Speakerphone,*

Tamani realized. He felt a laugh bubble up in his throat and had to bite his lip firmly to tamp it down. Shar had figured out his phone enough to use it when it counted.

Klea's voice—more hollow, but crisp enough to understand—came through next. "Honestly, Captain, is this really necessary? You've already blown my schedule all to hell by knocking out poor Yuki."

Knocked out a Winter? Tamani thought, both proud and incredulous. *Wonder how he pulled that off.*

"I saw you burn," Shar said, his voice simmering. "The blaze was so hot, no one could get near it for three days."

"Who doesn't love a good fire?" she said, her tone mocking.

"I made them test the ashes. Academy confirmed a Fall faerie died in that fire."

"How diligent of you! But that's why I left my blossom behind. I don't think it would have fooled them if it hadn't been fresh."

Laurel laid a hand on Tamani's arm. "Is it—"

Tamani shushed her gently and pulled the phone away from his face, hitting his own speakerphone button, then muting the microphone just in case.

"Where did you find Yuki?" Shar's voice said clearly.

"Find? Oh, Captain, all it takes is a single seed, if you know what you're doing. Work was slow when I had to rely on cuttings, but in the past few decades humans have made remarkable strides in cloning. I quickly discovered that every sprout has its own destiny, no matter its lineage. So it was only a matter of time before I got a Winter."

"Where did you get the seed, then?"

"I really shouldn't tell you," Klea said, "but it's just too good to keep to myself. I stole it from the Unseelie."

"*You're* Unseelie, in case you've forgotten."

"Don't lump me in with those wild-eyed zealots," she snapped. "I never did find out where the Unseelie got the seed, not that it matters. One of them even saw me take it as I made my escape. Oh, she was so angry," Klea said in a low whisper. "But then, I think you're familiar with her, Shar de Misha."

Tamani closed his eyes, knowing how his friend must be feeling to discover the secret his mother had kept from him—the secret that might have saved so many lives. There was a long pause before Shar responded. "You have a pretty big stack of these vials here. The least you can do is tell me what I'm about to die for. You owe me that."

"The only thing you're owed is a bullet in the head."

"So I should dump these, then," Shar said. "You're going to kill me anyway."

As Shar baited Klea, his voice seemed to blare, filling the room with his careful prompts. Tamani could feel Laurel trying to catch his eye but now was not the time for one of their silent conversations. He forced himself to focus on the phone resting on the palm of his hand and did his best to breathe evenly.

Klea hesitated. "Fine. Don't think it will spare you. They took me a long time to make and I'd prefer not to waste them, but this is only the final batch. Most of it has already been used."

"Is this how you make the trolls immune to our poisons?"

"In Avalon, you treat the ill. Here, humans have learned to prevent illnesses before they happen. This is basically the same thing. An inoculation of sorts. So yes, it makes them immune."

"Immune to faerie magic, you mean. Fall magic."

Tamani hadn't heard the word *inoculation* before, but its meaning was sickeningly clear. Klea was making an entire horde of trolls immune to Fall magic. All their troubles over the last few years—the dart that hadn't worked on Barnes two years ago; Laurel's serum that had knocked out four trolls in the lighthouse, but not Barnes; the caesafum globe that had no effect on the trolls after the Autumn Hop only a few short months ago; the tracking serums that stopped working. It was all Klea's doing.

"That upper troll," Shar said, catching on as quickly as Tamani had.

"Oh, yes. You remember Barnes. He was my guinea pig, way back when. That didn't pan out so well and he decided to turn on me. But I find it terribly soothing to have a contingency plan or two in place. Don't you?"

A forced laugh from Shar. "I could do with one of those about now myself."

"Well said!" Klea chirruped in a tone that made Tamani want to smash the phone. "But we both know you haven't got one. You're either stalling because you're afraid to die—which is dreadfully unbecoming—or you think you're going to miraculously get this information back to Avalon before I invade, which isn't going to happen. So if you'd be so kind as to step out here where I can kill you—"

"What do you think you're going to do?" Shar interrupted, and Tamani forced himself to focus on Shar's words instead of the terrifying images running through his head of what was about to happen to his best friend. "Torture Laurel until she tells you where the gate is? She won't. She's stronger than you think."

"What the hell do I need Laurel for? I know where the gate is. Yuki plucked that tidbit out of Laurel's head almost a week ago."

Startled, Laurel looked up, her eyes pools of shock, but comprehension dawned on her face as Tamani made his own connections. *Those headaches.* The terrible one after the troll attack—when her mind would have been vulnerable and possibly turned to Avalon. Yuki's phone call from Klea, the glittering look in her eyes—that must have been Klea's plan the whole time, her motivation for sending trolls after them that night. And in addition to the smaller ones, Laurel had mentioned another massive headache in front of her locker, the last day of school—had even voiced concerns that Yuki might be the cause. But Tamani had dismissed it because they were about to capture her anyway. No wonder Klea had been so furious when Yuki insisted on staying for the dance—she'd completed her mission. She really had stayed out of misguided affection for Tamani.

Tamani closed his eyes and forced himself to breathe deeply, evenly. Now was not the time to lose control.

"Then I just have one last request." Tamani's eyes flew open. There was something in Shar's voice he didn't like. An edge.

"Tell Ari and Len I love them," Shar said, coming through with increased clarity despite the quaver in his voice. "More than anything."

Icy fear filled Tamani's chest. "No." The barely audible plea slipped through Tamani's lips.

"That's very sweet, but I'm not running a messaging service, Shar."

"I know, it's just . . . ironic."

"Ironic? I don't see how."

An incredible clattering sounded in the background, like a hundred crystal goblets shattering against the floor, and Laurel clapped a hand over her mouth.

"Let's ask Tamani," Shar said, and Tamani's head jerked up at the sound of his own name. "He's the language expert. Tamani, isn't this what humans call irony? Because I never expected my last minutes in life would be spent figuring out how to use this damned phone."

"No!" Tamani yelled. "Shar!" He gripped the phone, helpless. The unmistakable blast of gunfire filled his ears and his stomach lurched as he slumped to his knees. Four shots. Five. Seven. Nine. Then silence as the phone went dead.

"Tam?" Laurel's voice was barely a whisper, her hands reaching for him.

He couldn't move, couldn't breathe, couldn't do anything but kneel silently, his hand wrapped around his phone, his eyes begging the screen to light again, for Shar's name to pop back up on the display, for his biting laugh to sound through the speakers as he tried to convince Tamani that the joke had actually been funny.

But he knew it wasn't going to happen.

Despite his shaking hands, Tamani managed to slide the phone back into his pocket as he stood. "It's time," he said, surprised at how steady his voice sounded. "Let's go."

"Go?" Laurel said. She looked as shaky as Tamani felt. "Go where?"

Yes, where? When they were hunting trolls, Shar had lectured him about sticking to his role as Laurel's *Fear-gleidhidh*. Should he take Laurel and run away? His head spun as he tried to decide what was *right*. But the sound of the gunshots—the mental picture of bullets ripping into Shar—it was blocking out everything else.

Tell Ari and Len I love them.

Ariana and Lenore were in Avalon. Those weren't simply tender last words; they were instructions.

Tamani had received his final orders from Shar.

"To the gate," he said. "To Jamison. Shar didn't have to tell Klea we were on the phone, but he did. You heard Klea—she was done with us. Shar made us a target again, to divide her attention and throw her off balance. He bought

61

us the time we need to warn Avalon, so that's what we do." The pieces were coming together in his mind. "Now!" he added, already pulling his keys out of his pocket.

He headed for the front door, but David stepped in front of him. "Whoa, whoa, whoa," David said, putting up his hands. "Let's wait for just a second here."

"Move," Tamani said darkly.

"Avalon? Now? I don't think that's a good idea."

"No one asked you." Of course he would pick *now* to fight over this.

David's eyes softened, but Tamani refused to acknowledge it. He didn't want pity from a human. "Listen, man," David said, "you just heard your best friend get mowed down. I barely knew him and *I'm* feeling pretty sick right now. Don't make any rash decisions so soon after . . . after what just happened."

"What just happened? You mean Shar getting *murdered*?" The words were salt on his tongue and he tried not to let David know how much it ripped him apart to even say them. "Do you have any idea how many of my friends I've watched die?" Tamani demanded, even as he pushed the memories away. "This is hardly a first. And you know what I did? Every single time?"

David shook his head, a convulsive shiver.

"I picked up my weapon—hell, sometimes I picked up *their* weapons—and I kept doing my job until it was done. It's what I do. Now I'm going to say it one more time: get out of my way!"

David stepped hesitantly back, but stayed close by his side, wedging a foot in front of the door as Tamani reached it. "Then let me come with you," he said. "I'll drive. You can sit in the backseat and think for a while. Decide if this is really the right choice. And if you change your mind . . ." He spread his arms in a shrug.

"Oh, so *now* you're the hero? Now that Laurel's here to see you?" Tamani said, feeling the grip he had on his temper begin to slip. "Last night you *left*. You ran away instead of doing what needed to be done with Yuki. I've been doing what needs to be done for *eight years*, David. And I haven't failed or run away yet. If there's one person who can keep Laurel safe, it's *me*—not you!"

When had he started yelling?

"What's going on?" A groggy voice made them all turn to the stairs, where Chelsea stood, her T-shirt wrinkled, the wild curls around her face a halo of darkness.

"Chelsea." Laurel pushed between David and Tamani, her arms steady and strong, forcing them both to take a step back. "It's Shar. Klea . . . Klea got him. We have to go to Avalon. Right now."

Tamani couldn't help but feel a sliver of pride that Laurel had sided with him.

"You can go back to sleep, or home, or whatever you want. I'll call you the minute we get back."

"No," Chelsea said, the weariness in her voice gone. "If David's going, I'm going too."

"David is *not* going!" Tamani insisted.

63

"I just . . . I don't want you guys to get hurt," Laurel said, and Tamani could hear the strain in her voice.

"Come on," Chelsea pleaded softly. "We've been through everything with you. We do it together. That's been our motto for months."

The last thing Tamani wanted was more passengers, and time wasn't a luxury they had. He opened his mouth to declare exactly who was and was not coming, but the expression on Laurel's face stopped him. She had her car keys in her hand and was giving them a strange look.

"Tamani, my car is back at your apartment. And so is yours."

Tamani felt the fight drain from him like rain off maple leaves, leaving only the jagged sharpness of grief.

David had the good sense to not smile.

"Fine!" Tamani said, crossing his arms over his chest. "But they won't let you through the gate, and in a couple hours, tops, those woods will be crawling with trolls and faeries and *I won't be there to protect you*." He gave Chelsea a look that begged her to stay. Stay where it was safe.

Saf*er*.

Where at least there were sentries to watch over her. But as he met her determined gaze, he knew she wouldn't.

"I guess that's a chance we're going to have to take," she said calmly.

"My car's in the driveway," David offered, pulling his keys out of his pocket.

Tamani lowered his chin. With the exception of Laurel,

and possibly his mother, he didn't think there was anyone in the whole world he loved as much as Shar. Even having Laurel here, looking up at him with empathy, couldn't lighten the weight he felt pressing down on him. She moved closer, but he turned his face away; if he looked into her beautiful eyes one second longer, he was going to crack and lose it entirely. Instead he stood stoically and nodded, blinking a couple times.

"Okay. We have to move, though. Now."

EIGHT

"WAIT," LAUREL SAID AS DAVID STARTED THE engine. "I have to call my mom." She went to open the car door, but Tamani stopped her with a hand on her thigh.

"Use this," he said, handing her his cell.

It felt morbid to touch the phone, but Laurel braced herself and reached out to take it. She dialed the shop and silently begged for her mom to pick up.

"Nature's Cure!" her mom said. Just the familiar sound of her mother's voice made her want to cry.

"Mom," Laurel said, realizing she didn't even know what to say.

"We're busy helping customers right now, but if you leave a message we'll call you right back."

Laurel's throat tightened. Just the machine. She waited for the beep and took a deep breath. "H-hi, Mom," Laurel said, clearing her throat as her voice cracked. "We . . . we're leaving. We're going to Avalon," Laurel said quickly, glad her mother was the only person at the store who had the voice-mail password. "Shar—Shar got caught, and we have to go tell Jamison."

She wasn't sure what else to say; hated that it was a recording. "I'll be back as soon as I can. I love you," Laurel whispered before jabbing her finger against the End Call button. She stared down at the phone in her hand for a long moment, knowing that if she looked anywhere else or tried to speak, she would start to cry. She hoped, prayed, that those weren't the last words her parents would hear from her.

Tamani reached out his hand.

After a shuddering breath Laurel returned the phone to him. He flipped through his contact list and put the phone to his ear.

"Aaron. Shar is dead. Klea has Yuki and an army of trolls. They're immune to Fall magic and they know where the gate is. I'm taking Laurel to Avalon. When you've finished cleaning up at the apartment, I suggest you gather everyone who isn't watching Laurel's parents and head to the land. You'll probably end up nipping at Klea's heels. Goddess protect you."

Every word came out evenly, tonelessly. But when Tamani ended the call, he turned the phone off and dropped it on the seat as though it had burned him. Laurel wondered if he would ever pick it up again.

Two final messages—one a heartfelt good-bye, one a seemingly calm business call, despite its devastating message.

Laurel shuddered. It would almost have been better if Tamani had shouted, raged. But he was hiding everything, even from her, as he sat, his head pressed against the window. She felt helpless.

About five miles outside Crescent City, though, he ran one hand down Laurel's arm and laced his fingers through hers, pulling her very subtly closer. His eyes remained fixed on the scenery outside his window, but his tight grip was sign enough that he needed an anchor. She found herself strangely proud to be the one he finally reached for. Even if her fingers were starting to ache.

No one said anything for most of the trip, at least in part because Chelsea had gone back to sleep, curled awkwardly in the semi-reclined passenger seat. It was probably good she hadn't heard Shar's call; no doubt sleep wouldn't come easily if she had. Eventually, a rough stretch of asphalt jostled her awake, and she unbuckled her seat belt so she could turn around and talk to Laurel and Tamani.

"So, um, when we get there, what do we do?" Her eyes dropped briefly to Laurel and Tamani's joined hands, but she said nothing.

Tamani turned from the window for the first time, his face—even his eyes—calm. "We go to the gate, we explain our urgency, request entrance, and if we're lucky, they let us in. And by *us*, I mean Laurel and me. No human has set foot in Avalon in over a thousand years."

"We want to help," David said. "You don't think they'll let us?"

Tamani's hand slid out of Laurel's as he leaned forward. "We've been over this," he said, not unkindly. "Your help is not the kind they're going to want. I suggest you drop us off and drive away as quickly as possible. Go south—not back to Laurel's house. The sentries there will protect your parents," he said, turning briefly to Laurel, "but the last thing they need is more people to confuse everything. Go to Eureka, or McKinleyville." He hesitated. "Go . . . Christmas shopping or something."

"The mall the week before Christmas. Sounds awesome," Chelsea drawled.

"Go eat pie in Orick, then. Point is, don't go back to Crescent City, preferably until tomorrow or the next day."

"How are we supposed to explain *that* to our parents?" David asked.

"Maybe you should have thought about that before you insisted on coming," Tamani said, his tone somehow sharper without gaining the slightest bit of volume.

David just shook his head. "We're on the same side, man."

Tamani looked down and Laurel heard him take a few sharp, shallow breaths before raising his head and saying, more calmly now, "Even if they let you in, you'll probably be in Avalon for at least that long. Trust me, you'll have plenty of time to decide what to say to your mother."

"I'm going to tell *my* mom that David and Laurel tried to elope," Chelsea deadpanned. "I only came along to try and talk them out of it. She'll forgive just about anything if she thinks I'm protecting Laurel's virtue."

Laurel realized her mouth was hanging open and she slapped Chelsea on the shoulder.

"I've been saving that one for an emergency," Chelsea said proudly to no one in particular, facing front and putting her seat belt back on as David turned off the main road.

The sight of the cabin, nestled among the mighty redwoods, sent a fresh wave of sadness through Laurel. The last time she'd been here was with Tamani, and it had been one of the most wonderful days of her life. Even now, the memory sent shivers through her body. Life suddenly seemed so fragile and uncertain; she wondered if she and Tamani would ever have another day like that. And, Laurel realized, she desperately *wanted* one. She looked over at him; his gaze was fixed on the cabin as well. Then he turned and their eyes met, and she knew they were both thinking the same thing.

"Where should I park the car?" David asked. "They'll see it when they come."

"If they arrive before you're gone, it'll be too late to worry," Tamani said, breaking his stare. "May as well leave it right here."

They started walking toward the forest when Tamani stopped them, his face deadly serious. "David, Chelsea, as I said before, there have only been the barest handful of humans admitted into Avalon. But those who have . . . sometimes, they don't come back. If you come with us into the forest, I don't know what will happen. And I don't know what would be worse—if they turn you away at the gate, with no time to get back to your car, or if they were to actually let you in."

He held David's gaze for a long time before David nodded once. Then he turned his eyes to Chelsea.

"I can't stay here," she said softly. "I would hate myself for the rest of my life."

"Fair enough," Tamani said, almost under his breath. "Then let's go."

Tamani led the way down the serpentine path, moving through the forest with such confidence and determination that Laurel and her friends almost had to run to keep up. Laurel knew there had to be sentries marking their progress, and around every corner she expected them to appear, as they had often done when she'd entered the forest with Tamani. But the woods remained eerily still.

"Are we too late?" Laurel whispered.

Tamani shook his head. "We're with humans," he said simply.

When they at last came into sight of the ancient ring of trees surrounding the gate, a sentry finally showed his face, popping up practically in front of Tamani and placing one hand on his chest. Tamani stopped with such grace, an onlooker might have thought he had intended to stop at that exact spot all along.

"You're on dangerous ground, bringing them so close, Tam," the sentry said.

"I will be treading more dangerous ground when I ask permission to bring them into Avalon," Tamani said flatly.

Shock splayed across the other sentry's face. "You—you can't! It's not done!"

"Step aside," Tamani said. "I don't have time."

"You cannot do this," the sentry said, refusing to move. "Until Shar returns, we can't even—"

"Shar is dead," Tamani said, and a hush of reverence seemed to ripple through the trees. After waiting a few seconds—perhaps to let the news sink in, perhaps to gather his own courage—Tamani continued. "As second-in-command of this assignment, his authority falls to me, at least until the Council meets. Now I say again, step aside."

The sentry shrank back and Tamani strode forward, his chin held high. "Sentries, my . . ." His voice faltered ever so slightly. "My first twelve to the front." Those words were Shar's words, the beginning of a ritual that would transform a gnarled old tree into a shining golden gate. Words Laurel had heard often enough to know their significance.

Eleven sentries joined the one that had stopped their progress, and Chelsea gasped softly as they formed a semicircle in front of the tree. They were quite a sight; all wore armor that had been meticulously camouflaged, and most carried dark-shafted spears with diamond tips. Several had hair tinged green at the roots, as Tamani and Shar used to wear. Out of their element, they would probably look quaint—perhaps even silly. But here in the forest, Laurel found it impossible to think of them as anything but mighty guardians.

As each sentry approached to place one hand on the twisted old tree, Laurel realized her friends were seeing it for the first time, and remembered her own first time witnessing the transformation. How different things were now. Then, Tamani had been shot and Shar had summoned Jamison to save his friend's life. Now, Shar was dead, and Tamani was trying to save . . . everyone.

The familiar low, melodic hum filled the forest as the tree shook, the light of the clearing gathering around its misshapen branches, giving it an ethereal glow. The tree appeared to split in two, molding itself into some semblance of an archway. Then came the final flash, so bright the clearing seemed to burn, and they were standing in front of the beautiful golden portal that barred the gateway to Avalon.

Laurel sneaked a glance over her shoulder. Chelsea seemed ready to explode with glee. David just stood there, his mouth slightly agape.

"Now I need to contact—"

Tamani stopped, looking puzzled. The blackness behind the bars of the gate began to resolve into shapes, and soon Laurel saw an old, withered hand curl around the bars, slowly pulling the gate open. Jamison stood there, his face lined with concern. Laurel wasn't sure she had ever seen such a welcome sight. It was all she could do not to leap forward and throw her arms around him.

But why was he already at the gate?

"Laurel, Tam!" He beckoned. "Please, come closer."

The sentries closed ranks behind them as Laurel, Tamani, David, and Chelsea all approached the gate. Jamison did not move from his spot in the middle of the gateway—was he going to turn them away?

"I received a most distressing message from the Manor,"

said Jamison. "Is it true that Shar has left us?"

Tamani nodded silently.

"I'm very sorry," Jamison intoned, laying a hand on Tamani's arm. "It is a devastating loss."

"He died to protect Avalon," Tamani replied, only the barest hint of mourning in his tone.

"From him, I would expect no less," Jamison said, straightening, "but the Manor only passed along a message sent by Aaron, who gave no details except to say that I should meet you here. I appreciate his discretion; we don't want to throw anyone into a panic. But now it falls to you to fill in the details so we can make sure our good captain's sacrifice was not in vain."

"The Wildling," Tamani began. "She's a *Winter* faerie raised by Klea." Jamison's eyes widened as Tamani continued. "She was sent to pull the location of the gate from Laurel's head—which she was able to do last week."

Guilt surged through Laurel as she watched concern deepen the lines on Jamison's face.

"It's not her fault," Tamani added. "We discovered Yuki's caste too late to prevent it."

"No, of course," Jamison said, smiling sadly at Laurel. "Not your fault at all."

"As we suspected, Klea is the Fall faerie who poisoned Laurel's father." He hesitated. "She is also the exile Callista."

"Callista," Jamison said, surprise on his face, then a look of regret. "That is a name I had not imagined I would hear again in this life."

"I'm afraid that's not the worst of it."

Jamison shook his head, looking decidedly weary.

"Klea—Callista—has been creating serums that make trolls immune to Fall magic. That's why we've had so much trouble tracking and fighting them. She apparently has an army of these trolls and"—he took a deep breath—"they will be here soon. Likely within the hour."

For a long moment, Jamison did not respond—he seemed scarcely even to breathe. Laurel wished he would say something, anything. Then his expression changed and he looked at Laurel with a strange light glowing in his eyes.

"Who are your friends?" Jamison asked abruptly, taking a small step forward. "Please, introduce me."

"David and Chelsea," Laurel said, confused, "this is Jamison."

Chelsea and David each offered their hands—Chelsea, breathlessly—and Jamison held onto David's for several seconds. "David," Jamison said pensively. "That is the name of a great king in human mythology, is it not?"

"Um, yes . . . sir," David said.

"Interesting. A Winter faerie, immune trolls, and possibly the most talented Fall faerie in Avalon's history are arrayed against us," Jamison said, his voice scarcely above a whisper. "Not in more than a millennium has Avalon been so threatened. And here are two humans who have already proven their loyalty." He glanced over his shoulder, off into Avalon. "Perhaps it is destined."

NINE

"THE QUEEN WILL BE WITH US SOON," JAMISON
said as they passed through the shadows from the branches
that shaded the gateways. "Quickly, tell me more of what
has happened."

While Tamani caught Jamison up, David and Chelsea
took in their surroundings. The armored female sentries that
made up the gate guard kept their distance, as did Jamison's
Am Fear-faire, but they were all standing at attention around
the gateway, looking quite splendid. Chelsea stared openly
and with undisguised wonder.

David's reaction was more reserved. He looked at everything from the trees lining paths of soft black soil to the
sentries eyeing the golden gates, with the same expression he
wore when reading a textbook or peering through a micro-
scope. Chelsea was delighting; David was *studying*.

When Tamani revealed that they'd taken Yuki prisoner,

Jamison stopped him with a tense hand on his arm. "What did Shar do to contain a Winter faerie?"

Tamani glanced nervously at Laurel. "We, uh, chained her to an iron chair, with iron handcuffs . . . inside a circle of salt, sir."

Jamison took a slow breath and glanced over his shoulder just as the great wooden doors to the garden swung open. Then he turned back and clapped Tamani on the shoulder, laughing loudly, but with obvious falseness. "Oh, my boy. Iron manacles. Surely you couldn't have believed that would work for long."

Queen Marion was making her way through the gate, surrounded by a passel of *Am Fear-faire*.

"It wasn't the chains that did it," Laurel corrected. "It was—"

"The iron chair was a nice touch. Still," Jamison said, with a hard look at the group, "I suppose you make do with what you have, in a situation like that. You are all lucky to have escaped with your lives," he finished, stepping back to greet the Queen.

Laurel didn't understand. Why did he want them to lie?

Without a word, Queen Marion raked Chelsea and David with her eyes, betraying only a touch of the shock that must have rippled through her. "You've brought humans through the gate?" she asked without greeting, and not only turned her back on them, but angled her shoulders so they were cut out of the circle, left to stand awkwardly on their own. Laurel flashed them an apologetic look.

"They were with Laurel and the captain, and their situation was so dire I felt I had no choice," Jamison said as though he had noticed neither the Queen's icy tone nor her blatant snub.

"There is always a choice, Jamison. Show them out," she added.

"Of course; as soon as possible," Jamison said, but he made no move to do as she asked. "Where is Yasmine?"

"I left her outside. You spoke of a threat to the crown," Marion said. "Surely you don't think the child should be exposed to such things."

"I think she is nowhere near a child anymore. Nor has she been for quite some time," Jamison said softly.

The Queen raised her eyebrows. "It matters not," she continued after a brief pause. "What is this supposed emergency?"

Jamison deferred to Laurel and Tamani and, with a show of great reluctance, the Queen turned to listen as Tamani gave a much-abbreviated version of the events of the past few days, skipping the circle of salt with only the barest glance at Jamison.

"We expect that Klea—or Callista, as she was known here—will arrive with her entire force within the next hour. Maybe less. With her ability to conceal gathering places, we have no way to know their numbers, but based on the vials Shar . . ."

Tamani's voice caught, and Laurel suppressed the urge to reach out a comforting hand. Now was not the time—but the pain in his voice as he spoke his mentor's name made her want to weep.

"Based on the shelf full of serum and Klea's claim that it was the last of many batches, there—" He paused. "There could be thousands."

The Queen was silent for a few moments, two perfectly symmetrical thought lines creasing her brow. Then she turned and called, "Captain?"

A young female faerie in full armor stepped forward and bowed low.

"Send runners," the Queen instructed. "Summon all the commanders and mobilize the active sentries."

Laurel took advantage of the Queen's momentary distraction to lean close to Tamani and whisper, "Why wouldn't Jamison listen to you about the circle?"

Tamani shook his head. "There are some things even Jamison cannot pardon."

Laurel's chest tightened as she wondered just what kind of punishment could provoke Jamison to encourage them to lie to his monarch.

"Shall we prepare for a military council then, Your Majesty?" Jamison asked as the young captain turned and began issuing orders.

"Goodness, no," Marion said, her tone light. "With a few instructions, the captains should manage on their own. We're leaving."

"Leaving?" Tamani said, clearly shocked. Laurel had rarely seen him speak so boldly in Avalon, and never in the presence of a Winter faerie.

Marion fixed him with a withering stare. "Leaving the Garden," she amended, before turning to Jamison. "You, Yasmine, and I will retreat to the Winter Palace and defend it while the Spring fae do their duty here at the gate." She turned to survey the milling sentries. "We will require some additional support, of course. Four companies should be sufficient to ensure our safety, along with our *Am Fear-faire* and—"

"We can't go," Jamison said firmly.

"We can't stay," Marion replied in an equally firm tone. "The Winter faeries always guard the palace and themselves in times of danger. Even the great Oberon stepped back to preserve himself when the battle raged its fiercest. Do you think yourself greater than he?"

"This is different," Jamison said calmly. "Trolls are already immune to Enticement; these trolls will be immune to Fall magic as well. If we leave the gate, our warriors will have *no* magic to counter their enemies' strength. There will be slaughter."

"Nonsense," Marion replied. "Even if the beasts have figured out how to evade tracking serums and some rudimentary defense potions, it's hardly the tragedy you're making it out to be. You there, tell me, how many trolls have you killed in your life?"

It took Tamani a moment to realize he was being addressed. "Ah, I don't know. Perhaps a hundred?"

A hundred? Laurel almost gasped at the number. So many?

But then, in almost ten years as a sentry outside Avalon, could she really be surprised? He had killed about ten just in her presence.

"And how many of those did you kill with the aid of Fall magic?" The Queen continued, not fazed by the number at all.

Tamani opened his mouth, but no words came out. Laurel realized there was no right answer; if the Queen found his reliance on Fall magic high, she would tell him he was incompetent—if it was low, she would use that to prove her point.

"Come, Captain, time is short and precision unnecessary. Would you guess half? A third?"

"About that, Your Majesty."

"You see, Jamison? Our sentries are quite capable of killing trolls without our assistance."

"And what of the two rogues?" Jamison asked.

"The Winter is untrained—aside from her power to open the gate, she is no threat at all. And the Fall is outnumbered, along with any others she might bring."

No threat?

"You always underestimated Callista," Jamison said before Laurel could speak up.

"And you always *over*estimated her. You were wrong then, and by the end of the day I expect you will discover that you are wrong now."

Jamison said nothing, and the Queen turned away from them; never in her life had Laurel felt so *dismissed*.

The Gate Garden became a hurricane of brightly colored uniforms as orders were given and messages sent. Jamison stood motionless until the Queen approached the gateway to Japan to let a messenger through. Then, at last, he frowned, and Laurel could almost see him gather his will.

"Come," he said quietly, turning his back to the flood of sentries. "Gather your friends. We have to get to the Winter Palace." His pale-blue robes flared out as he spun to face the far wall of the Garden.

"Jamison!" Laurel said, leaping after him, Tamani close by her side, David and Chelsea following with confusion written on their faces. "You can't honestly be doing what she said!"

"Quiet," Jamison whispered, pulling them a few steps away. "I beg you to trust me. Please."

Fear raced through Laurel, but she knew that if there was anyone in the world worthy of her trust it was Jamison. Tamani hesitated a moment longer, staring back at the California sentries now coming in through the gate, conferring with their peers. But when Laurel tugged on his fingertips, Tamani turned to follow the elderly Winter faerie.

"This way," Jamison said, indicating a tree with a barrel-shaped trunk and a wide berth of shading leaves. "Hurry! Before my *Am Fear-faire* realize I'm leaving."

Behind the tree they were out of sight of most of the Garden's occupants. Pausing only to take a deep, slow breath, Jamison placed his hands together, then swished them at the stone wall. The slim branches of the tree rose from beside

Laurel—one brushing her cheek as it passed—and vines snaked up from the ground to dig into the stones like spindly fingers, pulling them apart just far enough to create a small exit.

Once Laurel and her friends were through the wall, Jamison gestured again and the vines and branches retreated, returning the wall to its former pristine state. Jamison stood still for a moment, perhaps listening for some sign that they'd been spotted, but it appeared they had managed to get out without being seen. He pointed up to the Winter Palace and began the climb.

"Why are we sneaking out?" Chelsea whispered to Laurel as they scaled the steep hill after him. Without the benefit of the gentle, winding path that led out of the actual gate to the Garden, they were climbing almost straight up. It was a shortcut, but not an easy one.

"I don't know," Laurel answered, wondering the same thing. "But I trust Jamison."

"Once we find out what's going on, I'm returning to the Garden," Tamani said, his voice a low murmur. "I won't abandon my sentries."

"I know," Laurel whispered, wishing there was a way to convince him to stay somewhere safe.

On the long climb to the Winter Palace, Chelsea's eyes were practically popping from their sockets as she tried to take everything in. Laurel tried to imagine the scene through Chelsea's eyes, remembering her own first trip to Avalon—the crystalline bubbles far below them that housed the Summer faeries, the way the palace was held together by branches and vines, the footpaths paved with rich, dark earth.

Sooner than Laurel could have imagined, they reached the white archway at the top of the slope. Even Tamani was clutching his sides and sucking in deep, noisy breaths.

"Must continue," Jamison gasped after giving them only a brief moment to rest. "The strenuous part is behind us."

As they traversed the palace grounds, Chelsea eyed the broken statues and crumbling wall. "Don't they fix anything?" she whispered to Laurel.

"Sometimes retaining an item's natural power is more important than keeping up its outer appearance," Jamison said over his shoulder.

Chelsea's eyes widened—she had spoken so softly even Laurel had scarcely been able to hear her—but she said nothing more as they mounted the steps and pushed open the great front doors.

The palace was silent but for the footsteps of the small party; the white-uniformed staff were nowhere to be seen. Had they already received word of the attack? Laurel hoped they would be safe, wherever they had gone, but she had begun to wonder if "safe" was an option any of them had left.

Jamison was already climbing the enormous stairs that led to the upper rooms. "Please, follow me," he said, without looking back. He gave a small wave of his hands and the doors at the top swung slowly open. Even though she knew it was coming, the ripple of power that went through Laurel as she stepped through the gilded doors made her breath catch. Chelsea reached out and squeezed Laurel's arm, and Laurel knew her friend felt it too.

"We are not running away," Jamison said abruptly. "I suspect you are all wondering it."

Laurel felt a little guilty, but it was true.

"As soon as we have finished here, we will return and we will stand *together*. But this must be done first, and I alone can do it. Come."

At the end of the long silk carpet, they followed Jamison to the left and stood in front of a wall. But this wall, Laurel knew, could move—and it concealed a marble archway into a room with something Jamison had once called an *old problem*.

Jamison looked up at David, who had at least six inches on the wizened Winter faerie. "Tell me, David, what do you know of King Arthur?"

David looked over at Tamani, who nodded once. "He was the king of Camelot. He allied with you guys."

"That is true," Jamison said, clearly pleased David knew the fae version of the tale. "What else?"

"He was married to Guinevere—a Spring faerie—and when the trolls invaded Avalon, he fought alongside Merlin and Oberon."

"Indeed. But he was much more to us than a strong fighter with an army of brave knights. He brought to the Seelie Court one thing it could never furnish for itself: humanity."

Jamison turned and, with a wave of his arms, split the enormous stone wall down the middle. Vines slithered forth from the crack, curling around the faces of the rocks and dragging the two walls apart with a low rumble. "You see, in spite of his magician and his dealings with the fae, King Arthur was entirely human. And that was something we needed very badly."

As the walls parted, light streamed through a marble arch and into a stone chamber, illuminating a squat block of granite. Wedged into the granite was a sword that looked like it had been forged from solid diamond, its prismatic edges casting rainbows across the white marble chamber.

King Arthur, the blade of the sword wedged in stone.

"Excalibur!" Laurel whispered, understanding.

"Indeed," Jamison said, his voice low and hallowed. "Though it was called something else, in those days. But here it is, and here it has been, untouched since King Arthur himself drove it into this rock after his victory against the trolls."

"Untouched? But I saw you doing something with it when I was here last time," Laurel said.

"I was trying, as I have my entire life. I cannot seem to leave it alone," Jamison replied. "Excalibur is a unique combination of human and faerie magics, forged by Oberon and Merlin to seal the alliance with Camelot and ensure victory against the trolls. Its wielder is untouchable in combat and its blade will cut effortlessly through almost any target. But Oberon also sought to protect his people against a day when the sword might fall into the wrong hands: It cannot be used to harm fae. One could swing Excalibur at a faerie with all his might, and it would simply stop, a breath away."

"How?" David asked. "I mean, the momentum has to go somewhere, doesn't it?"

Trust David to bring science into it.

"Would that I could answer that," Jamison replied. "I cannot say whether Oberon intended to do precisely what he did, but I can assure you that the prohibition is absolute. No part of the sword can touch a faerie—and no faerie can touch any part of the sword. I cannot even manipulate it with my magic."

That's why you let David and Chelsea in, Laurel realized. Jamison's glance back into Avalon, his talk of destiny . . . he had shared last summer that the World Tree told him of a task he alone could perform. Only Jamison would be willing to place the fate of their land back in human hands, as it had been in Arthur's day.

"David Lawson," Jamison said, "Avalon needs your help. Not only are you human—with the ability to wield the sword—but I can sense your bravery, your strength, and especially, your loyalty. I know what you have done for Laurel in your world; standing by her when it meant risking your life. Even entering Avalon today took great courage. I suspect you have much in common with that young man Arthur, and I believe it is your destiny to save us all."

Chelsea was soaking up the scene with eager eyes.

Tamani looked horrified.

Laurel knew what Jamison was going to ask, and wanted to stop him, to tell David that he should refuse—that he didn't have to do this; that being around her had hurt him enough already. He didn't need to be a soldier for Avalon, too.

"David, with the name of kings," Jamison said formally, "it is time to discover if you are the hero Laurel has always thought you to be. Will you join us in defending Avalon?"

Laurel looked at Chelsea but knew instantly that there would be no help from her. Her gaze was fixed on the sword and she wore an expression not unlike jealousy, as though she wished there were a similar role she could play.

Then David turned to look at Tamani, and Laurel found herself hoping Tamani would say something, anything, that could dissuade David from accepting Jamison's offer. But a strange sort of silent conversation seemed to pass between them, and then Tamani, too, donned a look of wistful envy.

When David turned at last to Laurel, she closed her eyes, conflicted. Did David realize what Jamison was asking? The amount of blood he would be required to spill? But this was Avalon. Her homeland, whether she could remember it or not. So many lives at stake.

It wasn't a decision she could make for him.

She stood very still, then opened her eyes, meeting David's. She did not move, didn't even blink. But she saw his decision written on his face.

"Yes," he said, looking straight at her.

Jamison's outstretched arm was all the invitation David

needed. He walked through the marble archway and looked down at the sword. He touched the pommel, tentatively at first, as though expecting it to shock him. When nothing happened he stepped forward, bracing his feet on either side of the gleaming weapon.

Then, wrapping his fingers around the hilt, David pulled the sword from the stone.

TEN

THE AIR AROUND THEM SEEMED TO ELECTRIFY AS the crystalline blade emerged from the slab, and Laurel took an involuntary step backward as torrents of energy washed through the room. She felt Tamani's chest against her shoulders and his hands at her elbows, steadying her, and she was glad for the support. David stood motionless, staring down at the sword in his hand with a probing expression.

Jamison gasped and they all turned to see the smile spreading across his face. "I am not ashamed to admit I wasn't entirely certain that was going to work. After all these years, it's a bit of a dream come true for me." Then he cleared his throat and sobered. "We must work fast. The Queen will be here at any moment. Tamani, you'll want something as well." Jamison gestured invitingly toward a small selection of shimmering armaments hanging from the eastern wall of the chamber where the now-empty block of granite sat.

"They're beautiful," Tamani breathed, so quietly Laurel doubted anyone else had heard. He walked over and hefted a long, double-headed spear; the blades on each end looked razor sharp. It didn't give Laurel quite the same squicky feeling as she got when she was around guns, but it was close. Tamani turned and balanced the spear in his right hand, lifting it up and down a few times before nodding. "This is a good weight for me," he said, his voice serious. It was his sentry voice; a sign that he was officially in battle mode. And that frightened Laurel as much as the spear.

"Sir?"

Everyone turned to face David. Despite the unearthly power exuding from him, he looked rather lost. "Yes, David?" Jamison said.

"I don't . . . I don't understand. What do I do?"

Jamison stepped forward to place a hand on David's shoulder, but it slid away. David gave the hand a puzzled look, and Jamison pulled it back, smiling as though he'd just discovered something wonderful. "Believe me when I say it is as simple as swinging the sword. It will guide you, and make up for any and all of your deficiencies. But like Arthur before you, you must have the courage to step forward and the strength to remain standing." He paused. "I *am* asking you to do a hard thing, but it is well within your ability. I promise you that. Now come," he said, addressing them all again. "We should be going."

No one spoke as they traversed the upper chambers, descended to the foyer, and passed onto the palace grounds.

It was Jamison who finally broke the silence as they reached the white marble archway at the head of the trail.

"If we go back the way we came," Jamison said, turning to look back at the group, the wind carrying his voice to them, "perhaps we can avoid the Queen altogether."

"And why would you want to do that, Jamison?" Queen Marion's voice was soft and simmering as she stepped up to the white archway. Behind her, Laurel could see a long line of green-garbed sentries, their weapons shouldered, mingled with her *Am Fear-faire*.

Jamison drew up short, his confident posture slipping for the briefest moment before he recomposed himself. "Because you are going to be very angry with me," Jamison said simply. "And we don't have time for that."

Laurel could see the question on the Queen's lips, but she didn't ask it, searching each member of the party with her eyes instead. When her gaze fell upon Excalibur her expression betrayed shock. "Jamison, what have you done?"

"What the Silent Ones knew you would not," Jamison said evenly.

"You must realize the consequences of this."

"I am aware of what they have been in the past, but I also know that the past need not dictate the present."

"You will be the death of Avalon one day, Jamison."

"Only if I stop you from killing her first," Jamison said, his voice ringing with quiet fury.

The Queen's eyes flashed anger, then something Laurel thought might be pity. "You are so unbendable," she said.

"Even Cora spoke of how unyielding you are when you set yourself to something. Well, do as you will. But remember that the branch that will not bend is the first to fall before the storm. I refuse to bear any responsibility for your death. Come, Yasmine."

The young Winter faerie stepped away, taking Jamison's hands into her own. "I want to stay with you," she said, determination flashing in her eyes.

But Jamison was already shaking his head. "I'm sorry." After a glance at Marion, he bent himself close to Yasmine's ear. "If we were both there to protect you, perhaps. But I do not trust myself to do it alone."

"You don't have to," Yasmine said fiercely. "I can help."

"I cannot risk your safety," Jamison said, shaking his head.

"You won't actually die, will you?" Yasmine asked, looking reproachfully back at the Queen.

"I certainly don't intend to."

Yasmine glanced briefly at Laurel and Tamani before lowering her voice. "I can do great things," she said, so quietly Laurel scarcely heard. "You have told me for years, that I can and will do *great things*."

"That is precisely why you must stay here," Jamison said, lifting one hand to touch her face. "What we go to do now is not great—it is only necessary. It is more important than ever that you remain alive so that you can do those *great things*. Avalon cannot afford to lose you, or all our efforts will have been in vain, in the very moment they are nearest to blossoming."

Whether Yasmine understood Jamison's cryptic speech or not, she nodded her assent, then turned to catch up to Marion, who hadn't waited for her. Jamison's eyes tracked the two Winter faeries until they reached the palace and were safely inside with their *Am Fear-faire*. Only then did he turn back to the group. "Come," Jamison said, his voice strained as he led them down.

"There are . . . so many," Laurel said to Tamani as they trailed Jamison, passing lines of sentries still marching up the path that led to the Winter Palace.

"Two hundred, give or take," Tamani growled.

"Two *hundred?*" Laurel exclaimed, her breath catching in her throat. "Does she really need that many?"

"Of course not," Tamani said.

Laurel hesitated. "Can Avalon spare that many?"

"Of course not," he repeated, his eyes hollow. "Let's go."

He took her hand and together they followed Jamison, David, and Chelsea. Laurel's feet seemed to move of their own accord as gravity pulled her downhill along the path that led to the Gate Garden. The line of sentries finally ended and soon even their marching footsteps had faded away, leaving only the sounds of breathing and the scuffing of their own footfalls.

Laurel's head snapped up as the silence was shattered by a piercing blast of gunfire.

"We're too late," Tamani growled.

"They're here?" Laurel asked. *It was too soon!*

"And they have guns," David said, his face pale.

94

"It doesn't matter," Jamison said. "We have something better. Perhaps you young ones should run ahead. I'm afraid these old stems are slowing you down."

The others turned to look at the glittering sword and David's face paled. But Tamani's grip tightened on his spear. "Let's go kill some trolls."

The four of them ran the rest of the way to the Gate Garden, which was in an uproar. The tops of the walls were lined with sentries wielding bows and slings; others were passing around knives and spears. Most of the sentries seemed to be on the verge of panic, and the whole operation had an air of disorganization about it.

"The caesafum doesn't work!" Laurel heard one armored sentry shouting at a plainly garbed Spring carting a wheelbarrow full of potions. "*None* of that Mixer stuff works! Get back to Spring and tell them we need more *weapons!*"

"I—"

But the anonymous fae's response was drowned out by the roar of crumbling stone some fifty feet from the entrance to the Garden. Immediately, the cry went up: "Breach in the wall!"

"We've got to close that breach," Tamani said. "The Garden is a secondary choke point, after the gateways. We need to contain the threat until Jamison catches up. David, I want you on point."

David blinked.

"That means I want you in front. Nothing can hurt you."

"Are you sure?" David said, his voice shaking on the first

word before he steadied it.

Tamani fixed David with a determined look. "I'm *sure*. Just don't let go of the sword," he said seriously. "From what Jamison said, I don't think anyone can take it from you, or yank it out of your hands. But even so, whatever you do, *don't let go.* As long as you have your hands on that hilt, you'll be fine."

David nodded, and Laurel recognized his stony expression. It was the look he'd had when he pulled her from the Chetco River; when he carried her across the ocean to the lighthouse to rescue Chelsea; when he insisted on returning to guard Yuki last night.

This was the David who could conquer anything.

He plunged the tip of the sword into the earth and wiped his hands on his jeans. Chelsea bounced anxiously from foot to foot beside Laurel until Laurel wanted to grab her arm to make her stand still. After a deep breath, David cracked his knuckles—how often had Laurel watched him do that?—and reached for Excalibur again.

"Screw it," Chelsea muttered under her breath. "I am *not* going to die today without doing this. Wait!" she called out before David could touch the sword.

He scarcely had time to turn around before Chelsea grabbed his face and pulled him down, pressing her lips firmly to his. Laurel saw the moment more like a snapshot than an actual event. Chelsea. Kissing David. Not a moment of romance and seduction—rather of desperation and bravado. Still, Chelsea was *kissing* Laurel's boyfriend.

He's not my boyfriend, Laurel told herself. She looked down and forced back her weird jealousy. When she looked up again, the moment had passed.

Chelsea spun away from David, avoiding everyone's eyes—especially Laurel's—her face burning red.

David gaped open-mouthed for a moment before he composed himself and grabbed Excalibur, shouldering it, and turned to trail after Tamani.

He, too, avoided Laurel's eyes.

The dust was already clearing when they arrived at the breach, and all the trolls in sight were heavily armed. Laurel had expected Klea's soldiers to be carrying guns, but *guns* was far too simple a word for these weapons. They were semiautomatics, assault rifles, machine guns, the kind Laurel had only seen in movies. Sentries had pinned some of the trolls down in the gap as they tried to escape—arrow-riddled bodies outside the wall lay crumpled in testament to the archers' vigilance—but the remaining trolls were waiting for the faeries to give up their cover, to step away from the safety of the stone walls and bring the fight to them.

David scarcely hesitated before doing exactly what the trolls obviously wanted; he raised Excalibur and strode right through the hole in the wall. The first gun-toting troll spotted him and opened fire as Tamani pulled Chelsea and Laurel down behind a smooth-barked aspen, but not before Laurel saw David reflexively duck his head and raise an arm to shield himself from the assault. A second troll's gun joined the first, staccato bursts like a string of firecrackers assaulting Laurel's ears even louder than the shriek that escaped her throat.

She forced herself to peek around the tree at David, who was, she saw with relief, still standing. He studied his limbs and touched his face before holding Excalibur out in front of him and taking it in from point to hilt. Then he reached down and picked something up off the ground.

It took Laurel a moment to realize that the vaguely oblong metal bead in David's hand was a bullet. He stood there, deaf to the fray, staring at that misshapen bit of metal, awe blossoming over his face.

"Yes, the sword works!" Tamani shouted over the gunfire, flinching back as a bullet notched the tree near his face. "Now can you please *kill some trolls*?"

Shaking his head as if to clear his thoughts, David turned and charged his assailants. Several of them grinned menacingly; David looked like a child with a stick getting ready to try to beat up an oncoming freight train.

But when he clumsily swung his enchanted blade it cleaved the closest troll in two.

Laurel wasn't sure exactly what she had been expecting, but she most certainly had *not* been expecting the troll to fall to the ground in two cleanly severed pieces.

It didn't seem to be quite what David expected either. He stopped and stared at the bleeding corpse at his feet. The other trolls howled and attacked, their fists, knives, and clubs failing to so much as jostle David. With a jerky motion that looked more reflexive than purposeful, David brought the sword up again, and another troll fell to the ground in bloodied pieces.

"Snicker-snack," Chelsea whispered, awestruck.

With the corpses of *two* trolls at his feet, David was again stunned into inaction. Laurel could see his chest heaving as he stared at the carnage.

"David!" Tamani's voice was sharp, but Laurel thought she detected concern, as well. The remaining trolls had recovered from their shock and raised their weapons again.

Snapping to attention, David's eyebrows furrowed. He lunged forward, slicing one troll's enormous gun in two, separating another from its weapon by taking off its hands. His swings grew ferocious, indiscriminately cleaving metal and flesh alike with all the effort it might take to carve gelatin with a steak knife.

As David made a gap in the onslaught, Tamani stepped out of the protective cover of the trees. "Get some sentries into this breach!" he shouted. "Anyone without a weapon, I want you stacking rocks!"

The sentries were successfully cutting down many of the trolls that came pouring through the gateway, but *many* wasn't enough; the sentries were losing ground. Fighting had broken out in a dozen places throughout the Garden, and the archers on the walls were rushing to and fro in an effort to keep the trolls contained without wounding the sentries on the ground.

"There's too many," David called, shaking his head. "I won't be able to get to all of them before they break down more of the wall."

"Then let's at least stem the tide," Tamani said. "If you

can keep any more from making it through the gateway, maybe—"

But his words were cut off as a group of six or seven trolls emerged from the trees, making a run for the breach. Before anyone on the wall could react, however, thick roots erupted from the ground, spraying black earth into the air. They waved menacingly, and for a moment Laurel was afraid Yuki had arrived to finish them all off, but then the roots swept backward, throwing the trolls against the trees, where their howls of anger turned to cries of pain.

"I agree," Jamison said, approaching from the direction of the Garden entrance. Somewhere along the way he'd rejoined his *Am Fear-faire*, who were ready to fight beside him. "If David can defend the gate itself, I believe the sentries can clear the Garden."

Laurel didn't understand how Jamison could retain such an optimistic calm in the midst of such chaos, but the sentries close enough to hear Jamison's pronouncement were visibly encouraged by his words and Laurel realized it was deliberate.

"Most of these sentries have never seen a troll, much less killed one," Jamison whispered to Tamani and David, confirming Laurel's conclusion. "Tamani, your experience will be invaluable here. If you'll allow me to look after your charge, I promise I'll return her to you safely. I'd appreciate you joining David at the gates."

Tamani nodded, though his jaw was clenched; Laurel knew he didn't like leaving her, but he wasn't about to argue with Jamison. David also said nothing—though he did spare a glance back at both Laurel and Chelsea before following Tamani into the trees.

"Stay close," Jamison said without looking at them, his attention wholly focused on the battle.

With a nod, two of the *Am Fear-faire* shifted to include Laurel and Chelsea in their circle of protection.

Jamison set off down the interior perimeter of the Gate Garden as though he were on an evening stroll. When they encountered two black-clad trolls tearing chunks out of the stone wall, Jamison bent, stretching his arms forward. Mimicking his pose, two enormous oak trees also leaned forward, their mighty branches creaking and groaning as they wrapped around the trolls and then straightened, flinging the beasts up to such a height that Laurel knew they would never survive the fall.

Before Laurel could dwell too long on what it would feel like to be thrown to her death by an oak tree, they met a small group of sentries fighting desperately against several trolls that had armed themselves with massive tree branches, which they were wielding like giant clubs. Laurel guessed they were about to have their wooden weapons turned against them; but instead, when one of the trolls turned to charge Jamison, it sank into the ground, clawing madly at the dirt that closed over its head.

One by one, the rest of the trolls disappeared as if they'd stepped into quicksand. When the last one turned to flee, Laurel caught sight of the roots Jamison was calling up from the ground to drag the trolls under, burying them alive in Avalon's fertile soil.

Laurel tried to keep an eye on the guys as Jamison circled the Garden, assisting the sentries. David was easy; it was almost impossible to miss the arcs of blood being cast off his magical weapon with every swing. He looked less like a swordsman and more like a farmer at spring harvest, reaping a never-ending crop of howling monsters. He was truly untouchable. It didn't matter if he was shifting directions or actually aiming for a troll, every movement of the sword brought down bodies.

Occasionally, Tamani would emerge from the fray and shout an order at someone, but even dressed in her dad's shirt Laurel had a hard time following him as he blended in with the other sentries, all swinging their weapons, watching for each other, and fighting to keep the trolls at bay.

When they had first entered the Garden, Laurel thought there was no way this simple fighting force could beat the battle-crazed hordes pouring from the gate. But now—with the help of Jamison and Excalibur—the faeries were slowly, slowly, driving the trolls *back* through the gate.

They were winning.

Then, as abruptly as it had begun, the battle for the gate was over. The shouts of the sentries were deafening as they closed ranks on a handful of remaining trolls. As the final troll fell, everyone's eyes went to the gate.

But nothing else came through.

ELEVEN

AFTER THE RAGE OF BATTLE, THE QUIET WAS DEAF-
ening. Laurel's ears adjusted gradually, and soon she could
hear groans and murmurs of pain from the wounded faeries
and the buzz of the sentries on the walls as they spread the
news to those who couldn't see for themselves.

Tamani was favoring one of his shoulders and his eyes
were wary as he and David approached Jamison's circle of
Am Fear-faire.

"Did we win?" Chelsea whispered. "Can Jamison close
the gate?"

Tamani immediately shook his head.

"It's not over," he said softly. "If it was, my sentries would
have come through to tell us." He gritted his teeth. "Klea
and Yuki are still on the other side."

"Nevertheless," Jamison said, his gesture taking Tamani
and David in together, "if we do not take the battle to them,

they are sure to bring it back to us eventually."

"We have a decent force assembled here. I'll lead them through," Tamani said.

"Let me," David said softly, raising the sword.

Tamani hesitated. Laurel could see the war between pride and good sense raging in his eyes. But caution won out; Tamani nodded and began shouting orders to the assembled sentries, who again shouldered their weapons and began to align into formations.

But Laurel's eyes were on the gate. She could see the California redwoods through the gateway, the ones that ringed the clearing—which looked *empty*. Where were the sentries? Or the rest of the trolls? She thought she caught a flash of black leather, but convinced herself she was jumping at shadows.

Then something small and yellow came rolling through the gate.

It was immediately swallowed by the earth—Jamison's doing, Laurel had no doubt—even as several more matching canisters came hissing through the gateway, billowing clouds of sickly green gas that rose and expanded at an unbelievable rate.

Laurel managed to suck in a breath just before the smoke enveloped her. More canisters came streaming through, and Laurel blinked and squinted against the murk. She watched in horror as Jamison staggered, then collapsed onto the emerald grass alongside his *Am Fear-faire*. Those sentries still standing watched the Winter faerie fall, then turned in panic to flee the encroaching fog. But it was spreading faster than they could run. Klea's special recipe, no doubt.

Fighting the flow of retreating sentries, Laurel spun, trying to find her friends. She caught sight of David, who was standing like a stone in the middle of a raging river of faeries; Excalibur was in his hand and he was staring at it as if to ask, *What am I supposed to do now?* At the rate the gas was spreading, he had little choice but to run with them. Even with Excalibur, surely he still had to breathe.

It took Laurel only a moment to realize she could save him.

The same way she'd saved him once before.

Laurel rushed to David, grabbing for the front of his blood-soaked shirt. Her hand slipped away, as though she'd grabbed at a ghost; too late, she remembered that as long as he was holding Excalibur, she couldn't touch him. She felt herself being pushed away by the panicked throng and resisted the urge to cry out.

And then his hand was on her wrist, and he was pulling her to him. His eyes were hard and his grip on her arm was tight as he placed one hand on the side of her neck, the way he used to do. She could feel his heart racing in his chest as she brought her face close, then pressed her mouth to his.

Laurel heard a weird sound and opened her eyes to see Chelsea just a few feet away, her hand pressed over her mouth, watching them. Behind Chelsea, Tamani had paused in his task of dragging Jamison's unconscious form to stare at them in confusion.

Laurel sucked in a breath and peered around David,

catching their eyes. "Breathe!" she commanded, making sure she didn't let any of the misty air enter her mouth.

Realization sparked in Chelsea's eyes and she spun to Tamani with a smirk. She took a firm grip on his ears and pressed her lips against his.

And there they stood, four figures abandoned by the living, surrounded by the dead, clinging to one another. From their experience at the bottom of the Chetco, Laurel and David knew that they could share breaths for a long time. If they moved carefully, they could probably escape the smoke no matter how far it had spread. And David could still carry the sword between breaths.

But what will we do without Jamison?

Laurel pulled away from David and knelt by Jamison's side. She put both hands on his chest and—to her surprise—they moved up as the old faerie breathed. Laurel had almost convinced herself it was wishful thinking when he did it again.

Jamison was alive!

Laurel turned and grasped at Tamani's arm. She took his hand and placed it on Jamison's chest, her eyes fixed meaningfully on his. Tamani's shoulders slumped in what must have been relief as he understood.

That meant that the gas wasn't immediately deadly, and that most of the faeries around them were still alive—but for how much longer?

The sound of footsteps swishing through the thick grass indicated they didn't have much time. Laurel paused, peering through the mist. She could only make out shadows, but the hulking forms that were clearly not faeries were all the confirmation Laurel needed. The assault was about to begin again. Whatever this sleeping gas was, it was only intended to give the trolls back the upper hand.

After a quick pantomimed request for Chelsea's assistance, Tamani pulled Jamison onto his back and they began dragging him toward the wooden gates at the front of the Garden. As they approached the wall, the smoke thinned, and when they emerged through the heavy wooden entrance, it was into clear, breathable air.

"Aim!" The call was quiet—the faeries had discovered the trolls and were hoping to catch them off guard.

With his very first breath, Tamani called, "No arrows!"

The sentry who was giving orders to the archers atop the garden wall looked down from the battlements. "We can't fight them in there! We can't even see them. They'll breach the walls for sure this time. All we can do is rain arrows from above as fast as we can."

"It's sleeping gas," Tamani retorted. "Everyone who took a breath of that stuff is helpless but *alive*; if you fire now—especially blindly—you'll kill as many faeries as trolls. We need to fall back. Take up a more defensible position."

The sentry commander closed her eyes for a moment, her mouth a thin line. "We'll not abandon our post," she said. "I'll figure something out." She scurried to the nearest archer, clearly moving on to some kind of backup plan.

Laurel hoped it was a good one.

"David?"

Chelsea's voice was laced with concern, and Laurel turned to see David staring at his free hand—stained red—turning it this way and that. His clothing was equally bloody and he gingerly felt his face, which was streaked the crimson-brown of drying blood.

"David?" Chelsea repeated as his eyes seemed to lose focus and he put a hand to his forehead.

He gave no indication that he'd heard anything.

"David!" Laurel said, as sharply as she dared.

He looked up this time and Laurel's stomach turned at the hollow horror in his eyes. "Laurel, I—I don't—"

Laurel took his face in her hands, forcing him to look at her. "It's okay. You'll be all right," Laurel said. He must have only now comprehended what he had done. It took a few more seconds, but finally his eyes calmed. Laurel knew he was pushing his dismay away—he'd have to deal with it later—but for now it would have to do. Taking a deep breath, he picked up the sword again and repositioned himself in front of the Garden entrance.

Laurel turned her attention back to Tamani, who had laid Jamison on the ground and was listening at the old Winter faerie's lips. "He's really out. We need to find a way to wake him up."

"We have to go to the Academy," Laurel said. Surely someone there could wake Jamison. *Should have brought my kit,* she thought ruefully. And then, something else occurred to her. "They don't know about the immunity! They'll be helpless if the trolls get through." Thinking about the damage even

108

one elixir-immune troll would do in the Academy was horrifying enough. Get a whole group in there . . .

"They're not the only ones," Tamani said grimly.

"We have to go *now*," Laurel said, clutching at Tamani's sleeve. "We need to get to the Academy and warn them! They can wake Jamison, I'm sure of it."

"There's no *time!*" Tamani growled. "And zero cover. Carrying Jamison uphill, we'd be fruit ripe for the picking for any trolls that come through. Even if we get to the Academy, you're right—they're helpless. We can't risk losing Jamison. He'll be safest if we take him to Spring. There are sentries there and plenty of ingredients for you to try—"

"I appreciate your confidence," Laurel said evenly, wondering whether Tamani was trying too hard to protect *her*. "But if anyone can wake Jamison, it's Yeardley. And even if he can't, someone has to warn them!"

"All my men are back there!" Tamani snapped, pointing into the green mist that filled the walled Garden. "And the sentries here are refusing to fall back. There's no one to send. Unless . . ." His voice trailed off and he looked at Chelsea. "You're fast," he said.

"No," Laurel said softly.

"Chelsea," Tamani said, facing her fully. "I need you to run."

Chelsea nodded. "I'm good at that."

"Up this path, the huge gray structure on your right—covered with flowering vines, you can't miss it—go in the front gates, right up to the main doors. If you're fast—faster than you've ever been in your life—you can save them."

"No," Laurel said, louder this time.

"Tell them about the immunity, start them building a barricade at all of the entrances. As high and strong as possible. And the windows; bar them somehow. They're smart—like you—they'll figure it out."

"I'm gone," Chelsea said, rising from her crouch.

"No!" Laurel said, and felt David step closer behind her.

"She can't go alone," David said, brandishing the sword.

"She has to," Tamani retorted. "I need you to help me guard Jamison, and I need Laurel to try to wake him up. The Queen won't help until it's too late, so he's still our best chance at victory. We can't let him die."

"I'm doing this," Chelsea said, setting her jaw as she faced Laurel and David. "If you want to offer anything helpful, do it now. I'm leaving in ten seconds."

"Find Yeardley," Laurel said, hardly believing the words coming out of her mouth. "And Katya. Tell them I sent you; they'll listen." She hesitated. "Don't tell them you're human," she added softly, hating that she knew it would help. Hopefully they wouldn't see it for themselves in the commotion.

Chelsea nodded, then looked up the hill. "Runners set," she whispered. "Go."

Laurel's chin quavered as she watched her best friend looking very alone on the vast hillside. "I don't know if I can forgive you if she dies," Laurel said.

Tamani was silent for a long moment. "I know."

TWELVE

"I'LL TAKE JAMISON," TAMANI SAID. CHELSEA really *was* fast, and that gave him hope—but he couldn't spare another moment to worry over her. "We'll circle Spring through the trees. That'll keep us hidden long enough to get to my mother. Hopefully between her Gardening experience and Laurel's Mixings, we can do *something* for him." With a little help from Laurel, he maneuvered Jamison across his shoulders. "Laurel, follow me. David, watch our backs."

As they started toward Spring Tamani wondered—not for the first time—whether they should stick to the main road. But they'd seen how fast the trolls could overrun the Gate Garden; this time, there would be no one to push them back. The remaining sentries might keep them contained a while longer, but Tamani wasn't optimistic, and once the Garden fell, securing the main road would probably be Klea's next priority. As long as he was carrying Jamison, he couldn't really run, so that meant picking their way down the barely visible footpaths where he had played as a sapling.

He tried not to think about the sentries he was leaving to die.

They sacrifice themselves for the greater good, he repeated to himself, again and again, as they trudged through the woods, moving slowly but steadily downhill. For years Shar had pounded that concept into his head—*the greater good*—but he had never completely understood it until this moment.

Shar.

He couldn't think about that right now.

It took them less than an hour to reach the glade behind his mother's house, though each step felt like an eternity; Jamison wasn't a large faerie, but he seemed to grow heavier as the journey progressed, and Tamani struggled to stave off exhaustion. He was running on entirely too little sleep.

"Stay low," Tamani whispered, scanning the grassy expanse between them and the house. The streets were empty and the trolls didn't appear to have made it into this part of Spring quarter, but Tamani knew better than to let that lull him into dropping his guard. On his signal, the three of them launched into the open clearing and fairly flew to the rounded tree Tamani's mother lived in. When they reached the back wall Tamani twisted at the artfully concealed latch and pushed, but nothing moved. He pushed again, but still nothing. With a growl he raised one foot and kicked as hard as he could and the hidden door swung wildly on its hinges as it gave way.

He stepped forward and barely managed to stop before the knife at his throat pierced his skin.

"Cradle of the Goddess, Tam!" His mother withdrew her knife and made way for them to enter. As soon as they were through she glanced out at the field and pushed the door shut again. "I thought you were trolls. Young Sora just came through here, said trolls are making their way into Spring. I thought I'd go join the sentries at the barricades."

"I have a more important job for you now," Tamani said, striding to his mother's room and laying Jamison down on her cot.

"Earth and sky, is that . . . Jamison?" his mother exclaimed, already pulling off her arm guards and dropping to her knees by the side of the bed. "What happened to him?"

Tamani explained as quickly as he could. "We have to wake him up. I thought you might assist Laurel with that."

"Of course," his mother agreed, stripping off the rest of her armor. "It's a shame old Tanzer joined the Silent Ones, he'd know just what to do."

"I hadn't heard," Tamani said, his shoulders slumping in disappointment. He'd dared to hope . . . but Laurel would manage. She had to!

Seeing the confusion on Laurel's face, he explained, "Tanzer was a friend of my mother's. He . . . used to live near here."

"Finest Mixer I ever knew," Tamani's mother said, pressing her hands to Jamison's ashen cheeks. "Once upon a time I knew them all. Not many Mixers come to live in Spring, though."

"You mentioned barricades?" Tamani asked.

His mother nodded. "The main road—near the laundry huts. When the trolls breach that we'll be fighting in the streets."

Not if, when. Hopelessness threatened to consume him; the Queen had turned her back on them, Jamison was incapacitated, the Gate Garden had fallen.

At least they still had David.

And David had the sword.

"Do whatever you can for Jamison," Tamani said, meeting Laurel's eyes. "Any Mixer trick you can think of—just do it. We have to go to the barricade—do what we can."

Tamani's mother frowned at him, then stood and pulled him to the side where Laurel and David couldn't hear her. "I know who this is," she said in her mother voice, inclining her head toward David. "Do *not* go out there and get him killed to serve your own purposes, Tam. A dishonorable victory is no victory at all."

But Tamani was already shaking his head. "It's not like that. He has the sword, Mother. The one Shar used to whisper about. It's real, and I've watched him use it." He glanced up at David. "With Jamison down, he's our only hope."

His mother was silent for a moment. "Is it really so dire?"

Tamani squeezed her hand.

"Then go," she said. "Goddess protect you both." She started to step away, then reached out for his arm, pulling him close again and pressing one hand to his cheek. "I love you, son. No matter what happens today, you remember that."

Tamani swallowed hard and nodded. He turned to Laurel and she looked like she wanted to say something, but Tamani wasn't sure he could stand to hear it. He edged away from her to face David. "You ready?"

They had almost made it to the door before Laurel cried out, "Tam, David!" Tamani closed his eyes and steeled himself against her protests, but for a moment she said nothing. And then, to his surprise, she only whispered, "Be safe."

Grateful for her understanding, Tamani waved and led David out the front of the house, back toward the main road. It wasn't long before telltale sounds of battle reached their ears. "Blighted trolls are so fast," Tamani muttered under his breath. His fingers tightened around his spear; it was time to fight again. He had rarely fought—or even trained—with such a fine weapon. It brought down trolls so much easier than the small knives he usually carried. Good weapons meant dead trolls, and with every dead troll he felt like Laurel was that much safer.

And what could matter more?

"I want you to focus on trolls with guns," Tamani called over his shoulder to David. "If the fight at the gate was any indication, there won't be many, but most fae here won't even know what a gun is, much less to fear it."

"Sure," David said tightly. Tamani had to admit, for an untrained civilian, David was dealing well with everything that had been thrown at him.

Tamani gave a brief wave of acknowledgment as they passed under a rooftop full of archers shooting arrows over a sturdily constructed barricade. Sharpened stakes—repurposed fence posts, mostly—stretched across the main road where it dipped between two hills, atop which more archers had gathered and were raining arrows and sling stones on any trolls that tried to go around the long way. Most of the fighting was taking place in the slight valley at the mouth of the road, but some trolls had slipped through and were busy smashing as much of the barrier as they could manage.

Tamani raised his spear, but an arrow whistled through the air and struck his intended target square in the chest. Tamani shoved the misshapen beast to the side and kicked into a run, weaving through the barricade, David close behind him.

At all sides now he was surrounded by Ticers—and some of them even knew what they were doing, as retired sentries fought side by side with scythe-wielding Tenders and hammer-swinging Smiths. Still, it seemed to Tamani—as he stabbed a troll before it could kill the young Spring who was slapping at trolls with a long-handled shovel—that there were far too many green saplings in the mix. He almost opened his mouth to tell the kid to go home, but what would he do there? *Wait* for the trolls to come in and kill him? No, Tamani decided—he wouldn't discourage bravery. Even stupid bravery.

"David, this way!" Tamani called, directing him into the midst of the trolls. At such close quarters with the fae, he would have trouble swinging Excalibur; better to be completely surrounded by the enemy. "Almost there," he whispered to himself, stabbing a troll in the neck as it tried to wrap its meaty hands around him. He had lost count of the number of shallow, meaningless wounds he'd received today; none were even remotely life-threatening, but they were taking their toll on his reflexes. As the trolls crowded thicker about him, it became increasingly difficult to kill them as fast as they came at him. David was making up some of the difference, but trolls were pouring down the hillside by the dozens.

They were well beyond the barricade when Tamani heard a low rumbling and looked up to see several fae standing on the rooftops at the edge of the quarter, hands stretching out to the sky, then gracefully moving in as though pulling invisible ropes.

It took Tamani a few moments to realize what was coming. "David!" he warned. "Up the hillside!"

The hill was too steep to climb very high in the brief time they had, so David and Tamani pressed themselves flat into the dirt as the rumble grew to a near-deafening roar. From farther up the road, a huge herd of cattle came stampeding into the valley, trampling trolls as they rampaged down the road toward the barricade where their Herders had gathered on the roofs. At the thickest segment of the stampede Tamani had to push himself even flatter against the grassy hill to avoid the panicked cows and their long, deadly horns. Once the danger was past Tamani nearly laughed at David as he half stood, half sat against the steep hillside, his sword held limp in his hands, watching the spectacle.

"What the hell is up with the *cows*?" David asked, flabbergasted.

Tamani pointed up to the Ticers on the rooftops, swirling their charges into a wide circle now.

David followed his gesture and—though Tamani would have doubted it was possible—his eyes grew even wider. "Enticement on the cows?" he asked in disbelief.

Tamani nodded, but he wasn't smiling anymore. "Come on," he told David, "we have to strike while they're confused." The trolls were still bigger than most of the cows and they were getting the idea quickly, turning their blades against the herd. The distraction wouldn't last long.

"Why do you have cows in Avalon?" David yelled as he chopped down a lower troll that was covered in festering sores where it wasn't covered with coarse black fur.

Tamani dislodged his spear from a troll's chest with a savage kick. The name tag on its jumper said GREG, and Tamani wondered momentarily whether the mostly human-looking troll was Greg, or had just *eaten* Greg. "Can't depend on Mixers for *all* of our fertilizer," he said blandly.

The trolls were thinning out again, and David seemed to have found a rhythm that was working for him, so Tamani, his spear still clenched in one hand, took a few minutes to carefully pull some of the wounded fae back toward the barricade. They were still breathing, and if they could just avoid getting stabbed where they lay, they might be treatable.

There wasn't time to take them anywhere truly safe, but at least he could drag them away from the risk of being trampled.

"Tamani!"

It was David. He turned to thrust his sword at a troll that tried to jump on his shoulder.

"They're not coming down the hill anymore," David said, breathless.

Tamani tensed. Last time the trolls stopped coming, it was because they were preparing to unleash something worse. He certainly wasn't ready to trust *this* cessation.

He hesitated. "Let's keep fighting here until the Ticers have a better hold on everything—then we need to go back to my mother's." Though honestly, Tamani had no idea how long that would take. The Spring fighters were barely hanging on as it was.

David nodded, then jumped as something made of glass shattered by his feet.

"Finally," Tamani murmured, feeling his chest lighten a little. More tiny vials rained down from the sky, popping against the ground, splashing their sweet-smelling contents across the battlefield.

"Finally what?" David asked.

"The Beeherds have gathered their flocks," Tamani said, one side of his mouth ticking up in a grin as the telltale noise reached his ears. He pointed to the top of the barricade, where archers had given way to a cadre of Spring faeries, each with a crook in one hand and a sling in the other.

A buzzing cloud of darkness descended into the pass and the trolls began to howl in pain. The black and yellow insects swarmed across the battlefield, blanketing the trolls and stinging them with fervor. Their tiny bodies were dropping to the ground almost as fast as they flew in, and Tamani felt a twinge of sadness at the years it would take to rebuild their hives—but true to their nature, the bees were defending their home, just like the Spring faeries. Those trolls that refused to be brought down by the venom were blinded, both by pain and by the clouds of insects surrounding them, and became easy targets for the faeries.

A cry of alarm from David made Tamani turn, his weapon raised.

The bees were swarming over David, too. Thanks to Excalibur he remained untouchable—and unstingable—but the insects had clearly unnerved him, and he was thrashing about, swinging his sword like a flyswatter, trying to drive them off.

"David. David!" Tamani called, but if David heard, he gave no sign. "David!" Tamani yelled, finally catching his ear. "It's okay; I don't think they can sting you."

"No," David responded, calming at last. "But I can feel them. And it . . ." David paused, then spat, "It is *creeping me out.*"

That almost made Tamani smile. "I think the Ticers can take it from here," Tamani said, wishing he felt more certain. "We should go."

David muttered something that sounded like agreement and followed Tamani back through the barricades.

"Run," Tamani said, kicking into a jog. "In a while they'll be drawn back to the potions on the road and should leave you alone."

They jogged together down deserted side streets Tamani hadn't traveled since he was a sprout. The bees retreated slowly at first, but after a few minutes David was left with just a few stubborn stragglers.

"I thought magic didn't work on the trolls," David panted.

"Bees aren't magic," Tamani said, pausing for a moment to get his bearings.

"But that stuff they threw into the square—the glass things—those were potions, right?"

Tamani grinned now. "Yes. But potions for the *bees*, not the trolls. It stimulates them to attack animals. Unfortunately, that includes you."

David nodded, leaning over with his hands on his knees. "Brilliant," he said, taking one more deep breath before following Tamani, already a few strides ahead of him.

"Hecate's eye," Tamani gasped, throwing himself against a wall as they reached the corner across from his mother's house only to find a dozen trolls standing over the bodies of a handful of sentries. "They must have come in a different way," he said, peeking out quickly. They were making their way toward him—perhaps they had heard? Or—

"They smell us," Tamani said, shaking his head and looking down at his bloodstained clothes, cursing his carelessness. "They probably followed the smell of blood all the way here."

As the first troll came into view—an enormous lower troll

that looked like a hairless grizzly bear with a nose instead of a snout—it sniffed the air.

"Here we go," Tamani said, stepping around the corner to greet the attack. The big one loped toward them, closing the distance so fast that Tamani barely had time to raise his spear.

With a picture-perfect swing David stepped up and took the monster's arm clean off. At the sight of their comrade's vibrant red blood pouring from its shoulder, the others seemed to catch a kind of frenzy, sending the fight into a deadly fast-forward. David, his arms clearly growing weary of Excalibur's weight, could barely swing his sword fast enough to repel their attacks. Tamani did what he could, stabbing out at every weapon and limb that approached him, mostly just trying to stay alive until David whittled their number down to a reasonable ratio.

How about three to one? Tamani thought ruefully.

When he felt something grab at his ankle, pulling his legs out from under him, Tamani was afraid his luck had run out. He managed to regain his footing, but not in time to completely dodge the blow of a wicked iron mace. He yelled through clenched teeth as the iron spikes tore into his right shoulder and he felt his grip slacken on his spear. The troll behind him gave a kick to the back of his knees and though he tried to catch himself, his injured arm collapsed beneath him, unable to bear his weight. He rolled in time to see the first troll lift his mace again, aiming for his head this time. Tamani was powerless to stop him.

And then the troll's knees buckled and it lurched forward, collapsing onto Tamani, filling his mouth with troll flesh and burning his nostrils with its sickly scent. Tamani heaved against the crushing weight with his good arm, but it was only when he felt David's strength join his that the huge troll rolled away.

Tamani climbed back to his feet and David reclaimed the sword from where he'd plunged it into the cobblestones. He had a strange look on his face.

"I owe you my life," Tamani said, sweeping up his spear. "Again," he added.

"I didn't do it. I mean, that one I did," David said, pointing to the two halves of the troll that had kicked Tamani's legs out from beneath him. "But I turned to get this one and as I raised the sword he just . . . collapsed."

"Must have taken a poison dart," Tamani said, scanning the troll's body, then looking around the street for their concealed benefactor. Not finding one, he just waved his thanks to the empty streets.

He adjusted his arm, trying to find the position that was least painful on his shoulder, giving up after a moment and just dealing with it. "We'd better get to the house before any more trolls see us."

When they burst back in through the front door, Laurel was there to greet them, brandishing the same knife Tamani's mother had nearly killed him with earlier. Something in Tamani's core sank low to see Laurel holding a knife. She must have been terrified to be wielding a weapon, even if she didn't know how to do much damage with it.

"It's you!" she said, her voice heavy with relief as she tossed the knife from her the way Tamani might discard rotten fruit. "They've been outside for a few minutes, and all we could do was stay as quiet as possible." She threw her arms around them both and Tamani couldn't help but wish the embrace was for him alone.

"How is Jamison?" Tamani asked, but Laurel was shaking her head.

"How are you guys? Hurt?"

"It doesn't matter," Tamani said. He pushed past her and down the hall. He couldn't focus on himself for even a moment or he wouldn't be able to keep the pain at bay.

"He's stirring," Laurel said, following him. "But that's all we've managed."

"I was afraid of that," Tamani said softly, standing in the bedroom doorway and looking at his mother, who was sitting by Jamison's side. The room was heavy with so many scents that Tamani could scarcely breathe without coughing.

"Sorry," his mother said. "Laurel said humans have an elixir called smelling salts, and we thought we'd try something similar. It seems to be working, but slowly."

Tamani nodded. "Keep going, then. We held the road. Some trolls made it through, but it looks like everything will be under control soon." He looked forlornly at Jamison, wishing he were more awake. But there wasn't time for regrets. "I guess we need to go to the Academy after all," he said, pushing his emotions aside. "I'll take David. I just hope—"

No. Voicing hope that the Academy was still standing was *not* going to help Laurel, especially since he had sent Chelsea there. Had he made the wrong decision? Should they have tried to make it to the Academy in spite of the danger? Shar had warned him often against self-doubt, especially in the middle of a battle, but he had to wonder if his fears for the safety of Spring had influenced his feeling that Jamison was safest here.

"I hope we make it," he finished at last.

Then he turned and ran straight into Laurel.

"I'm coming with you."

"Not a chance."

"You can't stop me."

A surge of helplessness washed through him. He *could* stop her, but she knew he wouldn't. "You're safer here. And you can explain the situation if Jamison wakes up."

"I already told your mom everything. It's more important that I come with you and tell the other Mixers what's going on in his system. It's his best shot," Laurel said, her gaze steady.

Tamani hated that she was right.

THIRTEEN

AT FIRST, THEY KEPT TO THE TREES. THE FOLIAGE shielded them from view and almost made Laurel feel safe, even if it was just an illusion. Tamani waved Laurel and David forward, pointing through the lacy gaps in the leaves. "We can dash straight up the hill and probably get there faster—though the climb will be hard," he said. "Or we can take the road through Summer, where the trolls are almost certainly attacking in force." His brow furrowed like he wanted to say something else, but he was silent.

"We should go through Summer," David said, his voice firm. "We can help. Clean out some trolls as we pass."

Tamani nodded and his entire face relaxed. "Thank you," he said, and Laurel realized he had forced himself not to make the request, putting it in David's hands instead. "The Sparklers, they aren't warriors and they don't even have the strength of the Academy walls to help; their houses are mostly made out of glass."

"What about weapons?" Laurel asked. "They've got to have some, right?"

"Stage weapons," Tamani said dryly. "The kind specifically made *not* to hurt you."

"Is . . . is Rowen there?" Laurel asked.

Tamani nodded, looking at the ground. "And Dahlia, and Jade," he added. Laurel vaguely remembered the names of Tamani's sister and her companion, though she'd never met them.

It didn't take them long to reach the outskirts of Summer, but they heard noise before they saw anything. There were explosions, the ring of glass breaking, and a lot of screaming. Laurel braced herself for the gruesome sight as they approached the top of the rise.

They crested the hill and Laurel slowed in shock; Tamani paused as well. They were standing in front of an enormous stone castle with a moat full of fiery lava. By the time David realized they weren't with him, he was twenty feet ahead.

"You guys coming?" he asked warily.

"This isn't what Summer is supposed to look like," Laurel said.

"Not even remotely," Tamani said in awe.

"It's an illusion!" Laurel realized. "To intimidate the trolls."

As they looked at the huge structure one of the walls flickered and faded. For a moment, she could see a bright red silk covering, the kind used to cover the glass houses at night. Then the wall flickered back into existence, though it didn't look quite the same.

Had someone just lost their concentration . . . or died?

"Okay," Tamani said. "Illusions are completely substance-less, so we have to walk through anything that we know isn't actually Summer."

"That's helpful," David muttered.

"How about this," Tamani said. "If it's made of stone, it's probably not real. Almost everything in Summer is made out of sugar glass."

"We're still going to run into things," Laurel said, "because there *are* real structures in there. So be careful."

They walked up to the moat and David hesitated. "Is there actually a dip here of any kind?"

Tamani shook his head.

"Looks real to me," David said, edging closer and looking over the edge.

Steeling herself, Laurel stepped forward and reached a toe into what appeared to be thin air, but her feet felt the soft earth of the main path, right where she remembered it being. She took a few more steps until it looked like she was walk-ing on nothing over the steaming molten rock below. "It's okay," she said, beckoning to David. "You can just walk—" her voice cut off as something slammed into her, knocking the wind out of her and throwing her through the illusion-ary castle wall. She couldn't breathe enough to scream and when she connected with a cool, smooth surface, it shattered beneath her weight.

"Laurel!" She wasn't sure who yelled it, but as soon as she could move she scrambled to her feet, feeling sugar glass sharp against her palms as she pushed herself upright—only to trip on something she guessed was a low stool, rendered invisible by the illusory cobblestone floor.

"I'm okay!" she yelled blindly to Tamani and David, hoping they could hear her over the roar of battle. She was suddenly painfully aware of just how vulnerable she was— she had no weapons, and even if she'd had her kit, her potions would be useless against these trolls. Gingerly she made her way to a crumbling bit of wall she could see but couldn't touch, then crouched behind it.

Peering over the faux wall, Laurel realized that the inside of the Summer "castle" was even scarier than the outside. Creatures straight out of legend were running all over the place, but Laurel knew most of them couldn't be real—or, at the very least, not the creatures they appeared to be. There were fire-breathing dragons, armor-clad unicorns, even an enormous cyclops. There were also trolls and faeries, some of them exact copies of others Laurel could see, and a rather large number of boulders Laurel knew hadn't been there before. It was impossible to tell which were bespelled fae and which were illusions made from nothing.

They're trying to get the trolls to kill one another, Laurel realized.

And for the most part, it seemed to be working. Laurel winced in horror as a black-clad troll gunned down an orange-haired faerie—only to breathe a sigh of relief as the "faerie" shimmered and shifted, taking the form of a tusk-mouthed lower troll. Across the imaginary courtyard, trolls were trip-ping over hidden fences and running into invisible houses and fae, all while being blinded by sudden flashes of light. It was chaos, but Laurel had to admit, it was effective.

Still, it couldn't last forever. Some of the faeries that dropped *didn't* turn into trolls, and illusions were winking out where the trolls swung blindly and got lucky. And as each faerie fell, whatever the unfortunate Summer had been hiding was suddenly exposed and vulnerable for as long as it took for someone else to take up the illusion.

When Tamani and David failed to appear, Laurel tried to make her way back to where she thought she'd come in, her sense of direction skewed by the chaos around her. Taking care to avoid being seen, she carefully felt her way from faux boulder to faux boulder.

She realized she must be going the wrong way when she touched the curve of another bubble house, disguised as a half-destroyed stable. Swallowing her fear and wondering if she could risk calling out for David and Tamani again, Laurel tried to turn back, but the landscape had changed—the shifting illusion made navigation by sight impossible.

Suddenly the bubble house at her fingertips flickered and became visible, its translucent shell draped three-quarters with brilliant purple silk, a conspicuous target in a sea of artificial gray stone. A troll Laurel hadn't seen lurking behind the mirage turned and swung his ax at the glass, smashing through it—then went after the faeries huddled within.

Helpless to stop the troll, Laurel could only duck behind a

fake wall and curl up on the ground, her hands clapped over her ears as the screams—so close—filled her head. Where was Tamani? Where was David? Tears streamed down her face and her chest convulsed in sobs as the screams were silenced one by one.

It was a long time before Laurel stopped shaking enough to move. Forcing herself to find some semblance of control, she peeked around the corner. The troll had collapsed inside, its mismatched eyes glazed, its lips curled in a final sneer—but whoever had killed it was nowhere to be seen. The house remained visible. There was no one left to hide it.

"Help me!"

It was a small cry, the voice of a child—a child who would soon attract more trolls, yelling like that. No longer hindered by invisible obstacles, Laurel looked around for trolls, then approached the half-destroyed bubble of sugar glass, steeling herself against what she knew she would find there.

"Hello?" she called as quietly as she could. The crunch of sugar glass beneath her feet was her only answer.

Did I imagine it? She didn't think the Summer faeries could make sounds with their illusions, but she had to admit she didn't know for sure.

"Help!" came the voice again.

Laurel flew to the source of the sound, a hand waving from beneath a limp, headless body oozing thick, translucent sap. Laurel shuddered and tried not to think about it too hard as she braced her feet and rolled the woman's corpse over to reveal a tiny girl, clutched protectively in the dead faerie's lifeless arms.

She knew the child in an instant.

"Rowen!" Laurel pulled Tamani's niece to her chest, carefully tucking the girl's head behind her arm to protect her from the gruesome sight surrounding them.

"Laurel?" Rowen whispered. Laurel couldn't imagine the confusion she must be feeling.

"It's me," she said, holding back a sob of relief. "I'm here. Tamani's here too, somewhere."

"Where?" Rowen asked as Laurel continued to hide the girl's face while picking her way through the broken glass and ducking low to hide behind a small rock that was actually real, but too small to provide cover for long.

"I'll bring him soon," Laurel said, forcing her face to relax, her mouth to smile. "Was—was your mom with you?" she asked softly. Rowen nodded and stuck two fingers in her mouth. The darkening around her eyes told Laurel that she knew *something* had happened, even if she didn't comprehend quite what that was.

"How about your dad?"

She shook her head. "He said he was going to go fight bad guys."

"And that's exactly what he's doing," Laurel said, scanning the chaos around them, searching for someplace to hide. The castle was becoming a flickering patchwork, with wrecked Summer houses interspersed among the false walls and half-timbered illusions, but there were still a few places to hide.

"Laurel!"

Laurel had never been more relieved to hear Tamani's voice. She peered over the wall to see Tamani using his spear like a blind man's cane, scouting out the terrain by feel while guiding David along. Relieved of the chore of figuring out where to walk, David was swinging his sword freely since it wouldn't be able to harm any faeries.

"Tamani! I have Rowen."

Instantly, Tamani was running toward them. His feet found something he couldn't see and he tripped, sprawling to the ground on his stomach, David close behind.

"Watch that . . . thing . . ." Tamani said ruefully, scrambling to his feet.

He covered the remaining distance quickly and threw his arms around Rowen and Laurel together, burying his face in Rowen's soft brown curls. "Thank the Goddess," he whispered.

David was glancing about warily. "What do we do now?"

Tamani surveyed the confusion and destruction surrounding them and shook his head. "We're not even halfway through yet," he said. "I underestimated the Sparklers. Vastly. If we try to keep going we're never going to make it to the Academy in time, and I'm not convinced we'll actually do much good here." He hesitated. "I say we go back the way we came. To the woods. Follow them up as close to the Academy as we can."

"But everything keeps changing," Laurel said. "How do you know which way is out?"

"That way," Rowen piped, pointing one tiny finger.

Tamani smiled. "I was just going by the sun, but now we have a Sparkler. Perfect visual memory is good for more than illusions, you know."

Laurel and David nodded, and Tamani took up his spear, holding it in front of him like a cane again, just in case. "Are you okay with Rowen?"

Laurel nodded. The little girl hardly weighed more than an infant, which made it all the more awe inspiring that she appeared to have memorized the settlement's layout. Laurel wondered whether it was part of Summer faerie training, or if it just came naturally to them. With Rowen's help, it took them only a few minutes to retrace the short distance they'd traveled into Summer, but Laurel was more relieved to see the lava-filled moat than she would have thought possible. Without hesitation she ran right over the top of it and, clinging to Rowen, sprinted for the trees. She'd never imagined the beautiful illusions she'd seen at the Samhain festival or the cute familiars Rowen had made last summer could transform her favorite settlement into this nightmare-inducing terror.

As they all panted for breath Tamani gathered the little faerie into his arms, holding her as though she were his lifeline.

"Now listen to me, Rowen," Tamani said, pulling back and holding her face firmly in his hands. "I know you've been working on changing your appearance."

Rowen nodded soberly.

"Did you get a good look at any of the bad guys who came in here today?"

She nodded again.

"Can you show me?"

Rowen's tiny chin quivered for a moment. The she bowed her head and seemed to expand before them, becoming twenty times the tiny girl she had been, morphing into a misshapen man in black jeans and a tattered white shirt. A man with a huge ax.

"Holy crap," David said, jumping backward and nearly knocking Laurel over.

Laurel blinked away tears—Rowen had seen the troll who had killed her mother. Gotten a good enough look to replicate him exactly.

"Good girl," Tamani said, still clasping her little hand, now cloaked in a troll's enormous fingers. "I want you to go down this path until you get to Rhoslyn's house. Stay in the trees. Try not to let anyone see you—even another faerie. No one. Turn into a bush or a rock if you have to. When you get there, you knock on the hidden back door I showed you last summer, understand?"

"Back door," Rowen said, the wispy voice so bizarre coming from that massive body.

"As soon as the door opens, you show Rhoslyn who you really are before she can hurt you."

Rowen nodded.

Tamani hugged her again, his body sinking into the illusion, creating a grotesque Tamani-troll hybrid. "Now run," Tamani said, pointing the young faerie in the right direction. "Run fast." The Rowen-troll nodded and began picking its way down the twisting path with the quickness of the small faerie girl.

"What happened?" Tamani asked Laurel in a flat tone, his eyes trained on the swiftly disappearing form.

"Someone should go with her," Laurel said, avoiding Tamani's question.

"She'll be fine," Tamani said, though he didn't sound certain at all. Mostly, he sounded pained. "She knows the way, and we've already lost too much time. This is the best we can do for her."

Laurel nodded. "I found her in . . . someone's . . . arms. The trolls—"

But she couldn't bear to finish. *So much death.*

"Dahlia saved Rowen," Tamani said tonelessly. "She'd have been proud to die that way." He turned and gave the faux castle one more look through the web of branches. "Let's go."

FOURTEEN

AS LAUREL FOLLOWED DAVID AND TAMANI THROUGH the woods near the Academy, her breathing became ragged and clipped. They reached a copse of trees within sight of the Academy, and Tamani jerked to a halt, Laurel barely managing to stop before plowing into him. Through the breaks in the high wall surrounding the school, they could see a hundred trolls at least, wreaking havoc across the once-manicured grounds, tearing things apart, as far as Laurel could tell, for the sheer joy of it.

"I see a few sentries fighting in there," Tamani said, squinting at the small gaps in the outer wall. "But mostly there are a lot of bodies. Once the sentries are down the barricades won't last long. Not against this group."

"What? Then why did you send Chelsea?" David demanded. "I thought—"

"I hoped to buy them time while we got Jamison to

safety." Tamani said, shaking his head. "You were right, Laurel. We should have come here first."

"We don't know that for sure," Laurel said. *What's done is done.* And they'd saved Rowen—surely that counted for something. "How can we get in?"

"We could go around," David suggested. "Maybe there are fewer around the back?"

"Maybe. But those entrances will be barricaded too, and I'm more worried about them tearing their way in here," Tamani said, and sure enough, Laurel saw some of the trolls were beginning to attack the Academy itself, dislodging boards that had been fastened across windows, ripping down the ivy that crept over the structure, smashing their fists against the thick stone walls. There were a small handful of blue-armored sentries fighting to hold the front doors which, though battered and cracked, remained closed. But they were vastly outnumbered and it would be only a matter of time before the Academy was completely overrun. "We're going to have to charge through. David leads the way—if we stay close to him, I can protect Laurel from behind."

Moving as one, they stepped out onto the path. As they passed through the Academy gates Laurel could taste the tang of blood on her tongue; it was different from when they were in the Garden where—despite the deaths—they had been winning. The Academy lawn was strewn with bodies of trolls and faeries alike, their blood pooling together.

The trolls were on them in an instant, rushing from all sides at their fresh new prey.

"Keep running!" Tamani shouted as he speared grasping arms.

David was swinging his sword wildly, clearing their path. Each swing brought down more trolls, and soon they were picking their way over dead bodies as David moved closer to the front doors. The trolls continued to press toward them. Laurel had to avert her eyes and hold her breath to keep from retching. It helped to focus on the front doors, looking for a reasonable chance to make a run for them. As she and Tamani and David drew closer, two sentries managed to drive a group of trolls back and down the stone steps.

"I've got a clear path!" Laurel shouted to Tamani.

He turned to glance at the entrance for the briefest of moments. "I'll cover you. Go *now*!"

Laurel threw herself out of the protective sphere of David and Tamani and sprinted for the front entrance, expecting to feel a troll's claws pierce her back at any moment. When she reached the heavy doors she threw herself against them, pounding her fists and shouting, "It's Laurel! Let me in! Please! It's Laurel! We need your help!" She turned to see Tamani and David close behind her. More trolls were closing in like waves on all three sides, gaining ground every second.

"Please!" Laurel shouted again. "Let us in!" She didn't dare look again, just continued beating on the splintering wood, trying to ignore the ache of forming bruises on her fists.

A tiny crack appeared between the doors, so small it could

have been her imagination. Then the opening widened, fingers threading through, pulling on the thick wood until there was just enough room for them to fall through. The doors quickly shut again, closing them away from the battle with an ominous slam.

Laurel lay panting on the floor, only dimly aware of the hands and bodies around her pushing furniture and bookshelves back up against the doors—repairing their barricade. Laurel lifted her cheek from the cool stone, tenderly probing the scrape there.

Then Tamani's hands were lifting her gently, checking for injuries, and sighing in relief when he found none. "Are you okay?"

Laurel nodded, although *okay* was not exactly the way she would have described herself right now. She glanced around. "David. Where's David?"

"Calm down," Tamani said, a hand on each arm.

"I will *not* calm down," Laurel said, pulling away. "Where is he?"

"He's outside, fighting," he said, reaching for her arm again.

"No," Laurel said, trying to twist away. "We can't leave him alone! Not to face all of that." She threw herself back toward the barricade. "You left him out there to die!"

Tamani grabbed her around her waist now, pulling her back. "He's not going to die!" he said in a voice so sharp Laurel stopped panicking for a moment. "He has Excalibur and he's not letting it go. I know it's scary—I'm scared too. But—"

"You don't even care!" Laurel shouted, the panic edging back in. "You can't put this all on his shoulders. He needs us, Tam!"

"I would never let anything happen to him!" Tamani shouted back, his nose almost touching hers. He paused, his hands tightening on her arms just a little. "But if he wasn't out there fighting the trolls, there's no way we could have gotten these doors closed again. The trolls are too strong. He got us in, and now he's buying us the time we need. If you can't trust *me* right now, trust Jamison. David will be fine."

Something in his words brought Laurel back to the moment. She looked at Tamani and forced herself to take a few long, slow breaths. "I don't need to trust Jamison," she said finally. "I trust you."

"Okay," Tamani said. He stroked her hair, his eyes never leaving hers. "The best thing we can do is focus on our job in here—as soon as we can, we will get him back; I promise you that."

Laurel forced herself to remember the power of Excalibur—how invincible David was with it—and how binding a promise from Tamani was.

"Keep piling!" a voice yelled as a soft hand slipped onto Laurel's shoulder.

"Chelsea!" Laurel threw her arms around her friend. "I wasn't sure I was ever going to see you again."

"I ran so freaking fast!" Chelsea exclaimed. "I think I could have won state today. Apparently you put a troll on my heels and I turn into a superstar."

Laurel squeezed her hand and turned to survey the situation. She had to admit, things looked better than she'd feared. The doors had a stout beam thrown across them and were braced back with an enormous pile of furniture. A group of faeries were lined up replacing the area they'd torn down to let her in, and the barricade was so massive Laurel was surprised they'd been able to let her through it at all.

The windows were a little trickier, but they'd done a pretty good job, using stone-topped tables and securing them to the oak window sashes with thick boards. The unnaturally strong trolls would only be slowed a little by the setup, but a group of faeries on each side of the great barricade clustered around two massive guns aimed at the windows on either side of the entrance.

Guns?

One tall, older faerie who seemed to be supervising yelled a command to the gathered faeries, then turned his sandy-blond head toward her. Sap had congealed in a ragged cut across one side of his face.

"Yeardley!" Laurel said, running to her professor and throwing herself in his arms with no thought to decorum.

"Laurel, thank the Goddess you're safe. And you've brought us another sentry," he said, his voice heavy with unconcealed relief.

"Yeardley—Tamani. You met him last time I was here."

"I see Chelsea delivered the message," Tamani said, eyeing the barricade—and the guns—approvingly.

"We've been doing our best. Thank you for sending your

friend Laurel. She told us what happened at the Garden and before the trolls got here we were able to pull in all the students who had been working outside and gather the younglings into an inner chamber." He hesitated. "A few trolls did get inside, but we think we've managed to kill them all. The labs are a mess and . . . and we've had several deaths and more injuries. But you're here now. Were you able to wake Jamison?"

Before Laurel could answer, a mighty thud on the covering of one of the windows reverberated through the atrium.

"Be ready!" Yeardley called.

Another thump sent the stone table rocking askew and a huge hand pushed through, followed by a beard-covered face.

"Now!" Yeardley yelled.

The sound of gunfire and the sharp scent of powder filled the atrium as the troll stumbled back in a spray of blood. Several faeries rushed forward to resecure the table.

The faerie at the trigger burst into tears and another faerie took the gun from her and scooted into her spot.

"Your friend's idea," Yeardley said, answering Laurel's unasked question. "The trolls we killed had these . . . weapons. Chelsea suggested we turn them around on them. Brilliant, really." He paused. "Hard on our poor students. They're not killers."

"Nor would I want them to be," Tamani said. "I suggest they wear gloves when they handle cold iron like that, though."

A loud crash sounded at the front door and Tamani swore. "Sounds like they're using a battering ram," he growled. "It won't be long now. Yeardley, we need your help reviving Jamison. He's safe, but he's in the Spring quarter."

"I'm happy to help," Yeardley said, "but getting from here to Spring will be no easy task."

"We can make it—we have David. Or we will soon. Do you have a high window facing front, an overhang, something?"

A flicker of a smile crossed Yeardley's face. "Yes. We have a balcony we've been attacking trolls from; I'll take you right there."

"I need some rope—bedsheets, even—something to haul David up with."

Yeardley passed on the request to one of the faeries standing by. "He'll meet us there," Yeardley said, already turning. "Come."

"Do you have bows and arrows?" Tamani asked as Laurel and Chelsea followed them up a winding staircase.

"Why would we have those?" Yeardley asked, a trace of helplessness in his tone. "We're a school, not an armory."

"How are you fighting the trolls, then? They're immune to Fall magic."

"As your lovely friend warned us," Yeardley said, his jaw tight. "Still, there are many things we can toss at them that don't require magic at all. Acid. Hot oil." He paused. "Bookshelves."

The door at the top of the stairs was already open and led

to a large balcony two floors up, a little to the side of the main doors. As they stepped out Laurel saw several faeries lugging an armoire through a door on the other side of the landing and she watched with horror and fascination as they struggled to the railing with the beautifully carved cupboard, paused, and then, when someone shouted "Now!" pushed it off.

A small blond faerie brushed dust from her hands with satisfaction as she turned away from the railing. "Katya!" Laurel exclaimed, running forward.

"Hecate's petals, you're here!" Katya exclaimed. She pulled back, gripping Laurel's shoulders, then pulled her close again. "You *shouldn't* be! It's so dangerous. Oh, but I'm so glad you are!"

Laurel lingered in her friend's arms an extra moment. This past summer, when Avalon had been so lonely without Tamani, Katya had been Laurel's personal rock. She never asked for details, but somehow she intuited that Laurel needed *someone* and took special pains to keep her busy and entertained.

Katya squeezed Laurel's shoulders one more time then looked up at Tamani. Her eyes lit with recognition. "This is your sentry friend. Tim . . . no, Tam?"

"Yes," Laurel said.

Without hesitation, Katya threw her arms around him and kissed his cheek. "Thank you," she said. "Thank you so very much for bringing her to us safely."

"We're not yet half done," Tamani growled, but Laurel

could tell he was pleased. She turned and hugged Katya again, grateful she was alive. It was a bittersweet reunion, but one Laurel hadn't realized until now that she had been looking forward to so much. She even took a moment to laugh at their matching pink peasant-style shirts that looked like they must have been made by the same Spring faerie.

Katya's eyes fell on Chelsea, standing just behind Laurel's shoulder. Laurel looked at the two and grinned. She had told both of them so much about each other, it felt momentous to finally have them together. Gesturing to each one, Laurel simply named them, pleased that their faces lit as she did so. "Chelsea, Katya."

"Laurel," Tamani called, breaking into their momentary reprieve. He was at the far edge of the railing, pointing.

Turning from her friends, Laurel ran to him, and her eyes followed his finger. The trolls had felled a tree somewhere, stripped of its branches, and were now using it as a rudimentary battering ram. David must have realized that the battering ram was the greatest threat and was on one side of it, hacking away at any troll who tried to pick it up. It appeared the trolls hadn't yet figured out just how dangerous David was, though; they poured onto him like water and fell like autumn leaves.

"David!" Laurel yelled, almost not daring to interrupt his concentration, but needing to know that he was okay.

"David?" Katya whispered beside her. "Your human boy?"

Laurel nodded, not meeting Chelsea's eyes or bothering to fill Katya in on the specifics.

"He's amazing," Katya said in awe.

"He certainly is," Chelsea said under her breath.

Laurel had to admit it was true. Trolls were falling so quickly there was a pile around him and he was forced to shove bodies down the front stairs with his feet to avoid being buried. Everywhere he went, he turned the tide of battle, and yet watching him do it here only made Laurel sad all over again.

"David!" she called again, and at last he heard.

He glanced up at her, then his brow furrowed in concentration and he swung the sword in a particularly wide arc, picking his way across the piled bodies while still keeping his sword in front of him. He slowly made his way toward them and Katya halted the faeries still throwing things off the balcony so that they wouldn't hit David.

"It's okay," Chelsea said, a sparkle of pride in her voice. "He's untouchable. Keep tossing stuff."

"Guys," David gasped when he got closer. "I can't do this much longer. My arms—" He sucked in a breath and paused to swing the sword at another troll. "My arms are about to give out."

"Where is that rope?" Tamani demanded, an edge of panic in his voice.

Laurel scanned the balcony and caught sight of two faeries running toward them, tying sheets together as they ran. She leaned over the railing. "We're—" She paused, feeling her voice about to break. "We're here, David. We're almost ready."

Tamani grabbed the first sheet from the faerie and pulled out his knife, splitting the end into two strips that he tied into a stirrup. He met Laurel and Chelsea's eyes with gravity.

"We lower this and David has to get to it first or the trolls will pull it down and we lose it. He puts his foot into the loop and we pull him up. Understand?"

Laurel nodded as Tamani handed her the stirrup. She leaned over the railing and repeated Tamani's instructions, to which David—without looking at her—nodded his understanding. She worried about telling him what to do when all the trolls could hear, but he was killing them off so quickly she suspected none of the ones in earshot would still be alive when the loop descended.

"Grab hold!" Tamani yelled, gesturing to the handful of fae surrounding him.

Everyone grabbed on to the end of the tied sheets and Chelsea stepped forward as well, taking hold of the sheet right behind Tamani. "Aim carefully," he said to Laurel, then clenched his fingers around the material and planted his feet.

"David!" Laurel shouted, and he looked up at her.

"I'm ready," he called weakly.

Laurel closed her eyes, took a breath, then opened them and tried to apply every concept she'd ever learned in softball as she threw the knotted material toward David.

Removing one hand from the sword, David reached up and grabbed the material out of the air, pulling it down and against his chest. After taking a moment to catch his balance he leaned over and thrust his foot into the loop.

The trolls, seeing a moment of weakness, surged forward. If they somehow managed to pile on him . . .

"Pull!" Laurel screamed the instant David was ready.

As the sheet-rope went taut, David clung crazily to it, defending not himself but his tenuous escape line.

"We've got him!" Laurel called.

Several howling trolls made grabs at David's legs; each time they did they slid away, unable to touch him. One of them finally got smart and, just before David was out of reach, it jumped up and grabbed the sheet and began swinging its club at David.

The weapon couldn't hurt David, but it knocked him off balance and threatened his grip. David tried to swing Excalibur at the troll, but he was exhausted and at a bad angle. Laurel could see his white knuckles, the strain in his face as he worked to keep hold of the sheet and Excalibur both. The possibility that David would ever drop the sword had seemed remote, but now it was the thing Laurel feared most. Without Excalibur, David was as good as dead.

Abruptly, the troll released its hold on the sheet, dropped to the ground in a heap, and lay motionless where it fell.

There was no time for Laurel to question this; with more than half of the weight suddenly gone, David practically flew to the railing.

Tamani let go of the rope with one hand and leaned forward to extend the other to David. But their hands met and then slid away, and David fell back.

David took two breaths, then looked up and swung the sword, releasing it into the air. Laurel heard it clatter against the balcony floor behind her as she reached out to grasp his arm, her hands making contact this time. Tamani had a firm grip on his other arm and together they pulled David up and over the edge of the railing, all three sprawling onto the cool stone.

FIFTEEN

THEY LAY PANTING ON THE BALCONY FLOOR A moment before David reached instinctively for the fallen sword and pulled it close, cradling it against his chest. As he turned his face to Laurel, she almost didn't recognize him. Blood-striped sweat streaked from his temples to his chin, and his arms were stained a rusty red. The rest of him was a patternless mess of gore.

"Are you all right?" she asked, pushing up off of her stomach as Chelsea dropped to her knees beside David.

"Tired," he rasped. "I need some water. And rest," he added. "I have to rest."

"Is there someplace we can take him?" Tamani asked, turning to Katya as the other faeries resumed barraging the trolls from above.

"The dining hall," Katya said. "They've brought some medical supplies in there for . . . for the faeries the trolls got earlier," she finished, her lashes lowered.

"I'll take them," Laurel said, rising to her feet and helping Chelsea up too. They looked down at David, who had pushed himself up to his knees. He looked too tired to stand on his own, but he was clinging to the sword and neither Chelsea nor Laurel could do anything for him while he held it.

Chelsea leaned close, just a hairsbreadth away from his ear. "David," she said softly. "Let me carry it for you."

David blinked at her as though she were speaking a foreign language. Then comprehension dawned. "Thank you," he whispered, laying the sword down on the floor between them.

Wrapping both hands around the hilt, Chelsea reverently took Excalibur and held it close as Laurel and Tamani helped David stand.

Laurel kept a hand on David's arm and led him toward the stairs as a Fall faerie emerged bearing a tray of beakers filled with steaming chartreuse—a solution Laurel recognized as an acid derived from fermented limes. "Let's get you cleaned up," she said, pulling David around to put his back to the fighting.

"Do we have time for that?" David asked, his voice weak as he followed her through the doorway off the balcony. "They just keep coming—we've got to get Yeardley to Jamison."

"Let's think about that later," Laurel said, casting a concerned glance at Chelsea. It was easy to feel safe barricaded inside the huge stone Academy, but how much longer could they last?

The three of them descended the staircase slowly and Laurel paused at the bottom when she realized Tamani wasn't with them. He was still standing at the top step, one arm resting on the banister. His shoulders were slumped and he was clutching at the injury on his shoulder that he had refused to let her see at his mother's house. He seemed to be allowing himself a moment to feel the weariness and pain he'd been pushing aside all day. His eyes were closed and Laurel turned away before he could discover he'd been seen in such a vulnerable moment. She was glad to hear his footsteps catching up with them a few moments later.

"David," Chelsea asked haltingly, "are you—"

"Man, that thing is heavy," David said, cutting off her question as he stretched out his weary arms, flexing his wrists one at a time.

Laurel bit her lip and when Chelsea turned to look at her, she shook her head. Now wasn't the time for questions.

As they entered the dining hall they bumped into a faerie carrying masses of white cloth.

"Watch it," a cold voice said, and Laurel's eyes widened. Despite the deep gash across her face and the unruly state of her hair and clothing, it was, unmistakably, Mara. Tamani recognized her as well, judging by his glare. Mara raised her chin, as if to look down on Tamani from her slightly greater height. But he met her eyes unflinchingly and—Laurel noted—without the requisite bow. After a moment, Mara dropped her gaze and shuffled from the room.

"Nice to meet you, too," Chelsea said dryly.

"Go ahead," Tamani said stiffly when Laurel looked back at him. "I need to check a few things."

Laurel stepped away from David and Chelsea. "Come back as soon as you're done," she said in a tone meant to cut off any arguments. "I need to take a look at your injuries."

Tamani started to protest but Laurel interrupted.

"Five minutes."

Tamani set his jaw, but nodded.

The dining hall was bustling and Laurel saw Yeardley across the room, delivering serums and binding strips to several stations where healthy Fall faeries were treating the wounded. Laurel wondered how they must feel, using potions they had made and never expected to use for themselves. "Repetition work," as they called it, when they put their studies aside to make healing solutions and other potions for the Spring faeries, for sentries outside the gates who occasionally tussled with trolls, or Tenders who fumbled their scythes. The worst injury most Fall faeries got was a paper cut or perhaps an acid burn.

"Sit," Laurel instructed as soon as she found David an empty chair. Chelsea propped the sword against David's seat and he immediately picked it up and laid it across his lap.

Leaving him to Chelsea for a moment, Laurel fetched a tall glass of water—"Plain water," she insisted to the faerie who tried to add pinches of nitrogen and phosphorous—and returned to find Chelsea fretting over how bloodied David was.

"I'm fine," David insisted. "I just need—oh man, thank you," he said, taking the glass of water from Laurel and downing it all in one go, except for a few droplets that trickled down his chin. Absently, he wiped them off on his sleeve, leaving a smear of blood beneath his lips.

"Do you want more?" Laurel asked, trying not to look at the new streak as David relaxed in his chair, leaning his head back against the wall and closing his eyes for a few seconds.

"Is he really okay?" Chelsea whispered, staring at David's blood-flecked face.

"It seems like it," Laurel said. "But I should get the blood washed off to be sure. Can you go grab something to scrub with and meet me by the fountain?" She pointed to a table full of folded fabric where people were grabbing bandages and towels. Chelsea nodded and hurried off.

"Come on," Laurel said, gesturing to David. "Let's get you clean."

At first, David followed her numbly, dragging Excalibur along the ground, surely unaware of the perfect line its tip was scoring across the polished marble floor tiles. But when he realized what Laurel had in mind, he suddenly couldn't get there fast enough. He sank to his knees at the edge of the marble circle, set Excalibur reverently aside, and thrust his arms into the water, scrubbing vigorously. A murky red cloud spread away from him, giving the water a pinkish hue.

Out the corner of her eye, Laurel caught Caelin—the one male Mixer her age—watching them. *Perfect.* "Hey," she said. "Do me a favor? I need a clean shirt. For him," she added—pointing to David—lest Caelin return with a fluffy blouse.

Caelin eyed the strange new male—he'd always been comically territorial—and nodded, heading toward the dorms. Chelsea appeared a moment later with a small pile of clean handkerchiefs.

"Thank you," Laurel said, grabbing the top one. She looked at the sullied water David was still scrubbing his arms in and wrinkled her nose. Chilly, crystal-clear water was spilling from the top of the fountain, so Laurel reached up and wet the cloth there before scrubbing at the blood decorating David's face.

"I'll help," Chelsea said softly, wetting a cloth and going to work on the other side, tackling a particularly thick stream of blood that ran down his neck.

"Strip," Laurel said, when most of David's face was clean. "We're never going to get the blood out of that shirt. Just take it off and toss it."

David reached for the tail of his T-shirt and, careful to keep the blood away from his face, pulled it over his head, dropping it unceremoniously onto the ground.

At first Laurel thought she was imagining the hush that seemed to settle around her, but after another minute of scrubbing, she realized that nearly everyone in the room had stopped moving.

The silence was now a buzz of whispers that grew louder every second.

Chelsea had noticed too, and was looking around nervously.

But all eyes were on David. Specifically, on David's chest, where a small patch of dark hair was clearly visible against his skin.

They hadn't realized he was human.

They probably hadn't realized Chelsea was human either, between the fury of the battle and the fact that Chelsea had no obvious giveaways like visible body hair. Some of the faeries were now looking at the sword David had placed at the fountain's edge and whispering behind their hands.

David noticed them, too, and stopped washing himself off. He was glaring at those faeries who were bold enough to look him in the face.

With loud footsteps Tamani stormed across the dining hall, an angry look on his face and holding a white bundle of cloth. Behind him Caelin was looking all too happy to have someone else complete the task he'd been given.

"Here," Tamani said, handing David the dry, white piece of clothing. "A clean shirt is the least we can do for saving the Academy." Tamani shot a glare around the room before handing over the shirt. After a long moment of silence, David pulled the fabric over his head, looking like any other faerie boy as the Avalon-style shirt covered his chest.

As soon as he was dressed, the dining hall burst into activity again, though many of the fae continued to eye David with a mix of curiosity, condemnation, or fear.

"How are you feeling, mate?" Tamani asked, dropping into a crouch beside David.

"Better," David said. "I could use another glass of water, though."

Chelsea hurried off to fetch it.

"Any chance you might be ready to go back out there?" Tamani's tone was casual, but Laurel knew he was anxious to get Yeardley to Jamison.

David pursed his lips. There was something haunted in his eyes, but he looked down at the sword and, after a moment, nodded. "I think so," he said.

"Thank you."

David closed his eyes for a few breaths, then opened them and reached for his sword.

"Not yet," Laurel said, leaping to her feet.

"Laurel . . ." Tamani began, desperation in his voice.

"Let me bind your shoulder first." His gray T-shirt was ragged and the sap on it had dried, but without a handful of binding strips the wound would certainly open again.

"I'm fine," Tamani said, turning not so subtly so she couldn't see his shoulder anymore.

"You're not. You're in pain, and you will be more . . . effective," she finally settled on, "if you let me do something about it."

He hesitated, then looked up at Chelsea, who was returning with more water for David. "If you hurry," he said, relenting. Then, quieter, "We don't have much time."

"I'll be fast," Laurel promised.

She went to the nearest station and searched through the medicines that remained. "Can I borrow these real quick?" she asked, grabbing two bottles of clear solution and a handful of binding strips.

The faerie gave Laurel a nod, barely glancing up as he pulled a long cactus-spine needle through a deep cut on a small child's shoulder, stitching it closed.

Laurel ran back to Tamani. "Take it off," she said, touching his shirt.

Tamani glanced at David, then groaned as he lifted his arms and shed his T-shirt, pulling the sap-stained spots away from his wounds gingerly. He was oozing sap from a half dozen shallow cuts, and the deep gash across his ribs that Laurel had bound that morning was wet despite her patch job.

The wound on his shoulder wasn't a single cut as she had thought—there were about five deep holes peppered across his upper arm. He pulled a sharp breath between his teeth as she dabbed at them with a wet cloth. "I'm sorry," she said, trying not to lose her cool at the depth of the cuts that looked more like stab marks. "I'll make it feel better in just a second."

"Don't," Tamani said, stopping her hand as she reached for a bottle.

"What do you mean?"

"Don't make it numb," he said, his voice still labored. "I can't move as well if I can't feel it. Just put the healing tonic on and bind it. That's all I can let you do right now."

Laurel frowned, but nodded. There was no telling how much more fighting Tam would have to do today. "Just . . . just squeeze me if it hurts," she said, employing the tactic her dad had used when she was little.

But rather than gripping her hand, Tamani wrapped his good arm around her hips, burying his face in her stomach with a muffled groan. Laurel stole a moment to run her fingers through his black hair before reaching for the bottle of healing tonic, determined to get this over for him as quickly as possible.

She tried not to pay attention to his fingers pressing into her leg, his breath soft against the skin at her waistline, his forehead planted just under her ribs. She worked quickly, wishing she could savor the moment, but knowing her indulgence would only cost lives.

"I'm done," she whispered after a torturously brief span.

He pulled back and looked at his shoulder, covered in binding strips that would grow into his skin over the next week or so. "Thank you," he said quietly.

Laurel stared resolutely at the floor as she gathered her supplies and ran them back to the station she'd taken them from. By the time she returned, Tamani had taken up his spear again and was standing in front of David. "Ready?"

David hesitated for the barest instant before nodding.

"We'll need to clear a path—I don't want to risk anything happening to Yeardley—but I don't think we should try the doors again. Let's go out the same way you came in," Tamani said, his voice focused and emotionless again.

"Over the railing?" David said, one eyebrow raised.

"You got a better idea?" Tamani asked with not a trace of sarcasm.

David thought for a second and then shook his head. "Let's go."

"We'll help lower you," Laurel offered, even as her head screamed at her not to let them go.

David and Chelsea were already moving toward the doors, and Laurel made to follow them but paused at the brush of Tamani's rough fingertips on her arm. As she turned to him Tamani looked at her gravely, and reached up to tuck her hair behind her ear.

He hesitated for an instant, then his hands found the sides of her face, pulling her to him. He didn't kiss her, just held her face close to his, their foreheads resting together, their noses almost touching.

She hated how much it felt like good-bye.

The four of them left the dining hall and walked down the shadowy corridor, the sounds of the battle growing loud again with each step they took. The Academy was keeping the trolls at bay, but how much longer would the walls hold up against so many? And how many more battles could Tamani live through? Eventually, he would have too many wounds to survive. In spite of Avalon's advantages, the trolls were winning on numbers alone.

As they emerged onto the balcony, Katya turned to them with panic in her eyes. "Thank the Goddess, you're back! Something's happening."

"What?" Tamani asked, running to lean over the railing beside her.

"They're *falling*," Katya replied, studying the milling trolls beneath them. "I saw it happen a few times over the past hour or so, but I figured they had injuries I couldn't see. Now they're starting to do it in groups. Five, six, sometimes as many as ten. Look," she added, pointing as Laurel, David, and Chelsea stepped forward to see.

The trolls were still banging the felled tree against the front doors and Laurel could see the wood crumbling beneath the assault. But as they backed up to take another run, the tree trunk shifted and began to roll to the side as several of the trolls collapsed onto their knees.

"They just did it over there, too," Katya said, pointing to a group beneath the balcony.

"That's what happened to that troll in Spring," David said. "And on the rope, when you were pulling me up."

"I don't understand," Tamani said. But even as he spoke, Laurel saw several more trolls go down. Even the disorganized trolls were realizing it now, and they had turned from their task of breaking into the Academy to questioning each other and pointing. Panic spread like wildfire and the group on the balcony forgot their plans and watched, transfixed, as more and more of the trolls crumpled to the ground.

"They're running away," David said, with awe and more than a touch of relief in his voice. The remaining trolls had turned tail, heading to the gates now, but even retreat was fruitless. Soon everything was still and all of the trolls lay motionless amid the trampled remains of the once-beautiful Academy grounds.

SIXTEEN

"ARE THEY . . . DEAD?" CHELSEA ASKED AFTER A long spell of silence.

"That one in Spring was very, very dead," David said.

"So, what?" Laurel asked, staring out on the carnage. "It's over?"

"What's going on?" Yeardley said, bursting onto the balcony amid the tense silence. He was holding a cloth sack in one hand—his kit, Laurel realized. "Why did the fighting stop?"

"It's hard to say," Tamani replied, scanning the grounds. "They look dead, but the Goddess only knows why. I don't trust this."

"What's that?"

A blur of motion on the green hillside caught everyone's eyes—several figures were making their way up the path from the Gate Garden.

"More trolls?" someone asked from the crowd.

Laurel watched the approaching figures for a moment and found it suddenly hard to breathe. "It's Klea," Laurel said softly. "She's got Yuki with her."

"I don't understand," Yeardley said.

"The Wildling," Tamani said. "The one we were trying to figure out last time we were here; she's a Winter."

Katya gasped. "Are they coming here?"

"I don't know," Tamani said. "If not, then they're headed for the palace. I'm not sure which is worse. Either way, we're too late. This is why we needed Jamison—to fight her off."

"She's *hostile*?" Yeardley asked, a subtle fear filling his voice.

"It's hard to know for sure," Tamani said.

Laurel didn't think it was hard to know at all; Yuki was the only reason the trolls were even *in* Avalon, so that made her responsible for the death and destruction around them.

"But she *is* the puppet of an exiled Fall—Callista," Tamani said.

This time the horror in Yeardley's expression wasn't subtle at all. "Callista? That's . . ." He turned toward the Fall faeries gathered on the balcony. "We've got to get out of here. Now!"

"We can't just leave," Laurel said, following Yeardley as he threw himself back from the balcony railing. "We're barricaded here. It's probably the safest place in Avalon right now."

Yeardley stopped short. "And just how long," he said in a soft voice that chilled her to the core, "do you think it will take a Winter faerie to remove a barricade made completely of *wood*?"

"He's right," Tamani said from over Laurel's shoulder. "We should run. There's a pretty dense forest to the west—there's an exit that way, right?"

"There is," Yeardley said.

"Gather whoever you can and head that direction. Without Jamison, I—I don't know what else we can do."

Laurel hated hearing Tamani sound so defeated. All day he had fought trolls and won, and now two faeries were enough to destroy his spirits.

"Right. You there, run to the west barricade," Yeardley ordered a dark-eyed faerie Laurel thought she recognized from a more advanced class. "They need to take it down immediately!" Then, turning back to Tamani, he said, "Some of the staff are with the sprouts upstairs, and you saw how many students are gathered in the dining hall. Everyone else is busy securing their experiments and—"

"Their *what*?" Tamani asked.

"Their experiments," Yeardley repeated, with no indication that he considered this less than completely rational.

"Well, get them all together now," Tamani said. "To hell with their experiments."

"Tam," Katya called from the railing, "they've passed the turnoff to the Winter Palace. They're definitely coming this way."

Tamani was still for a long moment, then sprang into action as though someone had flipped an *on* switch. "Okay, everyone without a weapon, leave—now," he said, singling out David with a nod. "Evacuation time."

He began herding everyone on the balcony back into the Academy and down the stairs.

"I'm not going," Laurel said, planting her feet as Tamani tried to shoo her in with the others.

"Laurel, please. There's nothing you can do against her."

"There's nothing *you guys* can do against her either!" Laurel winced even as the words flew out of her mouth. "I—I didn't mean . . ."

Tamani was quiet for what felt like an eternity. "Maybe there's not," he finally whispered. "But perhaps we can buy you the time you need to get away. After we get you out, we'll go out the front and meet her, while everyone else heads for the trees."

Laurel looked at David, but he just nodded his agreement.

"Okay," she said softly. She hated feeling useless. "I'll go back to Rhoslyn with Yeardley. We'll bring Jamison here as soon as we can."

"Perfect," Tamani said, the slightest hint of relief on his face.

"Take Chelsea, too," David said, and he reached out a hand to nudge her forward before putting both hands back on the sword.

"Of course." Laurel nodded and took Chelsea's hand. "Come on. Let's see if we can help everyone get going."

"Thank you," Tamani said softly, squeezing her hand.

Laurel squeezed back, but didn't look up to meet his eyes—didn't want him to see how hopeless she felt. She knew what Yuki had done at the apartment building, what

Jamison had done to the trolls . . . how long could David and Tamani hope to last against a Winter faerie? Certainly not long enough for Laurel and Yeardley to revive Jamison and bring him here.

"We need to get all the sprouts out first," Yeardley was instructing as they trailed him into the atrium. "Get everyone to the west exit!" Faeries went running to spread the word, most of them obviously in a barely controlled panic.

"Laurel!" Tamani came barreling down the stairs, David close behind, as a series of shots sounded outside the front doors.

"Hecate's eye!" Yeardley swore. "What was that?"

"Soldiers at the entrance," Tamani said, panting. "They came from around back. Too small to be trolls, but they had guns. They've got to be Klea's."

"Klea's?" Laurel asked, confused. "But she's not even here yet."

"She must have sent them ahead," Tamani said, his voice flat and emotionless. "It's what I would have done, held back until they were in position. I should have realized. We're exactly where she wants us, and there's nothing we can do about it."

As if on cue from Tamani, the decorative colored windows fifteen feet over their heads shattered, raining stained-glass shards and a half dozen cracked plastic jars across the furniture-strewn atrium. Translucent liquid pooled around the open containers, saturating the air with the distinctive odor of gasoline.

"What do we do?" Yeardley asked. "Gather? Spread out? I—"

His voice cut off as the deafening roar of an explosion filled the air. Flames licked under the battered front doors, charring their finish and igniting the gasoline, sending a searing wave of heat rolling across the room. Those closest to the flames ignited instantly, their screams cut mercifully short by the intensity of the fire.

"Spawn of Ouranos!" Yeardley yelled. "Run!"

They fled the atrium ahead of billowing black smoke as flames skated over the puddles of gasoline and began licking their way to the carpets and tapestries that adorned the room.

As they ran toward the dining hall, Yeardley was almost bowled over by the dark-eyed faerie he had sent ahead to get the west barricade cleared. Her eyes were wide with fear as she spoke, her words almost unintelligible in their rush: "Fire! The west barricade is burning!"

Sure enough, Laurel could see wisps of black smoke snaking their way along the ceiling down the passageway to the west exit.

"Students! Please, calm yourselves!" Yeardley shouted, but Laurel knew it wouldn't do any good. Smoke was already gathering above them, thick, choking clouds spreading from the atrium and, she assumed, the other exits as well.

So panicked was the stampede of Fall faeries that Laurel almost didn't catch the strange hissing sound that came just before a reverberating explosion somewhere far above them.

"What was that?" Chelsea called, shouting to be heard above the noise.

Laurel shook her head and Tamani pointed at the ceiling. "What's up there?"

"Classrooms, dorms," Laurel rattled off automatically.

"No," Tamani clarified, "right there, specifically."

"The tower," Laurel said after a moment's thought. "Five or six stories high—you've seen it from the outside."

Tamani swore. "Probably more gasoline. She's got us trapped on all sides."

When they caught up with Yeardley again, he had opened a large closet and was tossing buckets to several older faeries— professors and Spring staff, mostly. "Use the fountain in the dining hall. Aurora, if we can't get the sprouts to the dining hall, we should get them to the windows. Jayden, take two faeries and get to the pulley deck—open those skylights."

"Air will feed the fire," Tamani countered.

"But it will also let the smoke escape," Yeardley said, tossing out two more buckets. "The smoke will kill us before the fire. Once it's under control, we should be able to organize an evacuation. We've plenty of windows and ropes, not to mention firewalls, throughout the Academy. Wouldn't be much of a research facility if we weren't prepared for a fire."

Tamani's brow furrowed. "Klea's soldiers are waiting out there, with guns. What's to stop them from killing anyone who goes out the windows?"

"I'm afraid that's not my area of expertise," Yeardley said with a meaningful look at Tamani's spear.

Laurel breathed and her throat was instantly burning, as were her eyes; the smoke was getting lower.

"The dining hall," Yeardley croaked, ducking low and waving for them to follow.

As they approached the double doors, Laurel caught sight of the bucket brigade, already passing water from the fountain down the halls to keep the fire at bay. Others were stripping the walls and floors of flammable material to halt the fire's progression. But their work was hampered by the acrid smoke, and for every faerie doing something useful, three were running blindly through the halls, clutching books and experiments to their chests. Others gathered in stairwells, arguing whether they should go up or down. Laurel tried to yell for them to follow her, but she gulped in a chestful of smoky air and began coughing uncontrollably.

"Faeries! This way!" David's voice rang through the murk like a lighthouse in fog. He was standing tall, seemingly heedless of the dark clouds that swirled madly around him and Laurel suppressed a gasp; the smoke was being repelled by Excalibur's magic. The layer of clear air that surrounded him couldn't have been thicker than an eyelash, but the air he inhaled was clean, and he shouted again. "To the dining hall! They're opening the skylights!"

At first, the faeries crowded on the stairs seemed paralyzed by indecision, and Laurel realized they were standing there, holding their breaths against the smoke, wondering whether they should follow David's orders.

Because he's human.

Then a Mixer Laurel didn't recognize began pushing his way down through the crowd in David's direction. For a moment Laurel's eyes widened and she wondered if he was about to pick a fight. But he simply stood in front of David for a moment, then nodded, and ducked down to enter the smoky hallway that led to the dining hall. The other faeries finally seemed to get the message, and slowly, so painfully slowly, flowed into the hallway, heading toward the dining hall, crouched low so they could breathe.

But not everyone was following. A handsome young faerie was fighting through the crowd to go the other way. He had placed a foot on the bottom step when someone called out from beneath the smoke, "Galen, stop!"

Galen paused.

Something dark was pouring very slowly down the stairwell. For a moment Laurel thought it was oil, but then she realized it was tinged red and had a strange wispy quality to it—not unlike the smoke gathering all around them. But it wasn't like the sleeping gas at the gateways, which had expanded and risen into the air; this mist was heavy and crept across the ground, like slow-moving dry-ice vapor, filling each step like sludge before a stream broke free and poured down onto the next step.

Galen's mouth tightened. "There are still fae upstairs," he called. "I have to warn them." And without another delay, he continued up the steps.

The instant the red, creeping smoke touched his foot,

Galen staggered and fell, his face going blank, his limbs convulsing. As he landed on the stairs, the deep red mist swirled out around him. Even through the hazy air, from ten feet away, Laurel knew he was dead.

Others saw it too; there were several shrieks as fae fled the creeping mist—some running straight toward the burning exits.

"Stop, stop!" Yeardley's voice was muffled in the choking smoke. "We must stop panicking," he pleaded. "The skylights are open in the dining hall; everyone get to the dining hall!"

"Galen was right; some of the staff is still upstairs! Can't we do something?" one of the lingering faeries asked.

Yeardley looked at the menacing gas pouring down both stairways that led to the upper floors. "Goddess help them," he said weakly.

At last, most of the faeries made for the dining hall, but a few remained stubbornly looking up the stairs. As Laurel watched, the reddish mist spilled over the landing above them, cut into long tendrils by the ornate rails, flowing downward like an oily waterfall.

"Look out!" Laurel shouted, pulling Tamani and Chelsea backward with her, barely missing the thin streams of mist that fell in the pattern of prison bars.

Not everyone was quick enough, and scarlet waves poured over them like rivulets of sand; without a sound, they fell where they stood.

"Let's go!" Tamani said, pulling at Laurel's hand. She

wanted to resist him—to pick up the fallen faeries, to carry them to safety. But Tamani's hand was firm in hers and she let him draw her backward.

In the dining hall, Yeardley was directing the students to line the bottom of the doors with wet cloths. Those in the bucket brigade who had escaped the deadly red poison were emptying buckets of water right onto the doors, soaking the wood. Thanks to the large skylights, now open to the dim evening sky, the smoke was higher here, and Laurel could stand up straight and still breathe. She looked over at Chelsea, whose face and clothes were blackened; Laurel assumed hers were the same. Glancing around, she was shocked at how few faeries were present, and even more shocked at how few were conscious. They'd been treating the injured here anyway, but now the injured were joined by dozens who had fainted from the smoke.

"Now what?" Laurel asked.

"David and I will head out first," Tamani said, waving his spear at the faeries who were situating a wooden ladder beneath one of the high-set dining hall windows. "It's not an ideal staging ground for an evacuation, but between the skylights, the firewalls, and the fountain, we should have time to get everyone out—*if* we can get in and out those windows without getting shot."

Laurel could tell something else was bothering him in the way he kept checking the sky. "What?" she said, laying a hand on his arm.

After a few seconds he turned to her. "There's no way

Klea will stick around—she knows she's won here. She's going to head to the Winter Palace next—someone has to stop her. I have to stop her."

He was right. "Take me with you," Laurel insisted.

"Laurel, please," he begged, but she was already shaking her head.

"Not with you to Klea—just get me out of here. Me and Yeardley. We'll get Jamison." She stepped closer so no one, not even Chelsea and David, could hear her. "You know he's our only shot."

"Will Yeardley even agree to come with you?" Tamani asked, and Laurel glanced at him where he was still organizing the panicked fae. He was the Academy's beacon, and she wanted to take him away.

"He'll have to, won't he?" Laurel said, the words choking her.

A commotion drew her attention as the light around her took on a strange, sickly hue. It took Laurel only a second to realize it was coming from the skylights overhead. The red mist must have spilled out the upstairs windows and was now making its way across the wide roof of the dining hall, coating the glass skylight and, as Laurel turned her eyes upward, spilling over.

The wide waterfall of deadly poison cascaded through the air for at least twenty feet before reaching the floor, striking an unconscious, soot-stained faerie lying on a linen-covered table. He convulsed silently before going still as the oily red gas spilled across the floor.

A collective murmur of dismay rippled through the gathered fae a moment before the panic set in. They turned almost as one and Laurel barely managed to stay on her feet as faeries pushed past her, hardly seeming to see her—to see anything beyond their desperation.

Laurel's eyes remained fixed on the ruby mist, her hand clutching Tamani's fingers as the truth slammed into her.

They hadn't escaped Klea's poison; they'd played right into her plan.

And now there was no way out.

SEVENTEEN

THE RED DEATH MOVED SLOWLY, SO VERY SLOWLY, its smoky tendrils more like a living thing than a simple gas. It curled around its victims, taking easy prey first—the fae who lay unconscious on the floor.

I have to save them! Desperation banished every rational thought from Laurel's head and she threw herself toward the fallen bodies only to meet Tamani's chest as he stepped in her way. "Laurel, you can't."

She fought against him, trying to get to the helpless, unconscious fae. Tamani's arms were tight around her waist and dimly she felt David's fingers on her face, caressing, trying to calm her.

"Laurel," David whispered. "Stop." The gentle word was so quiet it made her freeze as though he had yelled it. "We have to think," he said, and slowly Laurel forced herself to be still.

Everyone who could stand was up on tables, mostly at the edges of the room, wide-eyed with horror. Fire blocked the obvious exits; poison seeped in everywhere the fire failed to reach . . . Laurel could almost *feel* the contempt Klea had put into every detail of this elaborate assault. These people had been her teachers, her friends—her *family*, really. But it was clear from her actions today that Klea wanted them all to die, and what was more, she wanted them all to die *afraid*.

Laurel realized she was shaking with anger. Forget the trolls; the biggest monster in Avalon was Klea.

Laurel shoved David's arms away and strode to a faerie lying unconscious just a few feet from the creeping smoke. Laurel pushed her arms around the young faerie's chest and began to drag her backward, away from the danger.

Tamani grabbed her hand, but Laurel yanked it away. He reached out to grasp it again and held it tightly this time. "Laurel, what are you doing? Where are you going to take her?"

"I don't know!" Laurel shouted, angry tears burning her eyes. "Just . . . away from *that*!" She went back to her task, pulling another faerie out of immediate reach of the red mist. They would all die anyway, but somehow Laurel couldn't let them die *right now*, not when she could at least prolong their lives. She grabbed another faerie's shoulders and began dragging her back to join the first.

With a nod, Tamani stepped up and did the same thing, lifting another faerie and pulling him away from the smoke that was drawing nearer, inch by slow inch, as it filled the dining hall entrance and crept further into the room. It was pouring from the open skylights in earnest now, and the floor would soon be a deadly crimson swamp.

Chelsea and David pulled another faerie up onto a table and others began joining in, mimicking Laurel's futile act of service, dragging the wounded and the fallen back until there was a line of bare stone between the smoke and its next victims.

As David started on another faerie, Tamani stopped him with a hand on his chest. "You have to move the sword." The smoke was only a few inches away from where David had left it, with the blade sunk several inches into the marble tiles. "We cannot lose it."

David nodded and turned to retrieve it. His eyes widened. "Wait," he said, reaching out to grab Tamani's arm. "The sword. Laurel! Where does that wall go?" David yelled pointing to the wall at the back of the dining hall.

"Outside," Laurel panted, not stopping as she dragged another faerie backward. "Gardens and stuff."

"Is that it?" he pressed. "No, uh, overhangs or something?"

"The greenhouses are out that way," offered Caelin, and Laurel was surprised to see he was addressing David directly.

"Perfect," David murmured, almost to himself. "They'll hide us from anyone who might be back there."

"But you can't *get* to them from here," Caelin argued. "There's no door. They just share a wall."

"Thanks," David said, wrapping his fist around Excalibur's hilt, drawing it from its temporary sheath, "but I make my own doors."

Laurel watched as he ran to the wall, bowed his head for an instant, as if in prayer, then raised his sword and thrust it into the stone wall. Tears of hope sprang to her eyes as she watched him cut a long, vertical line in the stone. Two more cuts on the side and Laurel could see light bleeding through the wall.

"Help me push!" shouted David, and soon faeries were gathered around him, picking their way carefully over the unconscious fae they'd collected at the edges of the room. They heaved with all their might as David cut at the bottom and, with a loud scraping, the panel gave way and fell to the ground, the light of the setting sun pouring in.

The next fifteen minutes were like a fast-moving nightmare. Laurel's arms ached as she dragged faerie after faerie through the narrow passage David had opened into one of the greenhouses. Her legs, already weary from a long day fleeing trolls, threatened to collapse. But each faerie they dragged out of the dining hall was one more Mixer who would live.

A moment of chilling fear made all the fae halt in their tracks for a few moments when the red poison began pouring over the edge of the dining hall roof and onto the transparent glass ceiling of the greenhouse. They all seemed to collectively hold their breath as red coated the sloped roof, but the seals held; the faeries were safe.

Sweat poured down the faces of those who worked beside her—almost certainly a new experience for most Fall fae—but time was running out. In the dining hall the puddling gas had almost completely filled the floor and continued to pour in through the open skylights, no longer in single streams but waves as wide as the skylight itself.

"We have to stop," Yeardley said at last.

"One more," Laurel said breathlessly. "I can get one more."

Yeardley considered for the briefest of instants, then nodded. "Everybody, one more, then we have to find a way to seal this hole or all our work will have been for nothing."

Laurel ran to the nearest group of fallen fae. She had a good twenty feet to drag this one. With aching arms, she reached around the chest of the first faerie she came to, hating that there were so many others close enough to touch—so many she couldn't hope to save.

As she turned, a new line of mist fell from an overhead skylight, cutting off her view of the exit. When it hit the stone floor the ruby poison splashed, tiny wisps swirling so near that Laurel had to throw herself out of the way to avoid getting hit.

Gritting her teeth, Laurel hefted the body higher. She had to get out of here.

She dragged the faerie around the cascade, legs screaming in protest. She looked forward again and her path was open. Fifteen more feet. Ten. She could make it.

Then her legs tangled in something on the floor and she fell, feeling the skin on her elbow split as it hit the stone floor. She looked down at what she had fallen over.

It was Mara.

She'd been working in here before but must have fainted from the heat and smoke before the skylights were opened.

Laurel looked back. The creeping gas was inches away from Mara's feet.

I will not let you die.

With one more glance at the exit, Laurel turned and shoved one arm around Mara—she'd get them both; she *had* to! Her arms rebelled, shaking with fatigue as she awkwardly dragged them a few feet. A few more. She turned to get a better grip while staggering backward; other faeries—faeries who hadn't spent the day hiking and running—slid past her with their burdens. Laurel's chest and throat ached from the smoke still in the air—she'd been in here too long—and the mist seemed to be following her now, inching forward as quickly as Laurel could manage to flee.

It's her or you. The thought came unbidden, and though she suspected it might be true, she shook her head, yanking the two faeries a little farther.

I can't do it. Yes, I can! She glanced back at the exit. It felt so close and yet so very far away. Pulling with all her might, something made her look up just in time to see another cascade of smoke pour down from the skylight, splashing to the floor and sending a wave of poison rippling toward her.

EIGHTEEN

TAMANI HALF THREW THE UNCONSCIOUS FAERIE out of the hole in front of him and staggered over the stone lip, gasping for air. The gash in his side was seeping again and it was all he could do not to curl up in a ball and clutch at it. He had never put his body through so much torture before and wasn't entirely sure how he was still standing.

What doesn't kill you . . .

Shocked, Tamani stood up straighter and looked around him. The greenhouse was enormous, at least five times bigger than Laurel's entire house back in California. And through the glass walls he saw more, a long row of them just like the Mixer boy had said. Tamani vaguely remembered the greenhouses from his childhood days of roving the Academy with Laurel and his mother, but he had assumed they had only seemed gigantic in comparison to his tiny sprout self. This was a perfect place to harbor the survivors.

The parade of faeries had stopped emerging from the

smoke and Yeardley and some of the older fae were crouched at the hole, calling to the few who must still be in there. Where was Laurel?

His eyes found David, working with several faeries to raise the piece of stone wall upright, ready to push it back where it had been. Chelsea was kneeling beside someone who was on the floor coughing—probably a faerie who had breathed in too much smoke.

But no Laurel. Tamani scanned the crowd, then again, and a third time, but he couldn't find her.

Fear clutched him as he realized she must still be inside. All thoughts of weariness left him and he ran to the hole David had carved, elbowing through the crowd.

"No more," an older faerie said, laying a firm hand on his chest.

"I just have to see," Tamani said, pushing him away. "I have to . . ." But no one was listening. He stopped talking and focused on worming his way closer when he managed to get a quick look over a shorter female's head.

There she was! Just ten feet away from the exit, struggling to save one last faerie, her back to them as she pulled him toward the opening.

"Leave him!" Yeardley was yelling, but that blond head was shaking furiously.

Tamani cursed Laurel's stubbornness and tried to push forward again. "I'll go get her," he said. But no one seemed to hear him, the hands pushing back at him growing stronger as they all began to panic.

Why won't she leave him?

"I have to . . . I have to." Tamani continued struggling against the faeries, his words no longer coherent, only one thought in his mind. *I have to get to her.*

Tamani's breath caught as Laurel stumbled backward, the bulk of the faerie she'd been dragging dropping onto her legs, pinning her. She was kicking the weight away, but somehow Tamani knew those few precious seconds had tipped the balance against her.

"No!" he screamed, launching himself forward, making little progress in the crowded greenhouse.

She heard him—he could tell; she was scrambling to her hands and knees, turning her face toward his voice. But then she convulsed, silently, as the poisonous tendrils overtook her, her pink shirt seeming to glow in the darkness as the wispy red smoke enveloped it.

Everything inside Tamani shattered, razor-sharp edges that cut every inch of his body from the inside.

"That's everyone," Yeardley said mournfully, gesturing David and the faeries forward with the stone square. "We can save no more. Block it."

Tamani's feet seemed to have taken root in the ground. "No!" he screamed again. "Good Goddess, no!"

David heaved against the stone with all his might.

He must not realize; he would never let them leave Laurel like that. Tamani opened his mouth to warn David but his throat closed around his desperate words, blocking off the last rays of hope.

He couldn't say the words.

Couldn't say anything.

Couldn't breathe.

Couldn't see.

Blackness descended around him. He had to get to her—he couldn't live without her, didn't know how. Didn't know how to breathe in and out in a world she wasn't a part of.

Strong hands slammed him against the wall, the pain of his head hitting the stone bringing back the tiniest modicum of reason. Enough that he was able to blink and clear his vision—to see the face inches away from his nose. He didn't know the faerie—it was just another Mixer—but the pain in his eyes reflected Tamani's own.

"You have to let her go," he said. And Tamani knew this faerie had been forced to let someone he loved go too. "This fight isn't over yet," the faerie pinning him said. "That rebel faerie's still out there, and we're going to need you."

Klea.

She had taken everything—*everything*—from him.

She was going to the Winter Palace next. It was the only logical step.

There was no time to wait for the others. He had to go *now*.

She would kill him this time; he knew that. There would be no Shar to save him.

Maybe he could slow her down. *Then* she could kill him.

And, Goddess willing, then he would be with Laurel.

He forced himself to nod, to breathe evenly. To stop fighting against this faerie who held him back. He didn't want to wait for Chelsea to discover Laurel was gone—to see David realize what he'd done. Didn't think he could stand to share his pain with them.

The faerie in front of him said something—Tamani may as well have been deaf—and Tamani nodded, settling his forehead against the glass wall as if defeated. But his eyes roved the land outside, still just visible in the fading light. The steeply pitched roof of the greenhouse made the red gas slough off to the sides. This left the front door, just under the apex of the ceiling, safe. It wasn't guarded—who would think to guard it?

Only a crazy fool would want to leave right now.

Tamani edged closer to the door, trying not to draw attention to himself, putting more and more rows of plants between himself and the crowd of Mixers. He was almost there when the one who had spoken to him earlier glanced back. He met Tamani's eye, but he was too far away. Tamani slipped out the door, the glass frame closing and cutting off the protest.

Then he was running. He felt light, weightless, almost like he could fly as his feet pounded against the mud and grass and he ran for the Academy's living wall, heedless of any of Klea's minions who might still be watching.

He was going to kill Klea.

Or Klea was going to kill him.

In that moment, it didn't matter which.

Laurel's body ached and she hugged her arms to her chest. She'd barely gotten Mara out before collapsing on the floor in a fit of coughing. Then Chelsea was there, bending over her with concern on her face.

"It's okay," Chelsea was saying softly. "You're all right."

Several more faeries gathered around her as Laurel drew in a deep breath that filled her chest. "I'm good now," she said after a couple more coughs. "I'm good." But she didn't get up. For a few seconds she needed to just lie there, focusing on breathing in and out. Just for a second.

She heard screaming and shouts from the wall of the Academy, but she clenched her eyes shut and blocked it out. She didn't want to see them put the cut section of wall back in, or know how many they'd left to die. It was too much to even consider, so she lay with her eyes closed, trying to force her tears back until the commotion died down. Taking one more breath, she braced herself and opened her eyes, letting reality come crashing back.

"Where are David and Tamani?" Laurel said, pushing her sore body up and sweeping her hair out of her face.

"David's over by the wall," Chelsea said, pointing. "And I don't see Tamani right now, but he made it out a couple seconds before you did, I promise," Chelsea added. She must have seen the panic start to shine in Laurel's eyes.

"Okay," Laurel said carefully. *He's here—I'll find him.*

At the wall between the dining hall and the greenhouse, they were stuffing thick mud from the planter boxes into the cracks around the cut-out square to seal in the poisonous mist. A couple of faeries had taken off their shirts and were using them to fan the stone, not only to dry the mud, but to dissipate any tendrils of the toxic smoke that might make their way out.

Laurel looked around the garden at the surviving faeries, more than half of them wounded or unconscious and all coated in soot. She should have felt pride that there were probably about a hundred survivors but all she could think about were the hundreds inside. The hundreds dead. Sprouts, professors, classmates, friends. All gone.

Friends.

"Chelsea, where's Katya?" Laurel's eyes darted around the garden, looking for the blond hair and pink shirt that matched hers. "Where is she?" Laurel climbed to her feet, sure if she could just get a better look, she would find her friend.

"I—I haven't seen her," Chelsea said.

"Katya!" Laurel yelled, spinning about. "Katya!"

"Laurel." Hands were on her arms and Yeardley's voice was in her ear. "She didn't make it. I'm sorry."

Katya. Dead. Laurel vaguely heard David arrive at her side and felt his hand gentle on her arm. "No." She whispered the word. Saying it too loud would make it true.

"I'm sorry," Yeardley said again. "I tried . . . I tried to get to her to save herself. But you know Katya; she wouldn't."

Laurel had managed to hold back until now, but with Katya's face still so fresh in her mind—her smile, her determination on the balcony—it was too much. She collapsed against Yeardley and let the tears come raining down on his shoulder as he held her.

"She will be sorely missed," Yeardley murmured in her ear.

Laurel raised her face from Yeardley's shirt. "I'm going to kill her," she said, the bitterness in the voice that escaped her mouth not even sounding like her own. A spark of rage ignited within her and Laurel let it smolder, growing hotter. First Shar, now Katya . . . for the first time in her life, Laurel realized she genuinely wanted someone to die; wanted it so badly that she would strangle Klea with her bare hands, if necessary—

"Laurel."

Yeardley's soft, penetrating voice brought Laurel back to herself. She looked over at the fundamentals instructor.

"Laurel, you are not a warrior."

That was true. But did it matter? The Academy grounds were practically littered with guns just now—all she had to do was pick one up and shoot Klea in the back. It would be as easy as chasing her down.

"I have seen your work. You're no destroyer. You're stronger than that."

What's stronger than destruction? Laurel had seen strength. Tamani was practically built of it. Yuki was so strong she had almost killed them all. Klea was even stronger—she'd beaten Shar, who Laurel had imagined undefeatable. Even Chelsea and David had helped repel an invasion of thousands of trolls in one afternoon. So far today, Laurel had done nothing but run away.

"You're a healer, Laurel, you always have been. And even though you're angry right now, you don't have it in you."

"I could," Laurel insisted. "I could do it!"

"No, you couldn't," Yeardley said calmly. "Not like this. And that's not a weakness, Laurel. It is its own kind of power—the same power that makes you such a great Mixer, the kind of Mixer Callista could never quite be. Anyone can pluck a flower, Laurel. True strength is knowing how to give it life."

He pressed something into her hand. Laurel looked down at the bright red flower—*castilleja*. Her mom called it Indian paintbrush; common both here and in the human world. But, when cured correctly, it was one of the most powerful healing flowers in Avalon.

Laurel's anger melted away, leaving behind a deep, hollow grief. But sadness was familiar; sadness was manageable. It didn't transform her, the way the raging anger did. She could remain herself and still feel this aching grief.

With Chelsea and David flanking her, their arms around her shoulders, Laurel built up the courage to look at the Academy—her Avalon home. From the back she couldn't see any flames, but Klea's red poison was flowing over the dining hall roof and cloaking the entire greenhouse. Thick black smoke was still rolling off the stone, joining a murk as dark as heavy rain clouds that circled above her head. She wasn't sure she'd ever be able to look at the Academy again without remembering this devastation.

"Your friend Tam was quite broken up himself," Yeardley said, breaking the silence. "Tried to keep us from closing the wall, but we couldn't do anything else. They were all gone."

Laurel nodded, tears slipping down her cheeks again as

she looked away from the building. "He hates giving up," she said. "Where is he?"

As if in answer to her question, a handful of faeries came running up to Yeardley. "The Spring faerie, he's gone!" one faerie panted.

"Gone?" Yeardley asked, sounding truly panicked for the first time.

"When you were closing the wall, he went crazy," one of them said. "I've never seen anyone like that. I thought I had calmed him down, but the second I took my eyes off of him he ran. Slipped out the door and about took the fence in one jump." He paused. "I think he lost someone in there."

"But why would he . . . ?" Laurel looked down at her sodden pink shirt and the realization hit her with breath-stealing force. "He thinks Katya was me," she whispered.

"Oh no," Chelsea said, her hands gripping Laurel's arms. "He's gone for Klea."

"He's going to kill her," Laurel said.

"Or she's gonna kill him," Chelsea said, her face pale.

"Is there a gate?" Laurel said, spinning to look around the enclosure.

"Down in that corner," Yeardley said, pointing. "But, Laurel, I advise you not to go. What do you think you are going to do?"

"I don't know," Laurel said. "Something." She turned to David. "Come with me?" She had no right to ask, but she needed him. "The front door is still safe . . . after that, I—I don't know."

"Of course," David said, immediately taking up the sword

from where he'd plunged it into the ground.

"Chelsea—"

"Don't even start," Chelsea said, raising a hand. "I'm coming."

There was no time to argue—especially against something Laurel knew she would do—had often done—in Chelsea's shoes.

"Then let's go," Laurel said, nodding. "We have zero time."

Slowing just enough to dart through the trees on silent feet, Tamani pressed through the forest, catching up quickly. Klea and her entourage had veered onto the path that led to the Winter Palace, but they wouldn't reach it before he got to them. Ten more seconds and he could attack.

Nine.

Five.

Two.

One.

Tamani burst through the trees, his spear swinging, a primal scream he didn't recognize tearing itself from his throat. Two black-clad faeries went down beneath the spear's gleaming diamond blades; another stumbled to the ground. Her nearest bodyguards down, Tamani lashed out at Klea with his spear. With a yelp of surprise she raised a defensive arm; the heavy leather of her black outfit soaked up the brunt of the blow, but he thought he felt a stem crack in her lower arm.

Too bad it wasn't her right arm.

Klea whipped out a pistol and aimed it at him, but Tamani was ready, and a savage kick sent the gun flying. No cheating; it would be skill against skill this time.

"Tamani!"

In his peripheral vision Tamani caught sight of Yuki, looking almost human in jeans and a halter top that left the small flower on her back exposed to the air. Her cry distracted Tamani long enough for Klea to land a steel-toed kick to his jaw. He leaped back, then swept Klea's legs out from under her. Raising his spear to strike, Tamani took another kick, this time to the side of his knee. He was numb to her blows, but driving him back had given her time to scramble to her feet.

Several faerie guards were following the fight with the muzzles of their guns; Tamani doubted they would risk firing at him while he remained close to Klea. A few tried to get into the fight with knives, but Tamani lashed out with his spear, connecting with one faerie who didn't jump back fast enough.

Though Klea favored her broken arm, she was plenty fast with the other. She managed to pull a knife that snicked against his spear as he aimed for her throat, but she could only deflect the blow and it bit deeply into her shoulder. Sap seeped from the wound, but Klea paid no attention. "Yuki," she called, her voice hard and sharp. "Make yourself useful!"

Tamani saw Yuki raise her hands. A cluster of tree roots rose out of the ground, the same way Jamison had commanded them in the Gate Garden. The thick, soil-flecked coils shot toward Tamani and he braced himself for their stinging lash—almost welcoming it.

But it never came. The roots stopped inches away. When Tamani spared Yuki a glance, her face was contorted, as though she were trying to prevent the roots from attacking *her* rather than being the one in charge.

"I—I can't!" she cried, her words full of apology.

Klea swore and lunged at Tamani with her knife, but she had to leap back as he brought his spear around in a long, sweeping arc. He felt as though he were watching the encounter from outside his body, observing as some greater force took control of his limbs and threw him toward his enemy, blade first. He thirsted for justice; he would make her pay for what she had taken. Fueled by rage, he was as mighty as any Bender.

Beneath Tamani's onslaught, Klea gave ground; her knife was no match for his spear. He gave her an opening to his core, one she couldn't refuse; it cost him a shallow cut along his wounded shoulder, but it also put her neck between Tamani and the haft of his spear. Gripping it with both hands, he pulled Klea bodily against him, pressing the grip of his spear against her throat. Reflexively, she dropped her knife, bringing her hands up to ease the pressure bearing down on her windpipe.

"You," he gasped, his hands shaking but his mind filled with black clarity—with the hunger to kill. "You have taken everything from me, and you are going to die for it." Klea

194

made only a strangled sound and his mind barely registered the hint of fear that—for the first time—flashed in Klea's eyes.

"No!" Yuki's scream rent the air, and the universe ground to a halt as a second scream followed—

"Tamani!"

He tried to breathe, but his body was numb, paralyzed. His mind refused to believe.

"Don't do it!"

Closer now. He had to move. Had to see.

NINETEEN

"TAMANI, WAIT!" LAUREL YELLED, NOT ENTIRELY sure why. After all Klea had done, surely she deserved to die . . . didn't she?

Answers, she told herself. *We need answers.*

Laurel felt more than saw David step up behind her and with wide eyes, watched the guards raise their guns and point them at her.

"No!" Tamani's shout reverberated in her ears, but as the guns sounded David lunged in front of her. Laurel retreated, almost tripping over Chelsea, who was sheltered behind a thick oak. Laurel joined her as the guards continued to spray David with bullets, ripping the quiet air with the sound of gunfire. David didn't even flinch—just looked down as the bullets dropped into the dirt.

Laurel chanced a peek and saw Klea slip away from Tamani and pick something up off the ground. She stood with her signature semiautomatic leveled at David's chest and Tamani took the opportunity to run to Laurel, sliding onto the ground beside her and clutching her to his chest, his fingers shaking against her back.

"I suppose bringing your girlfriend in to save my life is going to have to make up for the fact that you've been making the rest of my day damnably inconvenient," Klea said dryly before unloading a clip at David, point blank.

Laurel and Chelsea both clapped their hands over their ears as Tamani tried to shield them, but David was beginning to look amused. He put his free hand on one hip and stared pointedly at the pile of jacketless bullets accumulating at his feet.

Klea got the idea and stopped shooting, smoothly snapping the gun into a holster at her side.

"David Lawson," Klea said slowly. "I saw your car back in Orick and figured Laurel had used it, but I admit, I'm surprised to actually see you here. There haven't been humans in Avalon—"

"For a thousand years. You know, everyone keeps telling me that."

"Yes, well, that's probably another one of their lies," Klea said. "Almost everything the faeries here tell you is a lie."

"This sword is no lie," David proffered, stepping forward again. "You saw the bullets dropping."

"And I see you coming my way, and can predict your intentions. But hear me out, human. I'm the only reason Barnes didn't kill you and Laurel last autumn, and you owe me."

"Owe you? Do you remember what you did to Shar, when he said those words this morning?"

Laurel felt Tamani's body tense beside her.

"A tragic waste," Klea said, not missing a beat. "He was probably the most skilled warrior I've ever met. But he was on the wrong side of history, David. This whole island is on the wrong side. Look around you! It's a tiny paradise, filled with effortlessly beautiful people who want for nothing, busily squandering their vast potential on petty social differences."

"Sounds like high school," David retorted. Yuki laughed, the bark seeming to surprise her as she flung her hand over her mouth—but Klea pressed on.

"Think what this place could offer to the world, David. And wonder why they don't. They hide themselves away—because they think they're better, purer, superior. And after this conflict is over and you give back the sword, what will you be? A hero? Maybe you want to believe that. But in your heart, you must know the truth. You'll go back to being a lowly human, unworthy of their notice. After all you've done for them—all the trolls you've killed?"

David tried to keep his face impassive but even Laurel could see the pain in his eyes.

"Do you have any idea how many years of nightmares you've earned today?" Klea said, clearly aware she was salting a wound. "And for what? A race that will cast you aside the moment they're done with you."

When David didn't respond, Klea continued. "If you

really want to be a hero, what you should do is help me fix this place. Avalon is broken. It needs a new vision, new leadership."

"He's not going to fall for this crap, is he?" Tamani whispered—but Chelsea just raised one eyebrow.

"What, *you*? Please," David said.

Chelsea shot Tamani a triumphant smile.

Klea sighed, but she sounded more annoyed than disappointed. "Well, can't say I didn't try. Enjoy your moment in the sun, David; it will be over before you know it. Now we really must be off. As the humans say, I have bigger fish to fry."

"I'm not letting you pass," David said, stepping onto the path in front of the group as Tamani drew himself to his feet.

Klea pushed her sunglasses to the top of her head and ran her fingers through her hair as if she had nothing better to do in the world. It was strange to see her without her ever-present dark lenses—to see the light green eyes rimmed by thick, dark lashes that gave her face a beauty and softness that contradicted everything else about her.

"David, you need to play more poker; you bluff like a child. Now, I've heard legends of Excalibur—which is what I suspect you've got there—and I can guess from the way you've been stalling that something about the enchantment prevents you from actually harming me with it. So I'm going to walk past you now. Stop me if you can," she said wryly, turning toward the Winter Palace and pulling her gun out again.

Excalibur glinted as David swung toward Klea. She didn't even flinch.

But he wasn't aiming for her.

With a clang the sword sliced through her gun, then David turned and made short work of the guns in her soldiers' hands as well. Several leaped back in surprise, but they were too busy protecting their skin to realize it was their *weapons* he was after. Some of them tried to shoot him again, only to have their guns severed in two. Barrels, stocks, and springs soon littered the ground, along with spent brass and deflected bullets.

Tamani took advantage of the confusion to lunge from the tree line and twist Klea's arms up behind her, his spear returning to her throat, but Klea kicked back and Tamani yelped as her heel connected with his knee. Laurel clenched her fists in frustration, hating that she couldn't *do* anything without getting in the way.

"Stop it!" Yuki yelled, flinging an arm toward David, palm up, fingers extended. She flexed her hand into a fist and several tree roots, as big around as David's chest, burst from the ground in an explosion of dirt and rock. They rocketed toward him and Laurel heard a strangled scream from Chelsea, but the instant any tendril touched David, it went limp, slumping back toward the ground.

Yuki gasped and thrust her hands toward the grass at his feet and the roots sucked back into the earth, scattering soil like raindrops across the clearing. She looked to Klea, but Tamani had her on her knees now, bent forward with his spear pressed against her back.

"Chelsea," Laurel whispered, never taking her eyes from Yuki, "stay here. Element of surprise. It's the only thing we have left." Aside from David, Chelsea was the only one who *could* surprise the Winter faerie, the only one Yuki couldn't sense at a distance. They'd used that advantage to capture her after the dance—*last night*, Laurel realized, though it seemed forever ago—perhaps they could accomplish something similar here.

Chelsea nodded as Laurel rose.

"Yuki," Laurel said, stepping forward tentatively with her hands held up in front of her.

"Stay where you were, Laurel," Tamani called, his voice strained. But Laurel shook her head. Yuki was too powerful for Tamani to fight without Jamison's help. Maybe Laurel could talk her down.

"Please, you can't really want this. You've been with us—all of us—for the past four months. We never wanted to hurt anyone, much less kill them. Yes, Avalon has its problems, but is it worth this?"

"Kill her, Yuki," Klea called.

Yuki's chin trembled. "It's a society built on lies, Laurel. You don't know what they do in secret. It's for the greater good, in the long run."

"Says who?" Laurel said sharply. "Her?" she asked, pointing at Klea, still fighting to get free of Tamani. "I've seen the way she treats you. She's not noble and strong; she's a scared bully. She *killed* all those faeries in the Academy. They're *dead*, Yuki."

But Yuki's eyes were narrowed. "It was just a fire, Laurel."

"And the red gas? Almost a thousand Fall faeries are dead because of her—never mind the faeries killed by trolls."

"They're not dead—they're just sleeping."

Laurel's jaw dropped and she spun to Klea now. "You didn't *tell* her?"

"I don't know what you're talking about," Klea said calmly.

"The red smoke? I know what it does," Laurel said. They were dead. She knew it; Klea knew it.

And Klea had lied to Yuki.

"Yuki, you have to listen to me—we're not the ones lying to you. *Klea* is. After the fire she sent that red stuff in and it *killed* everyone it touched. Not sleeping—dead. She's not what you think she is. She's a murderer."

Yuki blinked, but in her eyes, Laurel could see her decision was made. "She said you'd say that," Yuki said softly, steadily. She turned and looked at Tamani. Then, so low Laurel barely heard, Yuki whispered, "I'm sorry."

Roots erupted from the earth again, forming a dark, mossy birdcage around Laurel. Then the ground around David retreated, pulled back by a million tiny filaments of plant matter, forming a doughnut-shaped pit around him— too far to jump over without a running start, too deep to climb out of easily.

"Forget him!" Klea yelled. "He can't do anything."

Yuki turned and looked at her mentor and Tamani and, after a moment's hesitation, clenched one fist.

"Tamani!" Laurel shouted, but thick roots thrust up

beneath him, knocking his spear away and throwing Tamani to his knees, binding his wrists to the ground.

"Don't hurt them," Yuki said, even as Klea pulled a knife from a hidden sheath. "Let's just go."

But from the road, a familiar voice intoned, "I think you've gone far enough."

TWENTY

EVERYONE'S EYES WENT TO THE FIGURE LIMPING UP the path toward them, leaning heavily on a beautiful ebony cane.

"Jamison!" Laurel cried.

His face was haggard and he seemed to be dragging his body as much as walking. Yuki and Klea were momentarily stunned into inaction. The pit surrounding David filled itself in and Laurel's cage retreated back into the ground along with Tamani's bonds. Tamani tackled Klea—her remaining faerie guards were confused, and one of them seemed to be trying to put his ruined gun back together despite it being clearly beyond repair. Laurel ran to Jamison and took his arm before anyone could think to stop her.

"You're awake," she breathed.

"As awake as I am going to get for the moment," he said with a tired smile. He patted her shoulder. "But might I recommend that you stand back?"

Uncertain, Laurel took a step backward as Jamison raised his hand, almost casually; a thick oak root stopped with a smack right against his palm. Laurel turned to see Yuki, arms outstretched, her whole body trembling. Laurel couldn't tell if her expression was one of fear, fury, or sheer effort. Perhaps some of all three.

A crackling of leaves came from where Chelsea was hiding and Laurel knew she was about to step out.

"That's enough!" Laurel yelled as loud as she could, and though no one withdrew, they all stopped. For a moment. "Everyone needs to just *stay where they are*," she said, sparing a glance at the trees where Chelsea was, thankfully, still hidden. Even with Jamison back, Laurel wasn't ready to give up her one secret advantage, though she knew how hard it must be for Chelsea to look on helplessly.

The time it took to get those words out was all she got. Klea barked a laugh as she managed to throw Tamani off and Yuki advanced on Jamison.

"It has always been my destiny to face you," Yuki said quietly as David moved closer to Laurel, putting himself between her and the advancing guards with his sword raised.

"Subtle," he whispered out of the side of his mouth.

"It worked," Laurel retorted, returning her focus to Yuki, who was drawing closer and closer to Jamison.

"To face me? What kind of destiny is that?" Jamison asked calmly.

"I was created to avenge Klea," Yuki replied. "It has

always been my purpose."

"You don't believe that," Jamison said, and Laurel marveled at how the wizened faerie could be so firm and yet so gentle with every word.

"Why shouldn't I?" Yuki demanded, her eyebrows furrowed. She pushed her hands out and the earth beneath Jamison opened in a wide crack, very nearly swallowing Tamani and Klea as each struggled to subdue the other.

Latticework blades of grass hissed to catch Jamison before he had fallen even an inch, weaving a seamless, impossibly solid bridge over the pit Yuki had opened beneath him. His voice did not even waver. "No person's life should be defined by a single purpose, especially one they didn't choose. Who are *you*, Yuki?"

Yuki's eyes darted to Klea, but she had a knife out again and was busy lunging at Tamani.

"Yuki, you—"

But Klea's knife touched Tamani's throat, silencing whatever he'd been about to say. "You should have been dead the second you stepped into my Bender's sight," Klea spat to Tamani as he fought to keep the knife from cutting his skin. "Yuki could have killed you outright."

"I decided to take a chance on her," Tamani replied, flinging the blade away and reclaiming his spear.

"She's a poor bet. You got lucky." Klea's knife met Tamani's spear again and again, and Laurel realized that the erstwhile troll hunter was no longer trying to kill Tamani; she was trying to get *past* Tamani, to strike at

Jamison. Abruptly, as if waking from a dream, her guards turned their heads as one and pivoted away from David and Laurel to go aid their master.

"Stop them, David!" Laurel called.

"I can't hurt them," David said.

"I—I don't think they realize that," Laurel whispered. There was something very wrong with these guards. David stepped in front of them, holding his sword out in a threatening posture. They hesitated and Laurel caught another wisp of Jamison and Yuki's conversation.

"Don't act like you *care* about me, Bender," Yuki sneered, waving a hand above her head in a circle. "You pretended to care about Klea, and I know how that ended." She brought her arm down, pointing at him, and something blurred through the air toward Jamison.

"Do you?" Jamison asked, passing his hand in front of his face distractedly, as though shooing a fly. But at his movement a hundred wicked-sharp splinters of wood dropped harmlessly at his feet. "Because I would be most interested to hear what Callista told you."

"Shut up, old man!" Klea yelled, and Tamani grunted as the heel of her hand struck his cheek, reopening the cut she'd given him that morning. He cracked his spear against her broken wrist, eliciting a shriek of pain.

"She's not Callista anymore," Yuki said evenly, hardly sparing them a glance, her attention riveted on Jamison.

While David held Klea's guards at bay, Laurel looked over at Yuki's back and for a moment wondered if she could tackle her from behind. She glanced at Jamison, but he shook his head, almost imperceptibly.

"She will always be Callista to me. Do you know why?" Jamison said, his eyes on Yuki again.

Yuki hesitated, but Jamison didn't wait for her to reply.

"Because Callista was well intentioned and full of hopes and dreams and, above all, *brilliance*," Jamison says. "And I want to remember that—not the creature she has become."

"You made that creature. And that creature made *me*." One of the trees lining the road—thankfully, not the one where Chelsea had concealed herself—bent in two, shattering with a thunderous crack and falling, unnaturally fast, toward Jamison.

"Thank you, my dear," Jamison said with a sigh as the tree trunk flew over his head. "I do need to sit down." The mighty trunk crashed across what remained of the road to the palace, before coming to a stop right behind Jamison's knees. He lowered himself onto it with a quiet groan. "I confess, Laurel and Rhoslyn were only able to throw off the barest portion of the potion's effect. I am conscious, but only just."

Yuki's face screwed up in anger and she stretched her arms wide, swishing them forward. Laurel had to grab on to one of the trees beside her to keep from being swept away by the tornado of plant life that spun wildly around the two Winter faeries, sequestering them.

Laurel squinted against the haze of branches and leaves, but she couldn't see anything through the artificial storm.

The wind from the cyclone forced Tamani and Klea to the ground; Tamani appeared to have lost his spear again, and now the two were grappling, unarmed. Actually Laurel couldn't tell if they were still fighting or just using one another as counterweights against the gale. David kept to his feet, braced against the wind; the debris that bounced harmlessly away from him scattered Klea's mindless faerie guards onto the grass. David had to back up and sweep his sword at several to get them all together again in an exercise not unlike herding cats.

The whirlwind settled as abruptly as it had begun and neither Jamison nor Yuki appeared to have been affected by it in the slightest. With a strangled yell Yuki wove her arms in front of her and again a tangle of roots burst from the ground, lashing out to besiege Jamison.

But Jamison simply fixed the ground with a stare and the roots withered away. "I wanted Callista to stay—to mold her passion and intellect into a mighty force for Avalon's good."

"Avalon's *good*? You'd have made her into a puppet!"

"Instead, she made *you* into one."

Yuki gasped, her mouth opening and closing for a few seconds before she spoke. "I am not a puppet," she said, but her voice betrayed the tiniest tremble.

"Aren't you?" he asked. "Then stop this. Walk away from this pointless struggle. Go to Tamani and tell him you love him. After all, isn't that what you *really* want to do?"

Tamani's head shot up in surprise and Klea took the opportunity to twist his injured arm behind him. He cried out in pain, but kicked backward against a fallen limb with both legs, sending both of them sprawling.

Yuki's jaw shook at Jamison's words and tears sparkled in her eyes. "A true hero puts others first," she choked out.

"A true hero knows love is more powerful than hate."

She shook her head. "I love Klea—she's my mother."

"You *don't* love Klea; you fear her," Jamison said. "And she's not your mother."

"She made me."

"Making you doesn't make you a mother. Laurel's mother didn't make her—but she loves her."

Laurel felt a burst of pride for her human parents.

"Does Klea love *you*?" Jamison asked, so softly Laurel barely caught the words.

"Yuki!" Klea called desperately, but Tamani wrapped his arm across her mouth. Judging by his pained expression, she bit him for it.

"Of course," Yuki said, a tremble in her voice.

"If you walked away from me, from Klea's plan, from everything, right now—would Klea still love you?"

In answer Yuki put two hands up and thrust them forward as if pushing against an invisible barrier, and a wave of grass and earth moved forward to crush Jamison where he sat.

Jamison's face looked haggard and worn as he glared at the wave of earth, bringing it to a standstill with hardly a gesture.

Yuki screamed, a bitter, frustrated scream that pierced the evening air. The wave rippled again, slowly—so slowly.

Then faster.

Then it was rolling like an ocean wave and Laurel gasped in fear as it reached the trunk where Jamison was sitting.

The wave of earth and grass parted, rolling past Jamison, chewing both ends off the fallen tree. Jamison still sat on what was left of the oak log, breathing heavily but unharmed. "I wronged Callista, but not in the way she believes."

"How can there be any other way?" Yuki asked. "You lied to her, got her to trust you, and promised you'd defend her. But you didn't. You betrayed her and voted to have her exiled."

Klea's head jerked up and she stilled at these words, ceasing to thrash in Tamani's arms, where he had twisted her into a headlock.

Laurel held her breath, waiting for Jamison's answer.

"I did not," Jamison said, the words loud, almost echoing off the trees.

"You lie!" Yuki yelled.

Waves of earth came quickly now, emanating from Yuki in circles that tossed clumps of dirt and threw Laurel to the ground, where she clung to the grass to keep from being swept away. Even Tamani had to relinquish his hold on Klea to keep from being thrown.

"Yuki, stop!" Jamison said sternly, and the earth stilled. Jamison was on his feet now, leaning heavily on his ebony cane, staring down at Yuki with fire in his eyes. "I did *not* vote for Callista's exile."

"They told me the vote was unanimous," Klea shouted,

rising to her knees before Tamani could grab her, her face screwed up in fury. "You knew I was no Unseelie—you *knew* it! And you still voted to let them sterilize me and send me through the gateway."

Laurel gritted her teeth. She couldn't imagine why Klea would lie about this, but Laurel hated hearing that Jamison had voted in support of such a thing—Jamison, who had always supported both her and Tamani, who had welcomed her human friends to Avalon, and had always treated Tamani—a Spring faerie—with dignity and respect.

"*Every* vote of the Council is unanimous," Jamison said quietly, turning to Klea. "It is one of the secrets of our power; our united front. Behind closed doors, majority rules. But once it has, our vote is declared unanimous. I stood against Cora and a very young Marion for *hours*."

But Klea was shaking her head, making her way slowly toward him. "I don't believe you."

"That you do not believe does not change the truth."

"It doesn't matter anyway," Klea said, producing another knife from her seemingly endless supply and pointing it accusingly at Jamison. "Vote or not, you stood by and *let it happen*."

"And I regret that every day of my life," he whispered. "I'm so sorry."

Yuki's eyes widened and time seemed to freeze as Jamison and Klea stared at each other, now almost close enough to touch. Laurel held her breath, watching them, waiting for . . . she didn't even know what. Beside her, David lowered Excalibur. Even Klea's strange underlings seemed transfixed by the scene.

"It's too late for that," Klea said at last, and she raised a hand to strike. As Tamani moved to tackle her, Laurel felt the strong hands of one of Klea's guards lift her off her feet and she shrieked in surprise, the sound drawing Jamison's attention from Yuki for the briefest of instants.

No! Laurel bit off the scream, but it was too late. The log Jamison had been sitting on bucked and spun, sending him sprawling to the ground. Laurel winced as his head connected with a branch that threw him to the side of the road. He did not rise again.

Tamani spun from Klea and struck the guard holding Laurel square in the face; the black-clad faerie relinquished her easily. But the damage was done—Jamison lay powerless on the grass, his body restrained by a network of roots. Laurel slid to the ground and tore at his bonds with her fingernails, but they only seemed to pull tighter.

"Now, we finish him!" Klea screamed at Yuki, one arm cradled against her chest, her other brandishing her knife.

Yuki raised her hands but Laurel could see them shaking. The young faerie's chest heaved and her breathing was loud and labored as she tried to force herself to act. Laurel flung herself protectively over Jamison's fallen form, though she knew it wouldn't do much good against Yuki.

Tamani threw himself in front of Klea as Yuki seemed to gather her nerve. "Yuki, don't do it, please!" Tamani gasped.

Klea leaped at Tamani, full of crazy rage. He caught her knife arm and attempted to throw her to the ground, but she used her momentum to reverse the throw and bring him down instead. The point of her knife plunged straight toward his chest.

"No!" Yuki screamed, and the earth between Klea and Tamani ripped upward and drove them apart, tossing Tamani onto the ground and raining soil over Laurel and David. "You promised! You said he wouldn't be harmed. You swore!"

"Shut up, child!" Klea hissed. "There are bigger things at stake than your petty crushes! Kill them all!" she yelled.

At the loud command Klea's soldiers sprang to action again, their impassive faces taking on life almost as one.

"No!" Yuki yelled again. This time she reached through the air toward the men who were grasping for Tamani. In a flash of green and brown, thick, leafy vines burst from the ground, winding themselves around Klea's soldiers from their ankles to their necks. "I have done everything you asked me to do and this is the only thing I *ever* asked for in return and *I will have it!*"

Laurel watched, stunned, unsure what to make of Yuki's sudden change of heart, as the young Winter faerie ran to Tamani, who had managed to rise to his knees. She laid her hands on his shoulders.

"Tam, he was right, I—"

"Ungrateful *brat!*"

David lunged to disarm Klea, but his blade slid off her as she plunged the long, thin knife through the center of the rumpled white blossom on Yuki's back.

"Yuki!" Laurel cried, horrified, and tried to rise but David stepped in front of her.

"Stay back," he whispered.

Tamani lunged at Klea as Yuki collapsed to the ground with a cry of pain. Klea thrust her knife at Tamani's chest; he sidestepped and caught hold of her broken arm, forcing her toward him with a stifled whimper. Then he spun her around, bringing her knife hand up, and pressing her own weapon against her neck.

"Give up." His words sliced though the night air.

The road was silent except for Yuki's muffled cries. Laurel could hardly breathe.

Klea slumped against Tamani, defeated.

"Drop the knife."

Klea's hand twitched, and for a moment Laurel thought she would. But with a wordless yell, Klea drove the knife along the side of her neck, scoring her own skin and putting an inch of the blade through Tamani's T-shirt and into his wounded shoulder. Tamani released her in surprise and stepped back as Klea staggered away, dropping the knife and pressing a hand against her oozing wound.

A single slender root slithered up from the ground and wrapped around Klea's ankle, making her fall. Laurel turned to see Yuki's hand fluttering weakly. She was still alive!

Klea gave a high-pitched, almost mournful laugh from where she lay sprawled in the grass. "Well, now we can all die together."

"You, perhaps," Tamani said coldly.

"Look at your cut," Klea said.

Tamani hesitated, but when Klea's look sharpened into a glare, he pursed his lips and pulled down the neck of his shirt to expose his shoulder. "Eye of Hecate," he whispered. The edges of the wound were blackened, with dark tendrils radiating away from the gash.

TWENTY-ONE

"LET ME SEE," LAUREL SAID, RUSHING TO TAMANI and reaching out to him.

"Don't touch him," Yuki said, her voice soft but commanding. "It'll spread to you, too." She was on her hands and knees and black lines streaked out from the center of her blossom and sap dripped over her petals.

Klea glared at Yuki. "Years of conditioning unraveled by one stupid *Ticer.*"

Laurel stared in horror at the black tendrils tracing their way around Tamani's wound. She didn't know what it was, but it looked incredibly toxic—not unlike the red smoke that Klea had unleashed against the Academy. One more reason to be glad Chelsea was still hidden safely out of reach. Jamison, too, though how *safe* he was remained uncertain.

"A concoction I'm particularly proud of," Klea said, seeing Laurel's dumbfounded expression. "Something of a last resort, but this seemed like a special occasion. You should feel honored."

"What is it?" Tamani said, glaring down at Klea.

"Is it like the red stuff in the Academy?" Laurel asked, her voice shaking.

"Please," Klea said mockingly, "that potion is child's play compared to this. I wouldn't get too worked up, if I were you," she added, her eyebrow raising as she took in Tamani with a hint of a smile. "Sit down and relax, or it'll just spread faster."

"You've got it, too." Laurel could see the darkness spreading from the shallow cut on Klea's neck.

A sly smile spread across Klea's face. "But unlike you, *I* have the cure."

Hope burst to life in Laurel's chest as Klea held out a hand, two sugar-glass vials of serum on her outstretched palm. Laurel lunged forward, grasping.

"Not so fast," Klea said, yanking the vials out of Laurel's reach and closing her fist over them. "I want you to hear me out. And don't think you can get out of this by making a cure yourself," she added. "Nothing short of the viride-faeco potion can save them from this toxin. And that is *so* far beyond you." Klea chuckled. "So far beyond anyone at the Academy."

Viridefaeco. It was a word Laurel knew from her very first day in the classroom at the Academy, two summers ago. She had since learned that it was a healing potion no one knew how to make anymore—not even Yeardley.

"What do you want?" Laurel said.

"I want you to join me," Klea said, her voice almost casual as she spun the vials artfully through her nimble fingers. "Be my ambassador."

"Why would I do that?" Laurel spat. Klea had *lost*! She was dying! How could she still be acting as though everything was going according to plan?

"You mean, besides saving him?" Her head tilted scornfully at Tamani. "Because, when it comes right down to it, we both want the same thing."

Laurel narrowed her eyes and crossed her arms over her chest. "I don't see how that could possibly be true."

"That's because you're a shallow, gullible child," Klea said, sneering. "You only see what's on the surface; that's why it's been so easy to manipulate you over the years. For me, and for them." Klea nodded toward Jamison, still prone in the grass at the side of the road.

Laurel pressed her lips together against the insult.

"I, on the other hand, am the most talented Mixer Avalon has ever seen. Even you can't deny that. I made things beyond the wildest imaginings of those stodgy Academy lapdogs. Sometimes, things they didn't want to see. Poisons, like this one," she said, pointing to her own neck.

"What they never understood is that it's only by becoming familiar with poisons that you can make the best antidotes. It's true," Klea said when Laurel raised her eyebrows. "You can say what you want about the poison they had me mix for your mother, but that line of research led me to formulas that

219

could do for humans what we already do for faeries—treat any ailment, heal any wound, even reverse old age! Avalon has forgotten how much humans have to offer and would prefer to forget they exist at all—certainly no one wants to make potions to *help* them.

"The Council was furious. Told me I was *overstepping my bounds*. They called me Unseelie and exiled me." She leaned forward. "They do this kind of thing all the time. Lies, double standards. Avalon is built on deception—deception, and prejudice."

But Laurel refused to be manipulated by clever words and half truths; even if Klea had been legitimately wronged, nothing could justify the destruction she'd wrought. "So you decided to kill everybody? How is that better? All of those soldiers at the gate, the faeries in the Academy." *Tamani, Yuki,* she added in her mind, then had to push the thought away before despair overwhelmed her. Laurel had to keep Klea talking. She had to get her hands on that antidote.

"You're too sensitive."

Laurel thought of Yeardley's words and the tiny red flower in her pocket. "I'm no more sensitive than I should be—than *any* Fall faerie should be."

"Irrational, then. You think I'm a monster, don't you? That I simply go around killing people, thinking, *Huzzah, death!*" She shook her head with a smile. "I never sacrifice anything for nothing. The Fall faeries would have been the most resistant to change. They don't feel oppressed and they work for their high positions. They feel *justifiably* elevated.

But with most of them gone, Avalon will need me for my skills, and the Spring and Summer fae will be more likely to accept the change that's coming."

"You've destroyed the Academy, the labs, the gardens full of specimens; your Mixer skills aren't worth much without those."

"You really do think I'm stupid, don't you?"

Laurel forced herself to say nothing.

"One of my specialties is delayed effects. I was able to hide my research for years by Mixing potions that had no apparent effect—so later, when they kicked in, the effects would be blamed on the failure of some other Mixing. The mist I set off in the tower is short-term—it's neutralizing as we speak. The firewalls will preserve most of the structure—not to mention the components. The smoke damage will be extensive, I admit, but the labs will be completely useable in a quarter of an hour. I will have everything I need to rebuild Avalon."

"And the thousands you killed?" Laurel demanded.

"Even with the fae deaths, on balance I've done Avalon a huge favor. Thanks to my serum and my recruiting efforts, as of today trolls are effectively extinct on the entire Pacific Rim."

"It was your vaccine," Laurel realized, remembering the way the trolls had fallen so suddenly, dead where they stood. "It killed them."

"Like I said," Klea purred with a smile. "Delayed effects."

"Why kill them so soon? Why not keep them around to

help you with your *takeover*?"

"Trust *trolls*?" Klea laughed. "Those filthy animals just wanted to sack Avalon. They thought they were using *me* to get here, and they intended for me to die as surely as I intended the same fate for them. The second the trolls passed through the gate I couldn't have convinced them to protect me from a faerie *child*, much less a Bender. The timing was delicate and almost ruined by your stupid high-school dance, but in the end they had to die—that was *always* the plan."

"That's horrible," Laurel said.

Klea shrugged. "Well, you can't make an omelet without breaking a few eggs."

"And were the sentries some of your *eggs*?" Tamani demanded. "Do you have any idea how many faeries died today?"

"Thousands," Klea said, her voice deadly serious. "And their martyrdom is the foundation on which I will build a new order." She hesitated. "I admit things could have gone better. I never expected Excalibur—especially not with Marion in charge—so I had to change things up and send in some sleeping mist at the gate."

Was that *regret* in her voice? Over a *change of plans*? The woman really was stark-raving mad.

"But what's done is done. And I'm out of time to reminisce. The smoke from the Academy fire will keep the Sparklers' and Ticers' attention away from our little party here, but it is also likely to woo the Benders out before I'm ready. Laurel, look here," Klea said, opening her hand to reveal the two vials again—one containing a dark green solution, one a deep purple. "One of these is just a vial of the serum I injected into the trolls. The other is viridefaeco. Do as I ask, and I will give you the potion. Refuse and"—she clenched her fists, not quite hard enough to break the vials— "the serums will mix, their components will neutralize each other, and the cure will be useless."

Laurel hesitated. But at this point it didn't hurt to at least find out what Klea's terms were. "What do you want me to do?" she asked.

"It doesn't matter, Laurel. Don't help her!" Tamani called, his voice full of desperation.

"You think yours is the only life at stake here, Ticer?" Klea snapped at Tamani. "Even as we sit talking, looking so innocent and pathetic in the grass, this toxin is spreading right out of your skin—to the grass you're sitting on, to the roots Yuki has so kindly wrapped around me. To the trees in the forest, to Jamison lying over there at death's door anyway. It won't stop. In time, it will remake Avalon into a barren rock. And without me, you will *never* be able to make the antidote in time."

Klea turned back to Laurel. "Go to Marion and Yasmine," she said evenly.

"How do you know about Yasmine?" Laurel asked. "She sprouted after you were exiled."

"How many times have you spoken of her when you thought you were all alone?"

Laurel's jaw snapped shut.

"You'll be able to get past the sentries," Klea continued as if Laurel hadn't spoken. "Tell them about my poison, that all of Avalon is going to die. They can save their precious island by coming down and exchanging their lives for my assistance in curing everyone and everything."

"And if they accept?" Laurel asked.

"Then they will be executed in Spring Square—a public example declaring the end of the pathetic Bender dynasty. Avalon will live, and I will take over."

"Yasmine's only a child," Laurel said, her stomach writhing at Klea's brutality.

"Sacrifices, Laurel. We all have to make them."

"And Jamison?"

"I need *all* the Benders gone."

Laurel sucked in a breath but Klea continued smoothly.

"You know Marion isn't a good queen. I seriously doubt a child she trained could be any better. The Benders need to go. Avalon needs a change. With your help, I can still make that happen. Bring them, and I'll give you the cure for Tamani."

Laurel didn't think there was room in her body for the hatred she felt toward this smug faerie.

"Not only that, I'll make more—and as a show of good faith, I'll teach you how. Because you'll need it. This vial," she said, lifting her hand, "will cure, at most, two people."

"And if I choose to use it on them?" Laurel asked, pointing to Tamani and Yuki. "What then? You'll die."

"Then who will teach you to make the antidote to save everyone else?"

Laurel wanted to scream. No matter what she chose, someone was going to die. "You would kill all of Avalon, just to have your way?" Laurel said, her voice quivering.

"It's not my choice, Laurel. It's yours. Will *you* kill all of Avalon, just to get *your* way?"

Laurel forced herself to keep breathing. Now there really was no way out. Not through Yeardley, not through Jamison. If she didn't do as Klea asked, Tamani was going to die.

And slowly, so would everyone else.

If she delivered Marion and Yasmine to Klea, Tamani would live.

Everyone would live.

Three lives for all of Avalon.

And for Tamani.

There was only one thing to do.

"All right," Laurel said slowly, looking Klea squarely in the eye. "I will bring you the Winter faeries."

"Laurel, no!" Tamani said, lifting one knee as if to rise.

"Just don't move," Laurel said to Tamani, hearing the desperation in her own voice as she stepped toward him. "I need you alive when I get back!"

"Don't do this," he pleaded. "I would rather die than live under her rule."

"But it's not just you," Laurel whispered. "It's everyone."

"But Klea?" Tamani said, lifting one hand reflexively, as if to grasp hers, before clenching his fist and letting it drop to his side.

Laurel shook her head. "I can't stand to the side and let everyone die when I can do something about it." She realized she was talking loud—almost shouting—and took a deep breath, trying to remain calm. Then, a voice that didn't sound quite like her own said, "I can't and I won't."

"Laurel."

David's voice made Laurel pause.

"I'm coming with you."

"Not so fast," Klea said. "She goes alone, or I crush the vials and *everyone* dies."

"Stay," Laurel said, reaching out a hand that slid off David's arm. "Just in case things go wrong. Help Jamison. Do what you can for him." She raised her voice a little. "I'm going to head up the road—the wide one that leads to the palace."

She looked hard at David, hoping he would trust her just once more, and after a moment, he nodded.

"You'd better hurry," Klea said. "No telling how long it will take the Ticers and Sparklers to find us and come investigate—not to mention tromp around and get infected themselves. I'd say your friends here have an hour at the absolute most. Probably less. And, of course, you'll want to get back before I expire," Klea said with a sly grin that made Laurel want to slap her. "I trust you can convince two frightened Benders in less time than that?"

Wordlessly Laurel walked to Klea's captive minions. They were remarkably docile; none of them protested as she checked their belts, finding a six-inch-long blade on the third one.

"What do you think you're doing?" Klea asked.

Laurel looked over, her eyes wide and innocent. "I have

to convince a queen," she said simply. "I'm going to need a knife."

Before anyone could react, Laurel turned and headed up the long, sharply pitched pathway that led to the Winter Palace.

TWENTY-TWO

AFTER TAMANI WATCHED LAUREL DISAPPEAR INTO the trees, he turned his attention to Klea. It was all Tamani could do to not pick up his spear and finish her off, right here and now. But she had backed them into a corner, and seemed to know it. She was lying on her back, one hand tucked behind her head, looking for all the world like an idle stargazer except for the fist she had clenched against her chest. She wasn't even trying to worm free of the roots that Tamani was pleased to note still held her bound.

David was kneeling next to Jamison, trying to adjust him so he lay more naturally. He'd given Tamani a thumbs-up after checking his breathing, but even the confirmation that the Winter faerie was alive had trouble piercing through the gloom of their hopeless situation.

Tamani kept a sharp eye on Klea, more than a little afraid she would drink the viridefaeco potion the moment their backs were turned. But she seemed content to wait.

If anything, her faerie soldiers were even more docile than their commander. Their faces were slack and their frames hung limply against their bonds. The strange fae had bothered him since he'd first seen them.

Tamani looked over at Klea. "What's wrong with them?" he asked stiffly.

Klea glanced up and a little smile played at the corners of her mouth. "There's nothing wrong with them. They're perfect."

"They're not people," Tamani said, finally putting his finger on it. "They're empty shells."

"Like I said, perfect."

"You *did* this to them?"

"Genetics, Tamani. It's a fascinating field." Then she turned away, clearly ending the conversation.

"It doesn't matter when Laurel gets back," David said quietly, back near Tamani now that Jamison was taken care of. David pointed to the ground where Klea's knife had fallen; the poison that lingered on the blade had blackened the grass, and the blackness was spreading in a deadly sunburst. "If we don't stop this, I'm not sure that even Klea's cure will be enough."

"I don't know what to do," Tamani said, letting his gaze fall to the ground. He faced down the urge to rise to his feet and chase after Laurel. Even if Klea hadn't made him a plague bearer, what could he hope to accomplish? Surely Laurel didn't intend to help Klea, did she?

No, of course she didn't. She would do the right thing.

Assuming there was a right thing.

Tamani looked up as David plunged Excalibur into the ground, burying it to the hilt a few feet away. He set to pulling it through the earth like a plow.

"What are you doing?" Tamani asked.

"I'm digging a moat," David replied.

"A moat?" Tamani asked, lost.

"It won't stop the poison," David said, still digging, "but at least it will have to go down through the grass roots before it can spread farther. It'll buy us some time."

Tamani let himself smile, ever so slightly. "Brilliant."

David grinned back and returned to his task.

"Tam?"

Yuki's voice was soft and rasping. She had gotten to her feet with visible effort, but after only a few steps her legs collapsed beneath her. Tamani rolled forward to catch her, pulling her toward him to break her fall. He was surprised by how much energy it took to lower her gently to the ground, how breathless the simple action made him.

This poison is no joke. And he had barely been exposed at all; Yuki's wound was serious—potentially life-threatening by itself.

"Tam, I'm so sorry. For all of this." A single tear, glistening in the moonlight, slid down her porcelain cheek. She sniffled and looked away timidly, drawing a stuttering breath. "I didn't know." She hesitated. "I didn't understand just how much she . . ."

"Yuki—"

"When I saw the flames at the Academy, I thought . . . I was so afraid—"

"Yuki, please." He couldn't bear to relive it, the fear that had gripped him there.

"I just . . . I don't want to die with you hating me."

"Shh," Tamani said, bringing his hand to her cheek, brushing away the tear and leaving a tiny streak of glittering pollen. "I don't hate you, Yuki. I . . ." He faltered, unsure what to say.

"Do you remember, after the dance? When you brought me to your apartment?"

Tamani wanted to squeeze his eyes shut. When he'd lied to her? Betrayed her as deeply as he ever could? Oh yes, he remembered.

"I was going to confess everything. I was going to join you and fight against Klea. You were right—I was always afraid of her. But that night, you made me feel strong. Like I could do anything. And I was going to. I was going to try."

"I know," Tamani said softly. He reached out for her, drawing her in the way he had at the winter formal only the night before. But this time, he meant it. "I'm sorry I didn't let you."

"You were just doing your job," Yuki whispered. "When David put me in that circle, I was so mad . . . I should have just done what I was going to. Cooperated with you. Even after I was in the circle, I could have talked to you. But I didn't, because I was angry."

"You had every right," Tamani said. "I knew you were falling in love with me, and I used that against you. It's the most terrible thing I've ever done."

"Shh," Yuki said, pressing a finger to his lips. "I don't want to hear your apologies." It seemed like her voice was getting softer by the minute, and Tamani wondered if she was trying to conserve her energy or if this was all she had left. "I just want to lie here and pretend that I did everything right the first time. That I trusted you, and came over to your side before all of this happened. I want to imagine that hundreds of faeries didn't die because I wasn't strong enough to stand up to Klea. That . . . that you and I had a chance."

Tamani smothered his protests as he smoothed Yuki's dark, lustrous hair. Even with Yuki in his arms, it was Laurel in his mind. He wondered if he would ever see her again— if they would kiss and caress like they had that day in the cabin. But no—even if he lived until she returned, he would never touch her again.

He hadn't realized he was humming until Yuki pulled back and spoke. "What's that?"

"What? Oh, it's a . . . lullaby. My mother used to sing it to me; it was her favorite."

"A faerie lullaby?"

"I used to think so," Tamani said, smiling sadly.

"Sing it for me," Yuki said, folding herself into his arms.

In the darkness of the night, David, Klea, and her soldiers seemed to fade away as Tamani sang, softly, haltingly, a song of Camelot he'd learned at his mother's knee. He knew the words by heart, but as he sang them, he felt like he was hearing them for the first time.

> *"And by the moon the reaper weary,*
> *Piling sheaves in uplands airy,*
> *Listening, whispers, ''Tis the faerie*
> *Lady of Shalott.'"*

He met Yuki's light green eyes, filled with tears again, her chin quivering against the pain of both the poison and regret. Tamani knew exactly how she felt. He wished the song really would put her to sleep—that her life would drain away while she was dreaming, someplace the pain couldn't touch her. He was no stranger to death, but though he had watched friends die—more often than he cared to remember—he had never held someone as the life drained from their eyes. It frightened him to do so now.

But he wouldn't abandon her to suffer it alone.

> *"But Lancelot mused a little space*
> *He said, 'She has a lovely face;*
> *Goddess, prithee, lend her grace,*
> *The Lady of Shalott.'"*

"Alfred, Lord Tennyson," Klea said when Tamani finished singing, and Tamani's head shot up as if she had broken a spell. Even David had paused his digging to listen and he cast Klea an ugly look before turning back to his moat.

"Bowdlerized by some Sparkler hack, no doubt," she finished, her voice flat.

If Yuki heard Klea's acid commentary, she made no sign. Her eyes were closed, fingers relaxed on Tamani's arm.

"Tam?"

"Yes?"

"Is there any way this will end well?"

"There's always a chance," he forced himself to say. But he didn't see how either he or Yuki would live to see another sunrise. The poison was just too strong.

Yuki smiled wanly, then glanced over at Klea, who had returned to her silent stargazing. Tamani could feel the fear that still filled Yuki at the sight of her mentor. "I don't want her to win anymore. And I can make sure she never does."

"You can't kill Klea," Tamani said, though he was sorely tempted to let Yuki do just that. But he forced himself to trust Laurel, to let her make this decision.

But Yuki was already shaking her head. "Her plan can't work unless she controls the Winter faeries. When I die she'll kill the others and everyone will be stuck in here with her. And even if Laurel finds a way . . . You'll always be dependent on them. It isn't fair. I—I should have done something . . . before. But maybe this will make up for it." Her eyes seemed to focus on some distant point, then snapped back into focus as she looked up at Tamani. "Do you have anything . . . metal?"

"Metal?" he asked, confused.

"It has to match," she said, as if that cleared everything up.

"Um . . . maybe?" Pulling her against him with one hand, he pulled up the cuff of his pants and drew a small throwing knife from the sheath on his leg. "How's this?"

Yuki took the knife from his hand. "Perfect." Her breathing was shallow, rapid; tears were coursing down her cheeks and her voice quivered as she spoke. "This is going to take a lot of power from me. I . . . I don't know that I'll last much longer when it's done."

"Don't talk that way," Tamani whispered.

"No, I know. I can feel it." Her body shook as she clenched her teeth against her sobs. "Please don't leave me. Hold me till I'm gone."

"What are you—"

"*Shokuzai,*" Yuki said, closing her hands over the small blade. "Atonement." A warm glow began to shine from between her fingers and Tamani glanced at Klea, who was studying them with narrowed eyes. Tamani was pretty sure his body was angled enough to block her view, but he cupped his hand over Yuki's anyway, completely shutting out the strange light.

Yuki inhaled sharply and Tamani pressed his forehead to her temple as her brows knit and she pressed her hands together even tighter. Tamani felt like he was in the upper rooms of the palace again, so tangible was the power that pulsed from Yuki. His gut response was to leap to his feet and flee, but he made himself hold on until the feeling began to ebb, the light dimming until it was outshone by the star-light.

Tamani pulled back and looked at Yuki; her eyes were closed and her face was ashen. He was afraid she was already gone, but slowly—laboriously—her lashes rose. "Give me your hands."

Tamani obeyed her tiny whisper, and though he managed not to tremble, inside he was shaking with fear. What had she done?

She laid something warm on his palm—whatever it was, it was no longer a knife. Tamani peered down, careful to keep it concealed from Klea. He wasn't sure exactly what he was seeing. "I don't understand."

With soft fingers on his cheek Yuki pulled his head closer, whispering directions on how to use the object she'd just made. When the extent of the possibilities dawned on him he gasped and closed his fingers back over the infinitely precious gift.

Then despair washed over him and he shook his head. "I won't be able to use it," he said, squeezing her hand. "I'll be dead within the hour."

But Yuki shook her head. "Laurel will save you," she said firmly through her tears. "I'm the one who's out of time."

"Hang on," Tamani said, holding her tighter, wishing he could believe in his own future as much as she did.

"No," Yuki said, a sad smile crossing her face. "I have nothing left to live for. You do."

"Don't . . ." *Don't what?* Tamani didn't even know how to end the sentence; understanding for the first time how words could be so wholly inadequate.

"*Aishiteru*," she sighed, the words slipping from her as her chest fell, and then was still.

"Yuki. Yuki!"

But Yuki gave no response.

With a stab of fear Tamani looked up at Klea and the captive soldiers, watching for their bonds to unravel now that Yuki wasn't controlling them. But they didn't. Yuki had done . . . something . . . to make sure that even after her death, Tamani would be safe. He was beginning to think she was as calculating as Klea, in her own way.

He let her body slide down his chest until her head rested on his lap. There was no reason to move her farther. He had nowhere to go, nothing to do until Laurel came back. Assuming he lasted that long.

Could he last that long? He had to try.

Had the toxin killed Yuki, in the end? Or had it been her final act as a Winter faerie—the creation of a masterwork to rival the golden gates that Oberon had sacrificed his life to forge? Either way, Tamani knew his time was short. He had always assumed his life would end in a battle—at the tip of an enemy's weapon. Or, if he lasted that long, by joining his father in the World Tree. Not sitting idly on the grass, waiting for death to steal over him.

But there he sat beneath the slivered moon, Yuki's limp form draped across his lap, idly stroking her hair as he watched David, almost halfway done digging the trench that would encircle all the poisoned faeries.

Carefully—without attracting any attention—Tamani

reached his hand into his pocket and pushed Yuki's gift as far down as he could. He couldn't lose it; couldn't tell anyone else what it was.

Because there was no artifact, no single item in all of Avalon—including the sword that David was digging with— as dangerous as the one Yuki had just given him.

TWENTY-THREE

THE WINDOWS OF THE WINTER PALACE WERE AS
dark as the night sky, and as Laurel approached she closed her
eyes, desperately hoping her plan had worked.

"Laurel!" Chelsea's whisper sounded from a cluster of
honeysuckle.

"I knew you would figure it out," Laurel said, throwing
her arms around her friend as she stepped from her cover.

"What are you doing? You're not really going to do what
Klea said, are you?"

"Not if I can help it," Laurel said grimly.

"What can I do?"

"I need you to go to the Winter Palace. Tell the sentries
that Marion and Yasmine are still in danger and that they are
not to let them come out until you personally tell them it's
okay. Klea can't see them."

"But—"

"Even their Winter powers can't do anything because we need Klea alive and cooperative. We need what's in her head."

"Can't Jamison, like, read her mind?" Chelsea asked. "If he's okay, I mean," she added when a flash of fear went across Laurel's face.

"Maybe," Laurel said, pushing her dismal thoughts away. "But I don't think so. It took Yuki a long time to just get the location of the gate from me. Besides, even if he could just pluck a recipe from her brain, it's not enough." Laurel hesitated. It had taken her a long time to understand what Yeardley had meant when he taught her about the mixing process: *The most essential ingredient in any mixing is you.*

"It's hard to explain, but that's how Mixing works. I think Marion might kill her on principle, and we can't let that happen—just in case. After that I need you to run back to the Academy and tell Yeardley everything Klea said about her poisons, especially the red smoke. We may need to go back into the Academy, so they'll want to know the poison neutralized itself. Tell him I'm trying to find a solution, and tell him . . . tell him to be ready."

"Ready for what? What are you going to do?"

Laurel sighed. "I don't know," she confessed. "But I guarantee I'm going to need help."

"Where are you going?"

Laurel looked to the top of a far-off hill. "To the only place left to turn," she said.

Chelsea nodded, then took off like a shot, following the

back wall toward the crumbling archway they had crossed through earlier that day. It felt like an eternity ago. Laurel watched her for a few moments before turning and beginning her own journey.

Would Tamani last another hour? Could she do this in time? Laurel's energy was already sapped, but she pushed herself to run faster, even as breathing grew painful and she reached the bottom of the valley between her and her destination.

One more hill to climb. The thought was enough to bring tears to her eyes as exhaustion threatened to crumple her to her knees. The night air was chilled but her legs burned as she climbed.

When she crested the hill she allowed herself a moment to catch her breath before stepping under the expansive canopy of the World Tree.

She hadn't been here since Tamani had brought her almost a year and a half ago. She'd contemplated a visit this past summer, back when she didn't know where Tamani was or whether she'd see him again, but the memory of that day had been too painful to face. Now she bowed her head reverently as the power of the tree washed over her.

The time had come to ask her question.

Tamani had told her the tree was made of faeries—the Silent Ones. His own father had joined them not long ago. Their combined wisdom was available to any faerie with the patience to receive it, but getting an answer from the tree could take hours, even days, depending on the questioner.

She didn't have that kind of time.

She thought back to when Tamani had kissed her after biting into his tongue—the sensations that overwhelmed her, the ideas that had flooded her consciousness. It hadn't worked the way she'd hoped, and instead of figuring out how to test Yuki's powers, Laurel had learned Klea's secret: that potions could be made from faeries the same as any other plant. But Yeardley had taught her that she could do more than merely bend components to her will. That she could unlock their potential if she could feel their core.

Picturing Tamani in her mind, the black lines snaking out from his wound, the look on his face that told her he had resigned himself to death, Laurel steeled herself against the sacrilege she was about to commit. She walked up to the trunk of the tree and placed her hand on the rough bark, feeling the current of life that surged through the tree.

"This is gonna hurt me a lot more than it's gonna hurt you," she muttered under her breath. Then after a moment she added, "I'm sorry." She raised her knife and hacked at the trunk of the ancient, gnarled tree until a bit of green wick showed through. Even as she looked at the beads of sap beginning to ooze from the wounded trunk, Laurel knew it wasn't enough. *You give, I give,* she thought. Placing the knife's edge to her open palm, she gritted her teeth as she sliced her own skin.

Laurel pressed her self-inflicted wound to the exposed green treeflesh.

It was like stepping beneath an avalanche of voices, every

second a thousand hailstones of whispered knowledge bouncing sharply off her head, drumming on her shoulders, threatening to carry her into the abyss and bury her alive. She staggered beneath the weight of the assault, refusing to be swept away.

Forcing herself to submit her consciousness to the tree, the avalanche became a waterfall, and then a torrent, and then a part of her, running gently through her mind, rifling through her life and her memories. She almost pulled away at the intrusion, but tried to breathe evenly and focus on what she needed to know.

She pictured Tamani, relived the scene that had led to his poisoning. She recalled Klea's explanation and the impossible choice she had put before Laurel. Into the flow of thought she released Klea's final threat—that the toxin would destroy all of Avalon, the World Tree included.

Again the river of life became a storm of souls, but this time Laurel was standing in the calm, enveloped in the silence. Warmth spread up her arms and filled her from head to toe.

And then, the tree spoke. Laurel felt, rather than heard, a single voice cut through the numberless, formless silence.

If you can think like the Huntress, you can do as she has done.

What does that mean? Laurel pleaded, even as she committed the words to memory. But the warmth was already receding from her head, gathering in her chest, slipping down her arms.

"No!" Laurel yelled, her voice sounding sharp in the

silence. "I don't know what that means! Please help. I have no one else to turn to!"

The strange presence was draining from her hands and the roar of life beneath her fingers was picking up again, softer now that it wasn't inside her head. As her fingertips tingled and grew cold, there was a final pulse from the storm, and one almost-familiar whisper somehow made itself heard above the others.

Save my son.

Then the warmth was gone. The whispers were gone.

"No. No, no, no!" Laurel pressed her hand harder against the tree, pain shooting across her palm, but she knew it was pointless. The World Tree had spoken.

Laurel dropped to her knees, scraping them against the rough bark of the tree's sprawling roots and let the tears come. She had gambled everything, and she had lost. The World Tree—her one last hope—had not worked. Avalon was going to die. Whether from Klea's toxin or under her rule, it scarcely mattered.

If only Laurel had taken more interest in the viridefaeco potion! One of her classmates had been working on it obsessively for years; why hadn't Laurel studied with her? She didn't know where to start now! Couldn't even remember that faerie's name.

Klea knew. It was maddening to have the knowledge so close, and yet completely inaccessible. Another dead end. How could she possibly think like Klea? The very idea was revolting; Klea was a murderer. A manipulator. A malicious, sneaky, poisonous . . .

Poisonous. The word drifted through Laurel's head as her tears traced lines down her face.

It's only by becoming familiar with poisons that you can make the best antidotes. Klea's words less than an hour before.

But that was a dead end; Mara, the Academy's expert on poisons, had been forbidden from studying them further. And what could she teach Laurel in such a short time, even if she would?

Laurel leaned against the World Tree, wondering if there was any point in returning to Klea. To watch Tamani die? She wanted nothing more than to hold him in her arms right now, even if it was for the last time. She wasn't sure it mattered if the toxin infected her. Was her life worth living without Tamani? Was the risk worth one last kiss? One final embrace? Of course, then *she* would die alone, poisoned and untouchable. But—

It's only by becoming familiar with poisons that you can make the best antidotes.

An idea began to form in Laurel's head. She tried to envision a young, enthusiastic Klea—Callista—working by herself in the classroom, in secret. She would have needed test subjects for her poisons as well as her remedies.

Who else would she have used?

If you can think like the Huntress, you can do as she has done.

Laurel was on her feet and running almost before she realized it.

The stars were out in earnest, peeking through the forest

canopy, then filling the sky where the path cut through a clearing. The fire seemed to have gone out at the Academy—it was cloaked in murky darkness—but other lights were visible in Spring and Summer; Laurel tried not to wonder how those quarters had weathered the attacks before the trolls had all collapsed. If she failed, it wouldn't matter.

She stumbled a few times in the darkness, but soon she was approaching the strange, docile soldiers and David was reaching out for her, stopping her from falling into an enormous moat he had dug. She blinked in the darkness and, after a few seconds, realized what he had done for Avalon. Laurel threw her arms around him. "Thank you," she whispered. Before pulling back she softly asked, "Jamison?" not wanting to bring him to Klea's attention.

"Alive," David murmured.

Laurel nodded before bracing herself on the edge of the circle, and then hopped over.

It took her a moment to make out Klea, lying motionless in the shadows, and Tamani, who sat in the middle of the circle with Yuki's head resting in his lap. He looked up at Laurel with haunted eyes.

Laurel stared down at the unmoving faerie. "Is she . . . ?"

"I don't see the Queen," Klea drawled, pulling Laurel's attention away.

But Laurel gave her only a moment. She turned her back and crouched down next to Tamani and Yuki instead. Yuki looked like she was sleeping, but her features were waxen and she wasn't breathing. Laurel felt a stab of grief and a flash of panic; if Yuki was already dead, how much time did Tamani have?

"Take your shirt off," she ordered.

Tamani obeyed.

Laurel nearly gagged at the sight that greeted her. From the tiny scratch near his collar, the black lines reached out across his shoulders and up his neck. The wounds on his abdomen were weeping green-tinged sap—a sure sign Klea's infectious toxin was spreading through him internally as well. He didn't have long.

"You failed, didn't you?" Klea said, still motionless only a few feet away. "You failed, and now all of Avalon is going to die because of you."

"I didn't fail," Laurel spat. "I never went to the palace. Did you really think I was going to help you? Jamison was right to send you to the Unseelie." Laurel paused, her eyes shooting daggers at Klea. "I would rather die than live in your perfect world."

Laurel heard a crunching sound as Klea clenched her fist, and oily droplets of serum dripped through her fingers onto her black shirt. "Wish granted. It's a shame you felt the need to take everyone else with you."

"Not today," Laurel whispered under her breath.

It's now or never.

Her intentions must have been painted on her face, because Tamani pulled back slightly. "Don't!"

But her palm was already pressed to his blackened skin,

fingers splayed, eyes closed. She could feel the life beneath his skin, feel it fighting—could feel the poison it struggled against. Klea's toxin was like no potion Laurel had ever encountered, even more complicated and alien than the powder Klea had used to conceal the places she'd based her trolls. Laurel had successfully reverse-engineered that powder, but it had taken her a long time and no small amount of luck.

Fortunately, it had been a learning experience.

When she pulled back, Tamani met her gaze with tears in his eyes. "Why did you do that?" he asked, bringing his hands to her cheeks. "I'm supposed to be protecting *you*."

"You're the best protector a girl could wish for," Laurel said, leaning forward, pressing her lips softly, briefly, to his. "But it's my turn now."

She could feel Klea's poison working in her fingers and her lips, breaking down the chlorophyll and lysing her cell walls, commandeering her energy and turning it against her. She would have to work fast, but it was speaking to her, and she was ready to listen.

"Oh," she said, rising to her feet. "Your dad says hi."

Without waiting to see the look on Tamani's face, Laurel closed her eyes, repeating the World Tree's words in her mind. *If you can think like the Huntress, you can do as she has done.* "I'll be back," she said, hopping over the trench again.

"Laurel," David said, stopping her. "Where did you go?"

"I went to the World Tree," she answered, feeling time ticking away in her head.

"The tree that talks to you?"

Laurel nodded.

"What did it say?"

"It told me to save Avalon."

TWENTY-FOUR

THE GARDEN BEHIND THE ACADEMY WAS DIMLY LIT as Laurel crested the hill and let herself into the greenhouse. The remaining faeries were sitting among their fallen comrades, who were starting to wake. The sound of coughing and rasping breaths was loud, but so were the murmurs of the Mixers calming and comforting their friends.

Laurel noticed that they had removed the stone panel between the greenhouse and the dining hall, but it looked like few of the Mixers felt confident enough to re-enter the Academy.

She picked her way through the faeries, looking for Yeardley, careful to not so much as brush anyone as she passed. She wasn't sure the viral toxin had taken hold of her enough to be contagious just yet, but she didn't want to take any chances. She finally spotted the fundamentals instructor near the center of the greenhouse and was relieved, if unsurprised, to see Chelsea standing near him.

"Laurel!" Chelsea said, as Yeardley reached out a hand to grasp her shoulder.

"Don't touch me," Laurel warned, bringing her hands up in front of her. "I'm infected with Klea's toxin."

"Why do *you* have it?" Chelsea asked.

"Long story," Laurel said. "But don't worry; it won't hurt you, only faeries," she added. Her mind was being bombarded with the sensations of how the poison was killing her, and all of them had to do with chlorophyll. Both Chelsea and David would be fine.

She turned to her professor. "I need your help and I don't have much time."

"Of course," Yeardley said.

"Two summers ago there was a faerie—I think she was a little younger than me, dark brown hair—who was working on a viridefaeco potion. Do you know who she is?"

Yeardley sighed. "Fiona. She is so determined, but hasn't made any real progress since then. She decanted a promising base with the help of some old records, and I admit, we all had extremely high hopes. But since then, nothing."

"Is she here?" Laurel asked, hoping against hope that the young faerie had not been one of Klea's many victims. Thinking like Klea might save Avalon, but if the viridefaeco required lengthy fermentation or exotic curing methods, Tamani wouldn't live to see it happen.

Yeardley's face fell and Laurel almost couldn't breathe. "She's alive," he said softly. "She breathed in a lot of smoke and, honestly, she isn't doing well. But she's still conscious. I've been caring for her myself. This way."

Laurel nearly collapsed with relief. She followed Yeardley to the far end of the greenhouse where she recognized the dark brown curls and knelt beside a small faerie reclining against a planter box with her eyes closed.

"Fiona," Yeardley said softly, crouching by her side.

Fiona opened her eyes and, realizing Laurel and Chelsea were also there staring at her, struggled to sit up a little straighter.

"How are you feeling?" Yeardley asked.

"The viridefaeco potion," Laurel said, interrupting before Fiona could answer. She didn't have time for niceties. "Do you have a base made?"

"I—I—I did," she stuttered.

"What do you mean, 'did'?" Laurel asked, fearful of the answer.

"I was in the lab when the trolls attacked. I don't know if my bases survived."

Laurel tried to stay calm and cool. Klea didn't fly off the handle when the pressure went up. If anything, she rose to the occasion. Laurel had to maintain that kind of control too. "We need to go to the lab right away. Can you walk?"

Yeardley helped Fiona to her feet. She was a little wobbly but got her bearings quickly. "Can you help her?" Laurel asked Chelsea. "Please? I can't."

"Of course," Chelsea murmured, ducking under the faerie's arm and helping to support her as Yeardley led the way.

As they approached the entrance David had cut only hours earlier, Fiona drew back. "It's okay, the fire is out and the toxin is gone," Chelsea assured her, then added, "And I'm right here with you."

The young faerie nodded and took a deep breath before plunging back into the warm, sooty darkness.

Walking through the shadowed Academy hallways with a single phosphorescing flower felt like walking in a massive tomb. The hallways were scorched and decimated and bodies were everywhere, some whole, some burned, a few disfigured by the first wave of trolls. A fluttering panic settled in Laurel's throat; would there even be anything left to work with in the lab? As they turned down the last hallway Laurel was relieved that at least the door was still intact.

After a moment of hesitation Yeardley pushed open the door, leaving a wide handprint in the black ash. As they passed through the doorway Laurel heard Fiona gasp. The room looked like someone had picked it up and shaken it. Broken glass littered the floor, potted plants had been overturned, and instead of furniture there were only piles of splintered wood. Atop everything was a fine layer of soot.

Laurel tried not to stare at the faeries on the floor—or the dead troll at the end of the room. Yeardley's expression was stoic, his jaw tight, and Chelsea's face was a little pale. Fiona was actually managing pretty well, focusing on the task at hand in typical Fall fashion.

"My station is—was—over here," she said, hiking up her calf-length skirt as she stepped over and around the destruction. The floor was littered with broken instruments and shattered vials Laurel figured had once covered the top of the station, so Laurel was relieved when Fiona bent to open a cabinet set beneath the table. Several large beakers were nestled safely within.

"One was knocked over and cracked, but two are left," Fiona said, emerging from the cupboard clutching two bottles filled with a clear solution the consistency of fresh honey.

"Perfect," Laurel said, wearily resting against the table's edge, making sure only her skirt, and none of her skin, made contact with the surface. It was late, she was exhausted, and the toxin was taking its toll. She looked around the half-destroyed classroom. "Do you think we can find everything we need?" she asked, not really convinced.

"Over here." Laurel startled at Yeardley's voice and turned to find him wiping down a spot at one of the tables with a handkerchief. "You two discuss the base," Yeardley said. "I will gather everything I can find. The specimens on the shelves should still be clean." Laurel nodded and Yeardley set to rifling through cupboards.

Fiona put the two bottles on the clear bit of table in front of them and told Laurel how she had come up with the base. It was much the same as the explanation she had given in the circle the first time Laurel was in Avalon, but after two summers of study, Laurel actually understood much of what she said. Fiona rattled off a list of ingredients she'd found in an old text: cured Joshua tree nettles, blended ficus and cucumber seeds, passion-fruit extract. The list was extensive and after a few minutes of recitation, Laurel stopped her. "I need to *feel* it. Can you pour a few drops in a small dish for me? If I touch the base in the bottle, I'm afraid the toxin will destroy it completely." She looked over at Chelsea. "I'm going to need you both to be my hands."

Chelsea glanced around and found a small, shallow dish as Fiona carefully unsealed the top of one of her bottles. She poured a few drops and Chelsea handed the dish to Laurel.

"I know that I have the base right up to this point," Fiona said, shaking her head. "The text was very clear, and the whole thing came together perfectly. But the remainder of the instructions had been removed and no matter what I try next, I can't seem to complete it. There's something I'm missing and I have no idea what it could be." She sighed. "The things I've tried. It's ridiculous."

As Fiona outlined her experiments and failures, Laurel dragged her finger through the small puddle of solution in the dish in front of her. Her fingertips were black and a little swollen, and she focused on the way Fiona's mixture was reacting to the toxin in her body, how the toxin was reacting to the viridefaeco base. She felt the potential of the minor components, how they were suppressed by the major ones. There were several ingredients she would not have thought to put together—much like Klea's vanishing powder, the viridefaeco base was a mess of tension. What it needed was an outlet. And somewhere at the back of Laurel's mind, she felt like she'd encountered the proper element somewhere before.

It was the same feeling she'd had when she first analyzed the powder Klea had made from her own amputated blossom—not that the missing ingredient was part of a faerie, in this case. She remembered that day with Tamani, sensing the things she could make from him—toxins, photosynthesis blockers, poisons. The serum Klea had made to defend the trolls against faerie magic; that had used faerie blossoms, too. Potions that used faerie blossoms did not help faeries, but hurt them. That wasn't what they needed for the antidote.

Yeardley had told her when she first came to the Academy that knowledge was the essence of her magic—the place from which her intuition drew its power. The missing component was something she knew, something she'd encountered many times before—something she'd failed to recognize as a useful element, perhaps something Fiona had never encountered. That seemed to point to an ingredient that wasn't common in Avalon.

"Okay," Laurel said. "I think you were on the right track with dried wheatgrass. Are there any varieties you don't usually use? Maybe some they have to bring in from the Manor? Let's go in that direction."

Yeardley had gathered more herbs and supplies than Laurel would have guessed could survive the fire. But she didn't question it, just set to work, directing Fiona and Chelsea in gathering and preparing additives, letting them do the actual work and testing samples as the potion progressed.

"It's so close. Everything is here," Laurel said after adding a tiny mist of rosewater, the only other thing she felt it could possibly need. She traced her finger through yet another sample. "It's ready, it's just not enough. The toxin is still overwhelming it. It's like . . . like the ingredients are inert and they need something to activate them." She sucked in a breath. That felt right. "A catalyst," she said softly. "Something to unlock its potential." *But what?*

Fiona shook her head. "This is why I had to move on to other projects. I even had the same idea you did—I traveled to the Manor. They told me humans have driven many plants into extinction over the last few centuries. The final ingredient must be one of those."

"No," Laurel insisted. "No, I know the final ingredient. It's on the tip of my tongue. What grows in California that doesn't grow in Avalon?"

"Laurel," Chelsea said hesitantly. "Your face—it has dark spots on it."

Laurel reached her hands up to touch her cheeks, remembering the way Tamani had done the same thing. How long had it been? It didn't matter—she couldn't think about it now.

If you can think like the Huntress, you can do as she has done.

The viridefaeco potion had been lost for centuries. But Klea had figured out how to make it again. What made her so special? She was always willing to push boundaries. She had probably tested both toxins and antidotes on herself, risking everything for her work. And hadn't Laurel done that? Hadn't she taken the poison into herself, to better understand it? But the more she understood the poison creeping through her body, the more she feared she couldn't overcome it after all. Laurel picked up a fresh sample of the base and closed her eyes, continuing to run her finger through the solution, chanting her mantra in her mind. *Think like Klea, think like Klea.*

Avalon has forgotten how much humans have to offer.

Laurel's eyes popped open as Klea's words echoed through her head. "Chelsea," she said softly. "I need Chelsea!"

"What?" Chelsea said. "What do you need?"

"I need *you*. Some hair, some spit . . . no, better make it blood. Human DNA." She sorted through the supplies Yeardley had gathered. "The viridefaeco potion was lost after the gates were sealed—after all human interaction was cut off, right?" she asked, turning to Fiona, who nodded. "That's not coincidence—it's the *reason* it was forgotten; the reason they destroyed the second half of the instructions. The catalyst for this potion is human DNA. Chelsea," she said, turning to her friend with a small preparation knife, "may I?"

Chelsea nodded without hesitation, holding out her hand.

Laurel held the knife close to Chelsea's fingertip. *Just a tiny poke*, she told herself, but it was still difficult to lay that blade against her friend's skin and press down just hard enough to cut.

"Should I do this part?" Fiona asked quietly.

Laurel shook her head. "No. I have to do it," she said, strangely certain. She pulled the large vial in front of her, touching it for the first time. A tiny crimson bead was pooling on Chelsea's finger; she looked even more exhausted than Laurel, but too excited to see what happened next to suffer much pain.

"Avalon's last chance," Laurel said under her breath. *And Tamani's,* she added to herself. Then she tipped Chelsea's finger and carefully let one drop of blood fall into the vial, stirring it with a long-handled bamboo spoon.

As soon as the blood hit the solution, it *changed*. Laurel continued stirring and a sense of exhilaration spread through her as the translucent mixture took on a purple hue that matched the vial Laurel had seen ever so briefly in Klea's hand. It was working! All of the ingredients seemed to awaken as one and the potency of the base increased tenfold—a thousandfold! A giggle bubbled up in Laurel's throat and Chelsea grabbed her arm.

"Did it work?"

Laurel was so confident she lowered her finger right into the solution.

The toxin didn't stand a chance.

"It worked. It worked, oh, Chelsea it worked!" Laurel felt light-headed with relief. "Please," she said, turning to Fiona, "I need vials. Right now!"

She had to get to Tamani.

When Laurel burst through the tree line the dimly lit circle was so still she wasn't completely sure *anyone* was alive.

Tamani's head was propped on David's leg. "I think he's still breathing," David said when Laurel hopped over the trench and fell to her knees beside Tamani's body. "But he stopped opening his eyes about five minutes ago."

Tamani was still shirtless, his chest and shoulders swathed in black. Laurel held his face in her hands, feeling the toxin within him try to attack her, but the viridefaeco Chelsea had insisted she swallow before leaving the Academy repelled it with ease.

"Come back . . . to say . . . good-bye?" Klea asked, wheezing with laughter. Even swollen with infection, lingering on the brink of death, she was a bitter witch.

"Please live," Laurel begged under her breath as she poured the potion into Tamani's mouth and closed his lips over it.

She waited as the seconds dragged by, her eyes filling with tears as she gripped Tamani's arm, willing him to wake. The viridefaeco had started curing her almost instantaneously—why wasn't it working now? A minute passed. Two.

David touched her arm. "Laurel, I don't—"

"No!" she shouted, pushing his hand away. "It's going to work. It *has* to work. Tamani, please!" She bent over him, pressing her face to his chest, hiding her tears, wishing faeries had something like a heartbeat to assure her that he was alive. He *had* to be alive. She wasn't sure she could live another moment if he wasn't with her. What did any of this matter if, in the end, she was too late to save Tamani? She straightened, searching his face for some sign of consciousness. A lock of his hair hung partway over one eye and she reached out to push it back off his forehead, her hand heavy with despair.

Halfway through the motion, she stopped. The tiny black

tendrils that had begun to reach across Tamani's face were retreating. She squinted at them; had she imagined it? Was it a trick of the darkness? No, that line had been all the way across his eyebrow; now it was only halfway. She held her breath, hardly daring to move as she watched it lighten and disappear. His chest rose—ever so slightly—and fell again.

"Breathe again," Laurel commanded in a barely audible whisper.

Nothing moved.

"Again!" Laurel demanded.

His chest rose once more. This time he choked and sputtered against the viridefaeco caught in his throat and swallowed hard.

Laurel let out a shout of exhilaration and threw her arms around his neck, pulling him against her with glee. His breathing was still shallow, but it was even, and a few seconds later, he opened his eyes—those beautiful green eyes she'd feared would never look at her again.

"Laurel," he said, his voice cracking.

Tears fell on her cheeks, but this time it was tears of joy and she laughed, her voice echoing through the woods as if the very trees were rejoicing with her.

Tamani smiled weakly. "You did it."

"I had help."

"Still."

Laurel nodded and ran her fingers through his hair as he closed his eyes with a contented sigh.

But Laurel wasn't done yet.

Releasing Tamani, she stood and walked over to Klea. Her face was black and swollen, but her pale green eyes blazed with malice. She had to have heard everything—known her plan had failed for good.

"Viridefaeco," Klea whispered. Her breathing was ragged and she was still on her back—the same position she'd been in for an hour. Laurel wondered if she could even move anymore. "Well, aren't you . . . aren't you *something*. Bet you think you're pretty . . . smart."

"I think *you're* smart," Laurel said calmly. It was a strange truth to voice. "Open your mouth," she said, holding out the second vial.

"No!" Klea snarled, more fervently than Laurel would have thought possible from the dying faerie.

"What do you mean, no?" Laurel asked. "The toxin's about to kill you."

Klea rolled her eyes up to Laurel. "I would rather . . . die . . . than live in your *perfect world*."

Laurel felt her jaw tighten. "This isn't a contest—take the potion!" When Klea turned her head and pressed her lips shut, Laurel decided to just splash the potion in Klea's face— it was probably potent enough.

With lightning reflexes, Klea's hand closed over Laurel's wrist. Her grip was like iron as she forced herself into a sitting position, and Laurel struggled to tear herself away. Where had Klea found the strength?

"Laurel!" David took one hesitant step toward them, then stopped, giving his magic sword an exasperated frown.

"I will have . . . this . . . victory!" Klea said, every word a hiss through clenched teeth. With a mighty shove, she smashed Laurel's fist against the ground, shattering the sugar-glass vial, spilling the sticky serum into the blackened grass. Contemptuously, Klea shoved Laurel's captive arm away, collapsing back onto the ground. "Rot . . ."

Laurel was frozen with shock.

". . . in . . ."

The viridefaeco dripping off Laurel's hand might be enough. If she could just—

". . . *hell.*"

The expression that froze on Klea's blackened, swollen face was not one of anger or contempt. It was pure, malignant disgust.

Numbly, Laurel staggered back over to Tamani, dropping to the ground beside him. David joined them, planting Excalibur in the ground and sitting, cross-legged, at Laurel's other side. Tamani's eyes fluttered open again, and he lifted one hand to grip David's. "Thanks for staying with me, mate."

"Had nowhere else to be," David said softly, smiling.

Laurel let her head fall onto David's shoulder and twined her fingers through Tamani's. There was work ahead of them, recovery, viridefaeco serum to make, friends to mourn, and the Academy to rebuild. But for tonight it was over. Avalon was safe, David was a hero, and Tamani was alive.

And Klea could never hurt her again.

TWENTY-FIVE

"LAUREL?"

Laurel's eyes fluttered open in the murky predawn light. Her head lay on Tamani's chest, and David's arm was draped over her stomach. She wasn't sure just how much time had passed—snuggled in the cocoon of her friends' arms, she had let the world swirl around her unheeded, a tiny respite from the horrors of the last twenty-four hours—but with dusk only beginning to herald the sun's arrival, it couldn't have been too long.

"Laurel?"

It took her a few moments to focus through the dim morning light to find where the voice was coming from. "Jamison," she breathed. Raising Tamani's hand to her face, Laurel met his eyes and brushed her lips against his knuckles before leaving his side to crawl wearily over to Jamison.

Despite David's careful tending, Laurel was concerned

that Jamison had remained unconscious for so long. He was outside of David's circle and appeared to have been spared from the toxin, but still, Laurel tenderly probed his head where the log had hit him, then gripped his hands, feeling his skin for any sign that the poison had reached his cells.

"I fear I failed you," he said, his voice laced with disappointment.

"No," Laurel said, letting herself smile when she couldn't sense even a trace of the poison. "Everything is fine." *As fine as it can possibly be, at the end of a war.*

"Yuki . . . ?"

Laurel hung her head. "I didn't get back in time," she whispered, and was unsurprised to see tears glittering in Jamison's eyes.

"Callista too?"

Laurel nodded silently, the helplessness she'd felt during Klea's last moments filling her with sadness all over again.

"But Avalon is safe," he pronounced, not a hint of question in his voice.

Laurel didn't feel victorious.

"What happened?"

Laurel told the story as quickly as she could, trying not to overwhelm the weary Winter, wishing it had a happier ending.

"I'm proud of you," Jamison said when she was done, but his voice sounded as defeated as Laurel felt. Yes, the trolls were gone and yes, Klea and her toxin had been stopped, but the cost was almost incomprehensible. Hundreds of Spring and Summer faeries killed—perhaps more than a thousand. And the Fall faeries? It was painful to even think about. The Academy's population had been cut down to fewer than a hundred. It would take decades to restore their numbers. So many dead, and for what? For Avalon to return to its broken status quo.

Laurel heard a shout and the clatter of footfalls, and she and Jamison both turned toward the noise.

"I will not wait!" The Queen's voice sounded clearly above the arguments of her *Am Fear-faire* as she made her way down the path, Yasmine following more serenely a short distance behind.

Jamison's hands stiffened beneath Laurel's at seeing his monarch approach, but a small smile touched his lips when Yasmine caught sight of him and broke into a run.

"Wait!" All eyes turned away from the Queen and her entourage as Chelsea and Fiona burst through the trees in a scatter of leaves.

"Don't. Touch. Anything," Fiona said, gasping for breath, her arms cradling a large glass vial.

"Thank goodness!" Chelsea said, stepping around Fiona to sweep Laurel and Jamison into an exuberant embrace. "Doesn't that Queen listen to anyone?" Chelsea whispered and Jamison chuckled silently. "We saw them coming down the path just as we were finishing up another batch of the potion and we ran as fast as we could."

"At least the sentries were able to keep her back this long," Laurel said, one eyebrow raised.

"Wait, Yasmine, please!" Fiona called, trying to stop the young Winter faerie from approaching Jamison.

"It's okay," Laurel said. "Jamison's clean."

Reluctantly, Fiona let her pass.

Queen Marion stopped at the edge of David's trench and glowered, her hands crossed over her chest. Laurel ignored her stormy countenance and took Chelsea's hand, pulling her friend over the shallow trench, leading her to where David knelt, hand clenched around Excalibur, beside Tamani, who had managed to pull himself up to a half recline. His chest was still a smoky gray that looked like extensive bruising, but even that was fading.

"No matter what happens," Laurel whispered, "we do this together." She met each of her friends' eyes for several seconds and they all nodded. "And David, don't you let go of that sword." She glanced at the Queen. "I'm not sure we're through fighting the enemy yet," she finished grimly.

"Come over here, all of you," Marion commanded.

"Let me neutralize them first," Fiona said, and Laurel turned to see her duck in front of the Queen, holding the glass vial. She'd attached a spray nozzle to the top. "Just to be safe," she added, her eyes darting to the shadows that still lingered at Tamani's chest.

Laurel nodded and Fiona hopped over the moat.

"Hold your breath." Fiona misted them with a very fine spray of the viridefaeco. "I apologize that you will be a touch damp."

Laurel waved her concerns away and turned to help Tamani to his feet. "Can you walk?" she whispered.

His jaw flexed several times, but he shook his head. "Not without help," he admitted.

"Here," Laurel said. She laid his arm across her shoulders and Chelsea was quick to join her on the other side.

Though the Queen stood only feet away, Laurel and Chelsea took Tamani across to the opposite side of the circle, where Jamison and Yasmine were, and David straddled the gap and carefully helped Tamani over so they could all sit together.

"We'll talk over here," Laurel called to the Queen.

Marion pursed her lips and for a moment Laurel thought she would refuse to come. But she must have realized there was nothing more she could do. Flanked by her *Am Fear-faire*, she picked her way around the circular trench and stood over them, looking down on what might otherwise have appeared to be a cozy group.

The Queen made a show of counting them once, and then twice. "Well, Jamison, two humans and two faeries; a Fall and a Spring. Where is the Winter faerie you told me about?" Marion asked. "Or did she turn out to be a figment of a certain sentry's overactive imagination?" Her eyes rested accusatorily on Tamani.

"She's the younger one you see dead in the circle," Jamison said, pointing.

Marion looked over and her eyes grew large, realizing for the first time that the grotesquely shriveled black forms in the circle of dead grass were, in fact, fae. "You killed her," she said softly.

"I did not," Jamison said. "Yuki betrayed Callista when it was revealed that Yuki was nothing more than a pawn in the Mixer's plans. Callista killed her."

"A pawn?" the Queen asked, scoffing, clearly unable to take seriously the idea of a Winter faerie as anyone's pawn.

"Just like the trolls," Jamison said, slowly, deliberately.

Momentarily, Queen Marion looked like someone had slapped her in the face—as though she took the comparison as a personal affront. Her expression slowly settled into uncertainty. "I think you had better start from the beginning."

Slowly, and with many interruptions, Laurel shared with everyone the story of what they had done. When she got to the part about how she had discovered the final ingredient to the viridefaeco potion, Jamison beamed with pride and the Queen looked rather ill.

When Laurel finished, the clearing descended into tense silence. Marion looked over the circle where Klea and Yuki had died. The grass was blackened beyond recovery, but Fiona and two other soot-covered Falls were spraying the viridefaeco serum, putting a final stop to the poison's spread.

"Jamison," Marion spoke at last, sounding tired, "you obviously need to rest. I suggest you retire to the palace and show these two humans to their quarters as well."

"I agree. I think it would be best if David returns the sword before we reward him for his valor and escort him and his friends out of Avalon. I imagine they are all anxious to get home."

"Don't be foolish," said the Queen, rejecting Jamison's twisting of her command. "The humans cannot possibly be permitted to leave."

Chelsea made a small noise in her throat; Tamani reached out and grabbed her hand reassuringly.

"You know as well as I that the rule is not absolute."

"He has wielded the sword, Jamison."

"Just because it was done before does not mean it has to be done now. The circumstances were very different," Jamison said, his voice calm.

"I don't see how."

"Arthur had nothing to go back to. His life and kingdom were destroyed. This boy has a future ahead of him. I will not be part of trapping him here."

"What do you mean, trapping me here?" David said.

Jamison looked up at David. "King Arthur never left Avalon. Ever. And it may not have been entirely of his own volition."

"An unbeatable sword is too great a secret," the Queen said, her tone patronizing, but tinged with pity. "Surely you understand that."

"I can keep a secret," said David. "I'm real good at secrets."

"Not like this."

"I've kept Laurel's true nature a secret for over two years now. Not to mention the location of the gate."

The Queen didn't look impressed. "That makes *two* things

that should have been wiped from your memory, if Laurel d'Avalon's *Fear-gleidhidh* had been doing his duty. Please do not think us ungrateful. It is a matter of expedience. The leaders of your world—human or otherwise—would slaughter a great many to obtain this weapon."

"I know that."

"Then you understand that it is for your own safety that you remain here."

"I have a family. Chelsea too. We won't leave them."

"It is not your choice," the Queen said sternly. "We aren't monsters; you will be well cared for. But you cannot leave."

"It isn't *your* choice," David countered, before anyone else could speak up. "You can't keep me here."

The Queen's eyes narrowed. "I don't see why not."

"I have Excalibur."

"And you can carry it around Avalon till you die, for all I care," she said, her tone declaring an end to this conversation.

"What do you want to bet this sword would cut through the bars of those gates?" David said, his voice quiet, but piercing.

Laurel's breath caught in her throat; surely David didn't intend to destroy Avalon's most important defense—did he?

"Arthur never cut the gates," the Queen retorted, but there was uncertainty in her eyes.

"Maybe he didn't really want to leave."

"Perhaps not," Marion replied. "Or perhaps he realized the danger such rash action would pose to Avalon. Perhaps he was too noble for that."

David responded with a glare, which Queen Marion returned, measure for measure.

"I will not assist you in trapping them," Jamison said, interrupting their power struggle. "If they ask me to open the gate for them, I will."

"Then you will be executed for treason," Marion said without hesitation. "We may be one Council, *but I am still the Queen.*"

"No!" Yasmine shouted, clutching Jamison's arm, her young voice sounding strangely out of place in the midst of this particular conversation.

"Yasmine, the same fate for you," Marion said, not meeting her eyes.

"That's not fair!" Chelsea said, rising to her feet, her fists clenched. "She hasn't done anything."

"The choice belongs to the human," Marion said, staring steadfastly at David. "It would be a shame if, after all the work you've done, you decided to expose Avalon to even greater danger."

David was silent and still, his knuckles white on the hilt of the sword. Could he really cut down the gate? *Would* he?

David spun on his heel and presented the Queen with his back. Wordlessly he jumped the trench and stood looking at the bodies surrounding him. Klea, Yuki, Klea's mindless warriors, the still-blackened grass that filled the circle. Then he turned and, making eye contact with the Queen, thrust the sword into the earth, almost to the hilt.

But he didn't let go.

He just crouched, glaring at Marion for nearly a minute. Everything else was silent.

Then he released his hold on the sword, one finger at a time, until his arm fell and he stood and walked away.

When he reached them, David wrapped his arms around Chelsea and buried his face in her neck, his whole body shaking. "I'm sorry," he whispered. "I'm so, so sorry. After everything they've been through, I can't . . . I'm so sorry."

"I know," Chelsea said, holding him close. She squeezed her eyes shut and her voice quavered as she spoke. "You did the right thing. And hey, there are worse places to live, right?"

Laurel threw her arms around both of them; behind her, Tamani struggled to his feet and joined them, his weight leaning heavy on her shoulder. "Guys, I can—" he started to whisper.

"I will not stand by and let this happen."

They all turned to see Jamison on his feet, Yasmine tucked under his arm, bearing him up. "I will open the gate for them. And then I will accept my punishment."

"Jamison, no," Tamani said quietly.

"I've so little time left anyway—it would be an honor," Jamison said, his chin high.

But Tamani was already shaking his head. "No one is sacrificing themselves today. Not even you."

Jamison eyed Tamani appraisingly, but after a moment they seemed to come to some kind of understanding that

Laurel couldn't comprehend, and Jamison took one step back, silent now.

Tamani turned to Laurel, David, and Chelsea. "I will make things right," he said softly.

"How?" Laurel said. "We can't just—"

"If you have ever trusted me, any of you, trust me now," he whispered. He looked around the circle, meeting everyone's eyes. They all nodded.

With visible effort Tamani straightened, speaking loudly enough for everyone to hear him. "I have a few things to do. Laurel," Tamani said, turning to her, "will you help Jamison to the Gate Garden?"

"You can't let him do this for us," Laurel said quietly.

"Please?" Tamani replied.

She had agreed to trust him. She nodded slowly.

"Chelsea? Will you come help me?"

Chelsea mustered up a smile. "Of course."

"One hour—I want everyone together at the Gate Garden." Tamani looked up and met the Queen's eyes. "You should be there too."

"I am not accustomed to being ordered about like a—"

"You'll want to stop me if I'm better than you think I am, won't you?" Tamani interrupted with a raised eyebrow. Never before had he sounded so much like Shar's protégé. Laurel recalled how he once had trembled in the presence of Fall faeries, how he had cowered beneath the gaze of the Queen—it was as if a different faerie stood before her now.

Marion was silent and Laurel realized Tamani had caught

her in a trap. If she didn't come, Tamani might succeed. But if she did, it would prove she was afraid.

Control or appearances?

Queen Marion turned purposefully and departed without a word. But Laurel suspected that, in the end, Avalon's monarch would comply.

TWENTY-SIX

LAUREL WATCHED TAMANI LUMBERING DOWN THE road to the Spring quarter, one arm slung across Chelsea's shoulders for support. He was getting stronger every minute, but the serum cleansing the poison from his system would not change the fact that he was clearly exhausted.

They all were. Dark rings hung beneath Chelsea's and David's eyes, and Tamani's body had been badly battered even before Klea poisoned him. But Chelsea would take care of him—Laurel knew without a doubt that she could depend on her friend for that.

"That boy has something in mind," Jamison said, a twinkle in his eye. "And I am most anxious to see what it is."

Laurel nodded, though what she felt was fear. Tamani had proven his willingness to sacrifice himself for her and Laurel could only hope that wasn't what he was planning now. Not that she could see how it would change anything. She helped

276

Jamison to his feet and took one of his arms while Yasmine took the other.

David stood to the side, hesitating, then joined them, his arm linked with Laurel's.

"It feels strange for Klea to be dead," Laurel admitted as they walked slowly down the path. "I feel like I've been trying to figure her out and stay safe from her every moment of every day for . . . more than a year, I guess."

"I do wish things could have ended differently for her," Jamison admitted.

"I didn't like putting myself in her head, but it's the only reason I came up with that final ingredient," Laurel said.

"That is because she had a brilliant mind. And, perhaps more importantly, she had an *open* mind. She was willing to ask questions and pursue answers in ways other faeries simply could not fathom. In the end it was her downfall, but it was also her salvation."

"You told me once that I could be as good as someone, but you didn't say who. Were you talking about her?"

"I was indeed. I have thought of her often in the past fifty years, and how much Avalon lost when we gave up on her."

Laurel hesitated, then blurted out, "How can you remember her potential after everything she's done? When I think of Klea all I see is misery and death."

David squeezed her arm sympathetically.

"Then try to remember how often she has saved your family and friends."

"We were never actually in danger," Laurel argued,

remembering the first night they'd met Klea. The first time she'd "saved" them. "She sent those trolls after us to begin with. It's not the same. Even her saving us from Barnes was because *she* lost control of him."

"Ah, but you told me yourself that she said she made the best toxins *and* antidotes. I believe the healing tonic I gave you saved your father, and has also been administered to your human friends on occasion."

Laurel sucked in a breath, thinking of the small blue bottle she kept in her kit back home. "She made that?"

Jamison nodded. "I have encountered few truly bad seeds in my life. Even people who find themselves acting out of envy, or greed, or selfish pride, do not lose their ability to act out of love. In the end, even Yuki found her way back. I'm sorry that Callista was unable to do the same, but I still believe she had goodness inside her at one point."

"Yeah," Laurel said, but she was unconvinced. After watching Tamani nearly die, she was not inclined to think nice thoughts about Klea.

Jamison was silent for a spell, then said, "I do not know that I will still be here when you next return to Avalon."

"Jamison—"

"Please," Jamison interrupted, his face almost unfamiliar in its seriousness. "This is important. So very, very important." He paused and glanced around conspiratorially, then took both Laurel's hands in his and met her eyes. "It has been more than fifty years since we first decided to place a scion in the human world and began putting our plan into action.

I was reluctant. I did not think the timing was right. Cora was ready to wilt and I could see the kind of queen Marion was going to be. But I was outvoted. Then one day, many years later, they brought us a new Winter faerie, fresh from her sprout."

Jamison laid a fatherly arm around Yasmine and she smiled up at him.

"I looked down at this tiny Winter faerie—one who was doomed to never rule, as she was too close to Marion's age—and I thought of the potential in her that would be wasted. Just like Callista. And I knew at that moment that I could not let that happen again. Days later, they brought in the final two candidates for the human scion."

"Mara and me?" Laurel asked, and Jamison nodded.

"I realized I knew one of the young Mixers. I had seen her often when I was in the Academy, watching the Gardener care for the Winter sprout. This little Mixer was best friends with the Gardener's son."

"Tamani," Laurel whispered.

"And I realized that perhaps this was the answer. A scion—a good, kind scion with someone in Avalon who loved her, *truly* loved her, someone who could be her anchor, who could keep her coming back to our realm.

"But not empty-handed. I needed a scion who would not look down on humans, but who would love them—a scion who would reject traditions and prejudices so difficult to unlearn that I could not even trust a memory elixir to erase them. And what if this scion could show the fae of Avalon that there was another way? Might she prove a worthy advisor to the throne? Would it be possible to conduct a peaceful revolution—to bring new glory, a new way of life to our realm?"

"Jamison!" Laurel gasped.

"And while this scion was learning another way, *I* could teach that tiny Winter faerie to respect *all* the faeries in Avalon, not just those with power. And maybe, just maybe, when the time was right, she *would* have a chance to rule—a chance to make Avalon the place I always secretly dreamed it could be."

"You planned this!" Laurel said breathlessly, trying to grasp the scope of Jamison's involvement. "You picked me, you helped Tamani, you planned *everything!*"

"Not everything. Not this," Jamison said, gesturing to the evidence of the destruction that surrounded them. "Never this. But after Callista was exiled, I had to do something. I *had* to start a change. It is our secret," Jamison said, sobering as he looked down at Yasmine, then back at Laurel. "And now it is yours too. Move slowly, my no-longer-so-little sprout. The best, most lasting changes are those which come about gradually; to reach great heights, a tree must first put down extensive roots. But I promise you this, when it's time—when Avalon is prepared and when you're ready to join us here—Yasmine will be ready. Then we can have a true revolution. A peaceful one; one with the support of all the Avalon faeries behind it. And with you and Yasmine working together, Avalon can finally be everything we've always hoped it could be."

Her eyes wide, Laurel looked down at Yasmine, seeing all the goodness Laurel had always loved in Jamsion shining in this young faerie's eyes.

Avalon's future, Laurel realized, and her face broke into a smile. She looked at them both and nodded, silently joining their secret crusade.

They began walking again as Laurel tried to comprehend everything Jamison had done—the seeds he had planted, literally and figuratively, and the harvest he had planned even though he knew he would not live to see it. When they reached the gate Laurel numbly helped Jamison sit on the little stone bench inside the shattered doors to the Garden, Yasmine beside him, their *Am Fear-faire* standing at attention on all sides.

"I—I'll be back," Laurel murmured, needing a few minutes to digest everything.

With David at her heels, Laurel passed back out through the entrance and walked a ways before putting her back against the stone wall and sliding down to the ground.

"I can't believe he had everything planned," she said softly.

"And now he'll die to see it through," David said, joining her on the ground. "To make sure we get out."

But Laurel shook her head. "Tamani will think of something."

"I hope so."

They were silent for a long time as the sun started to peek over the horizon and a cool breeze tousled Laurel's hair. She cleared her throat and said, "I'm sorry you got stuck with the sword."

"I'm not."

"Well, then I'm sorry you were put in a position where you had to kill so many trolls."

He didn't respond, but she knew how tormented he must be on the inside.

"It was—it was great, though. You really saved the day. You're my hero," she added, hoping he would warm to the praise.

But David didn't crack a smile. "You can't even imagine what it feels like to take hold of that sword." He shrugged. "Actually, maybe you can. Maybe this is what it feels like when you do magic."

"Trust me, Mixing doesn't feel much different than home ec."

"You touch it," David continued, as though she hadn't spoken, and Laurel closed her mouth and let him talk. Clearly he needed to get it out. "And this surge of power just pours into you. And it doesn't go away as long as you're touching the sword."

Laurel thought of the World Tree and wondered if it was similar to that.

"And it's the most incredible rush in the world and you can't help but believe that . . . that you can do anything." He looked down at his hands, clenched in his lap. "But even the unbeatable sword can't give me what I really want."

He hesitated, and Laurel knew what was coming next.

"We're not getting back together, are we?"

Laurel looked down at her feet and shook her head.

She saw his face fall, but he said nothing.

"I wish," Laurel began tentatively, "I wish there was a way that no one could get hurt in all this. And I hate that I'm the one who has to do it."

"I think it's better to know, though," David said.

"I didn't know," Laurel said. "Not for sure. Not until I almost lost him."

"Well, staring death in the face does tend to put things in perspective," David said, leaning back against the wall.

"David," Laurel said, trying to find the right words. "I don't want you to think you did anything wrong, or that you weren't good enough. You were the perfect boyfriend. Always. You would have done anything for me, and I *knew* that."

David maintained his pose, but he wouldn't meet her eyes.

"And I don't know," Laurel continued, "if this is making things better or worse, but you have to know how much I loved you—how much I *needed* you. You were the best thing that could have ever happened to me in high school. I don't know what I would have done without you."

"Thanks for that," David said, sounding sincere. "And—it's not like I didn't see it coming. I mean, I hoped it wouldn't, but . . ."

Laurel looked away.

"I think Tam's the only person in the world who could

love you as much as I do," David said grudgingly.

Laurel nodded, but remained silent.

"So will you stay here with him?"

"No," Laurel said firmly, and David looked up in surprise. "I don't belong here, David. Not yet. Maybe someday. If— *when* Yasmine becomes Queen, she'll need me, but for now, what Avalon really needs is someone in the human world, just like Jamison said. Someone to remind them how great humans really are. How great *you* are," she added. "And I intend to do that."

"Laurel?"

There was an edge of desperation in his voice, a deep sorrow she knew *she* had put there. "Yeah?"

He was quiet for a long time and Laurel wondered if he had changed his mind when he blurted, "We could have made it. If it hadn't been for . . . for him, we would have had the real thing. Our whole lives. I truly believe that."

Laurel smiled sadly. "Me too." She threw herself into David's arms, pressing her cheek against his warm chest, the same way she'd hugged him countless times before. But there was something more in it, this time, as he wrapped his arms around her and hugged her back. And she knew, despite the fact that she would probably see him every day from now through graduation, that this was good-bye.

"Thank you," she whispered. "For everything."

A movement caught the corner of her eye; he was far away, but she knew him in an instant. Tamani was struggling up the pathway on his own, hardly able to put one foot in front of the other. Even as she watched he stumbled and barely caught himself.

Laurel gasped and was on her feet in an instant. "I have to go help him," she said.

David met her eyes and held her gaze for several seconds before he looked down and nodded. "Go," he said. "He needs you."

"David?" Laurel said. "Sometimes . . ." She tried to remember how Chelsea had explained it to her once. "Sometimes we're so busy looking at one thing, one . . . person . . . that we can't see anything else. Maybe—maybe it's time for you to open your eyes and look around."

That message delivered, Laurel whirled and headed for Tamani without a backward glance.

TWENTY-SEVEN

"TAMANI!" LAUREL CALLED, RUNNING TO HIM.

He looked up and for a second Laurel saw joy in his eyes. But then darkness clouded his expression. He blinked and looked down at the ground, running his fingers through his hair almost nervously.

Laurel tucked herself beneath his good arm, wanting to chide him for trying to do so much. Beneath her fingertips Laurel could feel no trace of Klea's virulent toxin, which was encouraging, but his wounds were grievous enough on their own. "Are you all right?"

He shook his head and his eyes looked haunted in a way she had never seen before. Yesterday she had been peripherally aware that he was pushing his emotions aside to accomplish the tasks before him. But here, with no one around but Laurel, with no lives to save, he had let all his defenses go and allowed himself to really *feel*. And it showed. "No," he said, his voice shaking. "I'm not all right. And I don't think I'm going to be all right for a long time. But I'll live," he added after a brief pause.

"Sit," Laurel said, pulling him off the path to a patch of grass where a large pine shaded them from not only the rising sun, but prying eyes. For just a moment, she wanted him all to herself. "Where's Chelsea?"

"She'll be here soon," he said wearily.

"Where were you?" she asked.

He was silent for a moment. "Shar's house," he finally said, his voice cracking.

"Oh, Tam," Laurel breathed, her hands gripping his shoulder.

"It was his last request," Tamani said, one silent tear tracing down his face for an instant before he broke her gaze and rubbed it away with his sleeve.

Laurel wanted to wrap her arms around him, to offer her shoulder for him to cry on, to soothe away those terrible lines on his forehead, but she didn't know where to begin. "Tamani, what's going on?"

Tamani swallowed, then shook his head. "I'll get you back to California—you'll see. You, and Chelsea, and David."

"But—"

"But I'm not coming with you."

"You—you have to," Laurel said, but Tamani was shaking his head.

"I'll tell Jamison I can't keep my life vow. He'll help me, somehow. I'll get you the best protector in Avalon, I promise, but . . . it's not me anymore."

"I don't want another protector," Laurel said, her chest feeling hollow, panicked.

"You don't understand," Tamani said, not looking at her. "It's not about us; I can't be your *Fear-gleidhidh* . . . effectively. In hindsight, I should probably never even have tried; if I was doing my job right, none of this would have happened. When I—when I thought you were dead, I went crazy. I honestly didn't know myself. I was *afraid* of who I had become. I can't live always knowing that I could lose you at any moment; that I could feel that way again." He hesitated. "It's too hard."

"No, no, Tam," she said, smoothing his hair, caressing his cheek. "You can't, not now, not—"

"I'm not as good as you think I am, Laurel," he protested, desperation filling his voice. "I don't trust myself to protect you anymore."

"Then find someone else to fill that role if you have to," she said, jaw clenched, "but don't you leave me!" She scooted closer and took his face in her hands, waited while he built up the courage to raise his eyelids and look at her. "Wherever we're going today, I want you with me, and I never want you to leave my side again." His ragged breath touched on her face now, her body pulled right against his chest, feeling his essence pull on her like a magnet. "I don't care if you guard and protect me—all I care is that you *love* me. I want you to kiss me good night before I go to sleep and bid me good morning the moment I wake up. And not just today; tomorrow and the next day and every day for the rest of my life. Will you come with me, Tamani? *Be* with me?"

Laurel lifted his chin until their faces were even. Tamani closed his eyes and she could feel his jaw trembling under her hands. She brushed her lips over his, reveling in the velvety softness of his mouth against hers. When he didn't pull away, she pressed more firmly, knowing, somehow, that she had to move slowly, convince his tattered soul so carefully that she meant every word.

"I love you. And I'm asking you . . ." She opened her mouth slightly and gently scraped her teeth along his bottom lip, feeling his whole body shudder. "No," she amended, "I'm *begging* you, to come be with me." And she pressed her mouth against his and murmured against his lips. "Forever."

For a few seconds he didn't respond.

Then a groan escaped his throat and he thrust his fingers into her hair, pulling her mouth back to his with a fierce hunger.

"Kiss me," she whispered. "And don't stop."

His mouth enveloped hers again and their shared sweetness tasted like ambrosia as he caressed her eyelids, her ears, her neck, and Laurel marveled at the strangeness of the world. She loved him, had always loved him. She had even known it, somehow.

"Are you sure?" Tamani murmured, his lips softly grazing her ears.

"I am *so* sure," Laurel said, her hands clutching at the front of his shirt.

"What changed?" He pushed her hair away from her face, his fingers lingering on her temples, just brushing her eyelashes.

Laurel sobered. "When I brought you the potion, I thought I was too late. And I had just taken it myself. And all I wanted right at that moment was to take my own cure away. To die with you."

Tamani pressed his forehead against hers and lifted one hand to stroke her cheek.

"I've loved you for a long time," she said. "But there was always something holding me back. Maybe it was that I was afraid of an emotion that was so consuming. It still frightens me," she admitted in a whisper.

Tamani chuckled. "If it makes you feel any better, it scares the daylights out of me on a regular basis." He rained kisses on her again, his fingers pressed against her back and her waist, and Laurel realized his chest was shaking convulsively.

"What?" she asked pulling away. "What's wrong?"

But he wasn't sobbing—he was laughing! "The World Tree," he said. "It was right all along."

"When you got your answer?"

He nodded.

"You said you would tell me someday what it said. Will you now?"

"Commit."

"What?"

"The tree just said, *Commit*." He ran his hand through his hair, smiling a little.

"I don't understand," Laurel said.

"Neither did I. I was already your *Fear-gleidhidh*; I'd committed my life to protecting you. When the tree told me that, I figured you were as good as mine. Easy."

"And then I told you to leave," Laurel whispered, sorrow at the memory settling deep within her.

"I understand why you did," Tamani said, threading his fingers through hers. "And it was probably best for both of us in the long run. But it hurt."

"I'm sorry."

"Don't be. I was listening to the tree, and to my own selfish desires, when I should have been listening to *you*. I think I know what the tree really meant now," he said, his voice rumbling against her ear. "I needed to commit my life to you—not to guiding you or protecting you, just to *you*, completely, in my core. I needed to stop worrying about whether you would ever do the same for me. In a way, I think that's what coming to the human world did, and why I wasn't sure I could bear to go back." He traced his finger down her face. "I was committed to an idea before—to the love I felt for you. But not to *you*. And I think you sensed that change or you'd have rejected me."

"Maybe," Laurel said, although at this moment she couldn't fathom rejecting him for any reason.

His fingers found her chin, lifting it so he could look her in the eyes. "Thank you," he said softly.

"No," she said, running one finger across his bottom lip, "thank *you*." Then she pulled his face down, their lips meeting, melting together again. She wished they could stay there all day, all year, all eternity, but reality came creeping slowly back in.

"You still haven't told me what you're up to," she said at last.

"One more minute," Tamani said, smiling against her lips.

"We don't need minutes," Laurel said. "We have forever."

Tamani pulled back to look at her, his eyes shining with wonder. "Forever," he whispered, before pulling her in for another long kiss.

"So, does this make us entwined?" Laurel asked, a sharp twinge of grief piercing her happiness as she repeated the word Katya had used, so long ago, to describe committed faerie couples.

"I believe it does," Tamani said, beaming. He leaned closer, his nose touching hers. "A sentry and a Mixer? We shall be quite the scandal."

Laurel smiled. "I love a good scandal."

"I love *you*," Tamani whispered.

"I love you, too," Laurel replied, relishing the words as she said them. And with them, the world was new and bright— there was hope. There were dreams.

But most of all, there was Tamani.

TWENTY-EIGHT

NOT SINCE SAMHAIN HAD LAUREL SEEN SO MANY faeries gathered into one place. While she had occupied herself with Tamani, they had crowded their way into the Gate Garden, lined its battlements, clustered around the entrances, and spilled back out into the trees where the trolls had breached the walls. Most wore the plain, practical garb of Spring faeries, but flashy Summers and even a few Falls were interspersed through the crowd. In fact, the only group Laurel didn't see represented in the crowd were the ceremonially garbed sentries whose job it would probably have been to clear the Garden of the rabble. With sadness she wondered if any of the Garden sentries had survived.

David had not moved from where she'd left him; he rose to his feet as Laurel and Tamani approached and Laurel tried not to see the sadness in his eyes. She couldn't protect him from that, and it bothered her deeply that she'd inflicted a wound she couldn't cure. But at least by realizing that the time had come to let him go, she wouldn't make his pain any worse.

"She should be here by now," Tamani said softly.

"Who?"

"Chelsea—ah! There we go."

Laurel turned to see Chelsea coming up the pathway with more Spring and Summer faeries in tow.

"Tamani," Laurel asked, feeing a nervous bubble of laughter building up in the back of her throat. "Seriously, you have to tell me! What did you do?"

"I had Chelsea tell the Ticers and Sparklers that Marion was about to either trap their hero in Avalon forever or execute Jamison, and that they should come . . . uh . . . *watch*."

"You didn't!" Laurel cried, delighted.

"Believe me," Tamani said ruefully, "what's about to happen should be witnessed by as many fae as possible."

As Chelsea reached them Tamani pulled her close, planting a fond kiss atop her head. "Thank you. And not just for this," Tamani said, his gesture taking in the crowd around them. "For everything."

Chelsea beamed as Laurel turned and beckoned to David. Together, the four of them passed through the destroyed Garden doors; the crowd parted to admit them with smiles and words of thanks, a few adding in a warning whisper that the Winter faeries were waiting at the gateways.

As they traversed the crowded enclosure, with its rich earth paths and enormous moss-covered trees, Laurel marveled at just how *little* it all had changed in spite of yesterday's battles. The grass was trampled and several of the trees looked like they'd been caught in a nasty hailstorm, but the bodies had been cleared away, the weapons disposed of. Avalon had suffered a serious wound, but like Tamani, it was already healing.

As Laurel had suspected, all three of Avalon's Winter faeries were waiting on a marble bench near the gateways, surrounded by a passel of *Am Fear-faire*—Queen Marion unable to relinquish her tight-fisted control. Remembering her conversation with Jamison Laurel smiled inwardly. It would take time yet, but Laurel looked forward to the inevitable day when she and Yasmine—well, all of Avalon, really—would wrench that control away from her.

All around them clustered many Springs and Summers, some swathed in bandages or exhibiting cuts and scrapes from the previous day's battles—and even here, a few Mixers were plying their trade, treating the wounded who were in need of care but who had presumably refused to miss the spectacle anyway. A murmur of conversation that was both excited and angry buzzed through the Gate Garden and electrified the air.

In the center of it all glittered the four-sided gates of gold, their tiny flowers twinkling warmly in the morning light.

"We're leaving," Tamani said to Jamison, not even acknowledging his Queen's presence.

"I don't think so," Marion said, rising to her feet. "I have already made my decree—if Jamison or Yasmine open that gate, it will be an act of treason punishable by death."

The milling faeries breathed a collective gasp.

"You've gathered quite a crowd," Marion added. "Did you think to intimidate me with their presence?"

"Not at all," Tamani said. His tone was casual, but Laurel could feel that his body was tense. "I wanted them all to hear for themselves the words of their Queen on this matter."

"I am not accustomed to making appearances for your *amusement*." Marion scowled. "Gate guards, do your duty. Clear the Garden; this audience is at an end."

From somewhere in the crowd, the gate guard's captain emerged with four other sentries. They looked like they'd crawled through hell on their bellies; they were still in the armor they'd been wearing yesterday and blood caked their hands. Laurel realized it was *they* who had cleared the fallen trolls—and their fallen friends—from the Garden. They must have been at it all night.

"I apologize, Your Grace," said the captain, her voice gravelly. "We are too few."

Marion's eyes were wide with shock. For a moment Laurel wondered whether the Queen could actually be ignorant of the number of sentries who had died protecting the gates.

"You will do as I command or I will strip you of your duties," she said at last, and Laurel realized that what had actually surprised her was that someone had told her no.

With a bow, the gate captain drew a gleaming, long-handled sword from the scabbard at her waist. The sentries behind her did the same, and for a moment Laurel feared they were going to turn their weapons against the gathered audience. She felt her fingers digging into Tamani's arm; she didn't think she could handle another day of fighting.

The captain held up her sword, crossed in front of Laurel's face and met Tamani's eyes—steely glare for steely glare.

Then she threw her sword onto the ground and stretched out her arm, beckoning for them to pass. The rest of the sentries stepped back into a short line and dropped their weapons as well.

Marion was too angry to speak, but it hardly mattered; anything she might have said would have been drowned out by the cacophonous cheering of the crowd. When at last she found her tongue, she addressed Jamison and Yasmine.

"Stop them," she said. "I command you. Take them into custody."

"No," Yasmine said, rising to her feet.

"Excuse me?" Marion said, turning to face the young faerie whose head barely reached her shoulder.

Yasmine raised one eyebrow and stepped up onto the stone bench so her eyes were even with the Queen's. "I said no," Yasmine repeated, but loud enough that the legions of "lower" fae who had gathered could hear her. "If you want them stopped, you will have to do it yourself—and somehow, I don't think that will win you any supporters here today."

"Tam," Jamison said, stepping forward. "Let me do you this final kindness. I don't mind dying, not for someone as noble as any one of you, much less all four."

"No," Tamani said firmly. "You've done enough. More than enough." He raised his voice and addressed the entire crowd. "There has been far too much death here in Avalon already. No one else is dying for me." He glared at Marion. "Not today."

"You are preserving Jamison's life in exchange for your freedom?" Marion said, but she sounded suspicious.

Before Jamison could respond, Tamani bent at the waist in front of the elderly Winter faerie. "I think it's time I fully take up my role as Laurel's *Fear-gleidhidh* and resign my station at the gate and as a sentry."

Jamison nodded, but he was eyeing Tamani warily.

Tamani returned Jamison's probing gaze for several seconds before gathering the old faerie up in his arms. "I know this is likely good-bye," Tamani said. "So thank you, for everything."

Chelsea was still holding on to David's arm on one side and Laurel's on the other, but Laurel pulled away to step forward and wrap her arms around Jamison too, beginning to believe she really might never see him again—whatever trick Tamani had up his sleeve, he seemed pretty sure of himself. She tried to speak, but words wouldn't come. It didn't matter. Jamison understood.

"As for you," Tamani said, looking up at Marion, who stood with venom in her eyes, "I suspect your days as Queen are numbered."

Marion opened her mouth, but Tamani spun away, leading Laurel, David, and Chelsea to the gate.

"I wasn't finished," Marion said shrilly, her tight control broken.

"Oh, yes, you are," Tamani said without turning around.

They had taken three steps when they heard Marion's growl of rage and Laurel turned to see enormous branches flying at them like deadly spears.

"Tam!" Laurel yelled, and he threw his arms over both her and Chelsea as they ducked to the ground.

Dull thuds sounded all around Laurel, and after a few seconds she raised her head. Every gate sentry had raised their shield and stepped in front of the limbs, bearing the brunt of the attack. If it was possible, the cheering from the crowd roared even louder as Tamani stood tall, glaring at Marion, her hands still raised, ready to command nature.

After a moment her hands fell to her sides.

But they hadn't won yet.

"Can you really get us through without help?" Chelsea asked when they reached the ornate golden gate and eyed the blackness within.

Tamani nodded. "I believe so."

"Why didn't you tell us sooner?" David asked.

Tamani unflinchingly met David's eyes. "I wanted to see you refuse to destroy the gates—knowing what it would cost you."

David swallowed. "Did you doubt me?"

Tamani shook his head. "Not for a *second*. Gather round," he said quietly. "I don't want anyone else to see this part."

Laurel, David, and Chelsea made a semicircle around

Tamani, who closed his eyes and inhaled deeply. Then he reached into his pocket and pulled out a heavy golden key, studded with minuscule diamonds like those at the center of the flowers adorning the gates. As he extended it toward the glittering golden bars that stood between them and California, the latch shimmered and shifted like a mirage.

And where there had never been a keyhole before, one appeared.

Laurel watched in wonder as Tamani inserted the key and turned it. With hands that were visibly shaking, he pulled on the golden gate.

It swung open and the entire population of the Garden gasped as one.

"Where did you get that?" Laurel breathed.

"Yuki made it for me," Tamani said simply, pocketing it again and holding the gate open for them all. "Come on. Let's go home."

Laurel paused. Then she took David's hand and wrapped it around Chelsea's. After a long moment he nodded and led Chelsea through the gateway and out of Avalon. Laurel took one look back before following. She saw Marion, her face the picture of shock; Jamison, his fist raised in triumph, a roar of cheers and applause surrounding him; Yasmine, still standing on the bench, looking every bit the queen Laurel had no doubt she would one day be.

Grinning, she twined her fingers through Tamani's and together they walked out into the glittering starlight of California. Laurel considered the words Tamani had just spoken.

They were technically true; soon they would be in David's car, headed toward the house where she lived. But she knew the truth now. With Tamani beside her—his hand in hers—she was already home.

AUTHOR'S NOTE

DESPITE THIS BEING A SERIES ABOUT FAERIES, ULTI-mately the question that has always driven the story is, *How would a regular human react to discovering real magic in the world?* And even more than Chelsea, this question was embodied in David's character. In some ways, the whole Wings story is about him. And at the end of such an epic adventure, what really does the rejected member of any supernatural love triangle have to look forward to? Especially a human.

What follows is the real and final end—the way I decided to conclude the series before the first book was even written. But because it's very realistic, it is also unavoidably bitter-sweet. So if you prefer your endings happy and without blemish, or if you simply love David as much as I do, maybe you should stop reading here.

You've been warned.

THE LAST WORD

Dear Chelsea,

Congratulations! I'm so excited for you and Jason. I can't believe you're already a mother; it feels like the wedding was just last week. And even though you hated them, I hope little Sophie gets your curls. I always thought they were beautiful. I've included a little gift for her. But it probably bears explaining.

Once upon a time, a faerie stole my heart.

What I didn't know at the time was that she hadn't stolen it from me. You'd had it on layaway for years. But before you could make the final payment, she carried it off. And something I never did understand was how easily you forgave her for that.

But of course, there were a lot of things I didn't understand about you back then. I treasure the time we spent together at Harvard—you were amazing, every single day, pulling my thoughts away from that faraway island and reminding me to just breathe. I needed that reminder. I still need it. I don't think you have any idea—especially on those hard nights, when I was afraid to go to sleep, afraid to face the nightmares, and you would just lie there with me, talking into the wee hours of the morning—how often you literally saved my life.

When you moved on—perhaps it's more accurate to say, when I drove you away—I didn't know how I was going to keep myself together. I tried to stay busy, buried myself in schoolwork . . . med school has been good for that! But I came to understand why you left, and eventually I had to face the things that were holding me back. I know how you worried about my attachment to Laurel, but in the end, it wasn't Laurel I couldn't get over.

It was Avalon.

When I woke screaming in the night, you never asked me why. I loved you for that. Of course, you could probably guess that trolls figured heavily in those dreams. But nightmares spent reliving that day in Avalon weren't the worst of what I suffered. Sometimes I dreamed that I brought that cursed sword home, and with it came to rule the world. Sometimes I dreamed that I conquered Avalon, too, and with the secrets of the faeries, eradicated sickness, hunger, and disease. In those dreams, I'm every bit the tyrant Klea aspired to be, and what's worse, almost everyone loves me for it.

Those are the dreams that are the worst upon waking. When I'm on my rotations and someone brings in a child who's sick or injured and I can see at a glance that their chances are slim, it's all I can do not to airlift them to Orick, knock on Laurel's door, and beg her to give me her little blue bottle of miracles. But I know that's not how it works. Can you imagine the wars that would be waged for control of Avalon, if its secrets were widely known?

I'm resisting the urge to start this letter over for the hundredth time. I don't mean to be bleak. I'm sorry. But Chelsea—the things we know! Faeries, trolls, magic! Things most people dismiss as childhood fancies. But we know the truth—we know they're real. That the world we see is just a shadow of what actually exists. I don't know how you keep from shouting it from the rooftops sometimes. But we both know where that would land us, and stark white has never been your color, or mine.

Anyway, I've met someone and I'm excited to introduce her to the gang back in Crescent City. I think you'll like her. We've actually been together, off and on, for more than a year, and I've decided to propose. Frankly, I think she's shown a lot of patience waiting this long for me to come around.

But after being with you I decided that, if love ever came back into my life, I needed to do it right. I had to find a way to let Avalon go—to stop dwelling on the past and let myself turn my face to the future. And there was one obvious answer. An answer I never, ever thought I would consider. And I suspect that even as you read these words, you know what I'm talking about. That's partly why I'm writing *instead of using the phone. I'm not sure I could stand up to one of your famous lectures. By the time you get this, the deed will be done, and I hope you'll forgive me.*

I went to see Laurel and Tam. Forgive her, too, for agreeing to keep this secret from you. If it helps, it took a lot of convincing.

Laurel has spent months perfecting a memory elixir that will strip Avalon from my mind. It's going to put a lot of gaps in my memories of high school . . . she doesn't think it will significantly change my memory of you, but she doubts I'll remember her very much, or Tamani at all. She thinks she can leave enough of herself that when Mom talks about her—as she sometimes does—I can nod and say, "Oh yeah, my high school girlfriend." But it won't be her.

It was hard to say good-bye to them. It's been years since I got over her in a romantic way—when you and I were together. You had my whole heart. But what we shared, the four of us, it can't help but bind you. And as much as I never thought I would say this, Tam has been a really good friend to me these last few years. In the end, it was he who convinced Laurel to make the elixir. He who convinced her that it was my right to choose.

I'm in awe of your strength, Chelsea, and hope you'll forgive my weakness. But before I take that final step: Sophie's gift. (Though maybe you will enjoy it just as much!) Erasing a memory seems so final, and I don't want everything to be lost. It's a damn good story, isn't it? So I've been writing it down and going to Laurel for her memories and the details I was never privy to. You'll see that she didn't hold back. She told me everything and I've tried to relay it here as faithfully as possible. It's way too long to make a proper book, but if a certain little girl grows up to be anything like her mother, she won't mind. She'll love it because it has faeries.

So I've enclosed the only copy of our story in the world. I've already erased it from my hard drive. I'm giving it to you to do with as you wish. Keep it, share it, hell, publish it, for all I care. But please accept it in the spirit it is given, and don't try to make me remember all this. I can't bear it any longer; please, please don't try to force me to. I can't get married carrying around the kinds of secrets I would have to keep from my wife. And I want to give Rose the kind of future—the kind of husband—I know she deserves. The kind of man I know I can be. The kind of man I used to be. The man you used to love.

It's hard to believe we've been friends for almost fifteen years. We're getting old! But, God willing, we'll get another fifty.

Love,
David

P.S. Introduce me to Tam someday, if you get a chance. I miss him already.

ACKNOWLEDGMENTS

KUDOS ALWAYS GO OUT FIRST TO MY BRILLIANT editors, Tara Weikum and Erica Sussman, who make me look good, and to Jodi Reamer, my awesome agent, who, well, also makes me look good! Thank you for being constants in my career. There are so many people at Harper whose names I don't even know who worked tirelessly on this book—thanks to every single one of you! And my foreign-rights team, Maja, Cecilia, and Chelsey, the degree to which you rock cannot be described! Alec Shane, trusty agent assistant, your handwriting on my mail always means something good.

Sarah, Sarah, Sarah, Carrie, Saundra (now aka Sarah)—I would go crazy without you guys. Thank you for everything! Especially the ninjas. I mean . . . what ninjas?

Just one new name credit for this book, Silve, my Facebook fan, like I said—I love your name. Welcome to the Wings universe.

To Coach Gleichman, though your name is also in the front of this book, I will confess back here that from the very first book, I always intended to dedicate this one to you. You taught me so much that has molded me into the person I am today: the importance of finishing strong, how to "flip the switch," and how to pronounce *fartlek* without snickering. But mostly you taught me how to make myself do hard things. And believe you me, this series was a hard thing! I wouldn't have had the discipline to finish if you hadn't taught me how to push myself further than I thought I could. Thank you, Coach.

Kenny—words cannot describe. Ever. You are my rock, and more than that, you rock my world! Audrey, Brennan, Gideon, and Gwendolyn, you are my greatest achievements. My family and family-in-law: I could not ask for better cheerleaders.

Thank you!

Don't miss the entire *New York Times* bestselling

WINGS SERIES

★ "Mixing a little bit of Harry Potter and a lot of Twilight,
Pike has hit on a winning combination. Yet it is her own graceful
take on life inside Avalon that is sure to enthrall readers."

—ALA *Booklist* (starred review)

www.epicreads.com